Praise to

"Poignant but never maudlin, sweet but never saccharine, *This Shining Life* gives us a heartbroken family, complicated and familiar in the best ways, going through the hardest of times but finding love and hope and, especially, one another."

—LAURIE FRANKEL, *New York Times* bestselling author of *This Is How It Always Is*

"An exquisitely beautiful and compelling novel about love, loss, and life."

—RACHEL JOYCE, *New York Times* bestselling author of *Miss Benson's Beetle*

"A beautifully written and endlessly touching debut that's sure to tug your heartstrings."

—PHAEDRA PATRICK, author of *The Curious Charms of Arthur Pepper*

"Harriet Kline masterfully captures how differently grief can manifest itself in each of us, how all-consuming and life-altering it sometimes can be. I felt deeply for each of these characters as they embarked on their journeys through Rich's illness and passing, and of course the aftermath. I loved Ollie and often wanted to reach through the pages to hug and comfort him. This story is sure to stay with me for a long time."

—RHIANNON NAVIN, author of *Only Child*

"Harriet Klin̶ gifts us with an authentic child's voice, and a sensitive ex̶ uty of grief."

NYAM, is Bliss

This Shining Life

A Novel

Harriet Kline

The Dial Press

New York

A Dial Press Trade Paperback Original

Copyright © 2021 by Harriet Kline

Book club guide copyright © 2021 by Penguin Random House LLC

Published in the United States by The Dial Press, an imprint of Random House, a division of Penguin Random House LLC, New York.

THE DIAL PRESS is a registered trademark and the colophon is a trademark of Penguin Random House LLC.

RANDOM HOUSE BOOK CLUB and colophon are trademarks of Penguin Random House LLC.

Published in the United Kingdom by Doubleday, an imprint of Transworld, a Penguin Random House UK company.

LIBRARY OF CONGRESS CATALOGING-IN-PUBLICATION DATA
Names: Kline, Harriet, author.
Title: This shining life: a novel / Harriet Kline.
Description: First edition. | New York: The Dial Press, [2021]
Identifiers: LCCN 2020044279 (print) |
LCCN 2020044280 (ebook) | ISBN 9781984854902 (paperback) |
ISBN 9781984854919 (ebook)
Subjects: LCSH: Families—Fiction. | Bereavement—Fiction.
Classification: LCC PR6111.L55 S48 2021 (print) |
LCC PR6111.L55 (ebook) | DDC 823/.92—dc23
LC record available at https://lccn.loc.gov/2020044279
LC ebook record available at https://lccn.loc.gov/2020044280

Printed in the United States of America on acid-free paper

randomhousebooks.com
randomhousebookclub.com

9 8 7 6 5 4 3 2 1

Book design by Simon M. Sullivan

For Nick

This Shining Life

Prologue

HE FELL OVER and lay in the grass, laughing. "I didn't think I'd had that much to drink."

The sky glowed golden above him. There were napkins and plates strewn in the grass, one with a smear of Stilton on the rim. How he loved cheese: Camembert oozing from a velvet rind, the fuzzy blue eyelets in a Saint-Agur.

Ollie came to stand beside him, shuffling his feet in and out of his Crocs. One trouser leg was tucked into a sock.

"Why are you lying down, Dad?"

"I'm not really sure, but I like it."

The summer term was over. There were six weeks of holiday ahead and a heat wave had been forecast. Rich planned to spend it lying down, on a blanket under the apple tree, on a towel at the beach, in the hammock that he had long been meaning to install by the river. And now it seemed he'd already started. Ruth leaned over him and offered her hand. Her skin was dry and warm and he brought her palm to his mouth, and kissed it.

"I'll kill you if you're hungover tomorrow," she said. Ollie looked from her to Rich and back again.

"You won't really kill him, Mum," he said. "That would be murder."

More people came to stand over him and he smiled at them all—Ruth's sister, Nessa, taking bites out of a gaudy cake, and their mother, Angran, her glasses flaring red in the sunset.

"You're right," Ruth said to Ollie. "But I could nag him so much he'll wish he was dead."

Rich laughed. "That won't happen." He attempted to sit, but his belly pitched. Black clouds churned across his eyes. He thudded back onto the grass. *Wait a while,* he told himself. *Just a moment more and the nausea will pass.* The sun was a red disk behind the trees and he watched it glinting on a wineglass beside him, gilding the rim. The scene around him felt like an idyll, the inky silhouettes of the oaks, children racing up the garden, the table on the patio still loaded with food. Ruth shivered beside him as the shadows crept up the lawn. He reached for her hand again and something clenched in his gut. But still he smiled at the people gathered around him. Their faces were ruddy in the enduring glow of the setting sun.

Part 1

Ollie

MY DAD DIED. He gave everyone a present before he died. He gave me a pair of binoculars. They smell of books that haven't been read for a very long time. When I put them against my face they feel heavy. I can feel them pressing on my bones. My dad hasn't got any bones. We burned them all and threw the ashes around by the river. When we'd finished we saw a heron flying out of the woods. Auntie Nessa sighed and said: "There he goes."

She said the heron was my dad, but it wasn't. I looked at it through the binoculars and saw its beak and some feathers sticking up on its head. My dad didn't have a beak, or feathers. He had yellow curly hair and big lines in the skin around his eyes that Angran calls crow's-feet. Everyone stood there watching the heron and Mum did that thing of crying and smiling at the same time, while she held on to Auntie Nessa's hand. I didn't really think it would be him. I knew it must be a turn of phrase, but I didn't know what it meant. When Mum says my bedroom is a bomb site I know she means it's messy, but I've never heard a saying about dead people and herons and that made me nervous. I was scared to say anything about it in case I got something wrong. I hate getting things wrong.

Mum had come to sit on my bed at the beginning of the school holidays and she said: "Dad's dying."

I thought she meant he was dying for a cup of tea or a bit of peace and quiet. It didn't seem likely that he was actually dying. I could hear him washing up in the kitchen, opening the cutlery drawer and not shutting it again. He wasn't in a bed with blood coming out of him, he was singing to the Beach Boys. So I said: "Dying for what?"

She said: "The brain tumor they found last week, love. They can't take it away."

So that time it wasn't a turn of phrase. I'd got it wrong. Mum had got it wrong too because I didn't ask what he was dying of, and she answered as if I had. People get it wrong all the time. But I don't like it. Especially not when people are crying and holding each other's hands. Then I know that getting it wrong makes things worse.

Ruth

NESSA DROVE THEM to the hospital, hurtling them there, it seemed, with the shadows of the trees on the valley road flickering through the car. They lived eight miles out of town at the end of a narrow lane, and the journey started slowly enough, with Nessa pipping the horn at the corners, giving one-finger waves to other drivers who had pulled into gateways to let them pass, but once they met the two-way road that followed the crease of the valley, she seemed to yank the car around each bend, hurling it over the humpback bridges.

"Please, Nessa, slow down," Ruth murmured to her sister from the back seat. She didn't really want her to hear, or to admit to anyone that she was feeling sick. It seemed wrong to voice her own needs at a time like this. She looked over at Rich, gazing quietly out of the window in the passenger seat, and she curled her fingers around her seatbelt. Heat built up in the car as they approached the town and she watched the steamy prints of Nessa's hands blooming and fading on the steering wheel.

"I'll come in with you, right?" Nessa said, swinging them swiftly into a parking space outside the oncology center. "I've got a list of questions for the doctor."

Rich climbed out of the car and stretched his arms above his head. "The more the merrier." He grinned, as if it were a party ahead of him, not a pronouncement on the rest of his life. Ruth stood beside him and reached for his hand. He'd been so frightened on their first trip here, at midnight, after their party at the end of term. He'd held a bucket between his knees then, and he'd rocked and groaned the whole way. Now, as they made their way along the corridors, he seemed to be giddy—high on the relief that steroids and anti-nausea medication had brought him. Giddy was better than scared, Ruth reckoned. She was terrified herself and glad to have Nessa with her, striding purposefully ahead of them into the consulting room. Someone, she thought, needed to concentrate on what was being said.

Ruth was actually thinking about hair, whether Rich would look old or broken if he lost his blond curls, and why her own hair, reflected in the windows, looked so much like a nest of spider's legs or a bulge of weedy foliage. Dr. Ahmed's hair, she noticed, was sleek and black, pulled into a gleaming chignon. She looked worthy of the serious facts that lay hidden in the file on her desk. Ruth felt too mad to comprehend them, too ugly to make sensible plans on Rich's behalf.

Dr. Ahmed showed them a patch of darkness on the brain scan. The tumor was sitting, she said, on the brain stem itself. *Crouching*, Ruth thought, not *sitting*. She was almost offended that Dr. Ahmed would use such a dull word to describe something so horrible. She glanced at Nessa, scribbling away in her book, and hoped her notes were closer to the truth. *A menacing shadow lurking on the scan.*

Rich leaned forward. He was wearing a Hawaiian shirt, pink with silhouetted palm trees, and he smiled at Dr. Ahmed. Ruth noticed a tiny quiver in his jaw.

"There will be chemotherapy, I suppose," he said.

Dr. Ahmed folded her hands. Ruth thought about her kitchen, the way the lids of her Tupperware boxes spilled out of the cupboards if she opened them too suddenly. It made her laugh, usually, or swear in creative ways. Now she wondered if others would begin to think badly of her. People undergoing chemotherapy had to live in spotless homes to eliminate the risk of infection. Nessa, in particular, would suspect her of failing Rich on this.

Dr. Ahmed put a hand to her perfect hair and explained that there would be no chemotherapy in Rich's case. She said that although there were treatments he could undergo to reduce the size of the tumor and to make the rest of his life more comfortable, what they really needed to consider was a plan for his palliative care. She let her eyes rest on each person in turn, to check that her message had been understood.

Ruth doubted that the comprehension was evident on her face. She was holding her mouth too rigidly, her tongue dry against her teeth. It came to her that this was all her fault. She had never let Rich rest. He was first out of bed each day, and if she heard Ollie stamping or shouting downstairs she didn't always go to help. Every morning was a rush for him—no clean cups for his coffee, his clothes crumpled in the washing basket, Ollie calling for fingertip checks of his socks lest the toes had turned crispy or any threads had come loose. On a good day, Ruth told herself there was something glorious in the chaos, but what if Nessa was right, and it was merely a symptom of her failure? What if, by hiding in her sewing room in the mornings, drawing up designs for a new sofa cover or searching out embroidery threads on eBay, she had scuppered him? She had withheld her everyday support and he had withered under the strain.

Rich turned to her and stroked her knee. His jawline quivered as he smiled. "It'll be all right," he said.

She put her hands to her face. "How can it be? You're going to die."

He didn't want to know how long he had left. He said he would take a walk in the sunshine while Dr. Ahmed gave her estimates.

No, Ruth wanted to say. *Don't leave me with this on my own.* Her breath stuttered in the hollow of her hands and she wanted to say it over and over—no to the illness and no to the dying, to her stupid jumbled thoughts about her hair and the state of her house. But she didn't dare with Nessa's eyes on her. She'd always told Ruth she was a quitter and it was true that, as a child, she'd been the one to faint in assembly, then later, as a student, the one begging for extensions in the tutor's office. She had abandoned her work at the theater wardrobe not long after Ollie was born, and still she left a stack of greasy plates in the sink at the end of the day. Ruth had never been able to persuade Nessa that washing the dishes didn't matter to her, or that her strengths lay elsewhere. What Nessa saw was Rich, rolling up his sleeves and gushing water into the washing-up bowl. She saw him dancing and whistling as he lifted the plates onto the drainer, bubbles popping merrily on his forearms, and she loved him for it. Everyone did. His blue eyes crinkled when he smiled, and he smiled all the time. He invited friends for dinner, to stay the night, to come camping with them on a sunny weekend. But he never knew if there was food in the house, any bedding for them to sleep in, or room in the car for all the tents and children he had gathered on the way. It was Ruth, supposedly so feeble, who made it all work.

Now she pictured him walking from the hospital in his ridiculous shirt, a breeze lifting the curls from his forehead. For a moment it seemed as if dying was just another of his misbegotten plans. It was almost reckless the way he had left her here in this airless room. He was keeping it all vague as usual, with only a broad fantasy of how things would be. She was the one with the details: she would have to plan it all out and make it work for everyone.

Ollie

MY DAD DIED. We had parties in the garden while he was still alive and loads of people came, like Michael Wardle from my dad's five-a-side football team, and our neighbors from the farm at the end of the lane. My dad sat in the deck chair and smiled at them all. Once, when they were all hanging around him, I heard him say: "I understand now, what it means to be alive."

Michael Wardle laughed, because he laughs at everything, even when it's not funny, but I noticed that everyone looked pleased when he said that. I asked him about it later. I said: "So, Dad, what does it mean to be alive?" That's how he used to put questions to me: "So, Ollie, what's the capital of Peru?"

I used to know every capital city in the world. That was when I was little and I thought it would be useful for going to school. Now that I'm nearly eleven I know it's better to learn the names of football players in the Premier League. The boys with the loudest voices play football in the playground. They won't let me join in because I'm rubbish at it but they like it when I list the players in their favorite teams. So I learn the names each season and after every transfer window. Dad used to say: "So, Ollie, who's in defense for

Liverpool this year?" I never got it wrong. He's dead now, so no one ever asks me. Mum says she doesn't like football. Nor do I, but I wish someone would test me on the names.

My dad died. I asked him what it meant to be alive and he laughed. Then he said, "Oh, Ollie," and looked out into the distance. There were binoculars hanging over the back of his chair so I borrowed them to see what he was looking at, but there was nothing there. Just the sky turning pink and some magpies in the trees. He said: "Why don't you keep those binoculars, Ollie? I'd like you to have them."

He started telling me then that being alive was like a puzzle and it was all falling into place. He was writing a list of names on an envelope and he said that everyone he loved would get a present.

I love puzzles. Killer sudoku are my favorite but I like word ladders and codewords too. They make me happy, but only when they're finished. If they go wrong or I have to rub something out and the page gets creased, I get itchy under my fingernails and Mum tells me off for throwing the puzzle book across the room. But when I complete a sudoku and I can run my eyes along the rows and up and down the columns, I feel happy because everything is neat and correct. I said: "Can I do that puzzle, Dad, the one that tells you what it means to be alive?" He laughed at that, but I didn't know why.

He said: "That's something we all have to keep working at, son."

He looked happy, writing names on that envelope. I think he was making up clues to the puzzle and he was smiling because the answers were falling into place. I want to do that puzzle now. I want to feel happy like he did. All I have to do is get the answers right.

Angran

A ROCKFACE ROSE snaggle-toothed out of the woods behind Black Coombe Cottage, a flat, gray edifice that shaded the garden in the morning so that the air smelled of moss and damp earth, even on dry days. The trees massed around it, dark and hunched. Crows flitted from the branches, like splinters knocked from the shadows.

The cottage had been Ruth and Nessa's childhood home and Angran, their mother, still lived there, tending her garden and chopping her logs while the crows cackled and the wind hummed in the trees. She was glad that her daughters had stayed close by, Ruth half a mile along the river, and Nessa in the village on the other side of the hill, but she thought they lived in noisy places—too many tractors or passing cars. Her cottage, in the sunken hollow of the woods, was at the end of a rutted track with grass cresting down the center. The only vehicles she encountered belonged to her visitors or people lost on the winding Devon roads.

She woke, on the day that Ruth and Rich were at the hospital, to the smell of drains in her house, thick and eggy in the warm air. Somewhere in the bathroom the pipes had backed up and she found herself staring down at last night's bathwater, the soap scum lying like lace over the surface.

"Caustic," she said to the empty house. "That'd be the thing." She was sure she had a carton of the stuff somewhere but she wasn't about to go marching around in search of it. Not in this heat. Already the air seemed heavy, like oil on her skin, and her feet were clammy against the lino. The drains were forever troubling her. It wouldn't hurt to leave them for another day or two.

She was a thin woman, with sharp elbows and sinewy limbs. She wore glasses with thick black frames and, regardless of the weather, shorts from the army-surplus shop that flapped around her knees as she tramped about. Not that she felt like tramping anywhere today. She wasn't sure if it was the smell of the drains that was making her nauseous, or the thought of Ruth at the hospital, head bowed as the doctor delivered the prognosis.

She had offered to drive Ruth and Rich to the hospital. She wanted Ruth to know there was someone on her side. So far, since the tumor had been found, Rich's friends, the whole chitter-chattering gang of them, had been reaching their arms toward him, sending him get-well cards and huge bouquets. They weren't thinking of Ruth, what a disaster this would be for her.

"But I'll be there to help her," she said now, and she tugged at the front of her T-shirt and wiped her face with it.

She could not stop thinking of the misery that awaited her daughter. She knew only too well how it felt to wake in the morning heavy with loneliness and dread. When her children were little, there had been days when she could hardly lift her head from the pillow. No one else understood this feeling, she was quite sure—not Nessa, clapping Rich on the back and talking about the power of positive thought, and not Rich either. Cancer certainly hadn't wiped the silly grin off his face. So Angran planned to stay close to Ruth and watch over her. She peered into the murky water in the bath. No one, she decided, was to think she had failed as a mother.

Outside, the crows were squabbling and she heard the thump and scuffle of their feet on the roof. She aimed an experimental kick at the side of the bath.

"Go on," she said, "get moving," but only the tiniest ripple flittered across the surface of the water. She moved to the window in search of cooler, odorless air.

Her real name was Angela, but Ollie, as a toddler, could not untie the knot of "Angela" and "Grandma" in his mouth. She had tried to separate the sounds for him but he had screamed in response, repeating *Angran* back at her, no matter what she said. In the end it was easier to accept it. Before long she began to invite others to use it, too, and she came to believe that it marked her out as a woman at the heart of a distinctive family. It had always been a matter of pride for her that she had brought up her children alone. She had let them go barefoot in summer, grubby-faced and tangle-haired, had baked her own bread and plumbed in the bathroom herself. The name "Angran" soon began to represent all her defiance in the face of convention: she wanted it shouted out in delight as she made her entrance at public gatherings, faces turning toward her, wondering who this lively and interesting old woman might be. But Nessa and Ruth seemed to favor Rich's friends, these days, ordinary folk with ordinary names, who looked surprised when she joined their conversations, thinking, no doubt, that a grandmother should be silent in the corner, knitting booties for babies.

At the window, she stared down into the garden at the crumbling wall along the edge of her lawn. The woods, rising around the rock, were dark, thick with dusky shadows, and she wondered if a walk would clear her head. There were plenty of paths she could take, most of them leading to precipices and tangles of briars, but if she could muster the energy, she thought, she could skirt the rock and clamber up to the famous viewpoint at the crest of the hill. She considered bringing her morning coffee in a flask. It was early enough to avoid the tourists, who would soon come yabbering up the track from the village. She could sit at the mossy picnic tables and watch the river rattling through the gorge, plunging over a series of waterfalls and swirling pools.

She waggled the latch on the window. The wooden frame was swollen with damp, and tiny shards of paint flaked away as it juddered open. She could hear the fizz of the waterfalls in the distance now, and the highest of them was visible, a finger smudge of froth springing away from the bald peak above the tree line. Nessa, as a child, had named this waterfall The Ravages. She had made a sign for it once, Gothic black writing painted onto an old floorboard, and she had wedged it between two of the rocks around the pool. She loved to see the tourists bending to read it as they struggled down the muddy steps from the viewpoint. Angran had laughed at them with her, pointing out their baffled looks as they consulted their guidebooks, but in truth, she'd never really liked the name. She felt it was aimed at her in some obscure way, an insult that Nessa, grinning, would never admit to. Even as she considered it now, something uncomfortable stirred within her, a kind of deep-down quiver, not unlike the jittery hiss of the water pushing toward her in the humid air. She propped her elbows on the windowsill and thought of all the times she had taken the girls to The Ravages when they were young, loaded with sketchpads and blackberry-picking tubs, pointing out the rare orchids and poisonous fungi on the way. She had tried to impress upon them how beautiful it was and how lucky they were to live here. But she found that it was not the sunlight stippled on the paths or the fluttering leaves that drew her attention when she was there: it was the black crevices in the rock, the clots of sodden moss, the rabid foaming of the water in the pool. It was worse at night. The rush and roar of it rattled through the darkness as she made her way there, stumbling over roots, blinded by tears.

"Don't think about that now," she said. "Irrelevant."

She was afraid that Ruth would forget to phone her from the hospital once the prognosis had been delivered. She pictured them all, Ruth, Nessa and Rich, in some bright hospital corridor, fingers interlaced. Angran couldn't remember the last time anyone had held her hand. Ruth and Nessa would have reached for her as children, she supposed, when they were crossing the road, or stepping from a train, but there had never been any comfort in it for her. John, the father of her girls, must have been the last adult to hold her hand. She tried to remember when this could have been—after the births perhaps, or at a party when he might have pulled her close. But now, as she turned from the window and peered down into the bath-water, she could not bring a tender moment to mind.

"Oh, forget it all," she said. Sweat prickled across her brow. She went to the basin to rinse it, and as the water trickled into the plughole she ignored the faint waft of decay.

Ollie

I THINK I'M supposed to cry because my dad died. Mum cries sitting up in bed and sewing at the same time. I'm supposed to bring her a tissue for her nose but I don't always do it. I don't like the sound of the tissues scraping against the oval hole in the box. It gives me a cold feeling at the back of my neck. I'm supposed to ignore that if someone is crying. There are lots of things I have to ignore when someone is crying. If I want to ask my mum a question I have to wait until she's blown her nose and looked at me. If I want her to help me with my socks I have to wait even longer. I hate ignoring things. It's too difficult. When there's a thread in my sock, wriggling against my skin, I'm supposed to act as though it isn't there. But it makes my feet feel blurry if the threads move around. I can only ignore it if I do a sudoku. Then I get told off for being rude because I'm ignoring everything else.

My dad died. I wish I could ignore that, but I can't.

My dad made up a puzzle and he said we should all be working on it. When it's done, I'll find out what it means to be alive. So I've been working on it for the whole month since he died. Mum says I've been spending too much time in my room. She's wrong. I've been coming out to look for clues. The first thing I need is the envelope with the list of presents on it and the names of all the people he loved. He carried that envelope around with him and I think each present gives a clue about being alive. I've looked for the envelope under the sofa cushions and in the big pile of papers on the hall table, but I haven't found it yet.

Yesterday, when Nessa came around with some pizza, I saw some screwed-up paper under Mum's bed. I thought it might be the envelope so I squatted down to reach for it. I saw a plate with toast crumbs stuck to it and lots of bits of foil from the backs of Tylenol packets. It wasn't the envelope. It was a letter my dad had started writing to me. It said:

Dear Ollie,
    One day you will be a man and I'm so sad I won't see that. I think you will be a brilliant man. You will be very funny, very clever, and also rather strange.

Then it stopped. Underneath it said *Dear Dad* but the rest of the page was blank. On the other side there was some scribbly writing about the color of the sky.

I showed it to Mum and she said: "Stupid idiot. He should have finished it. He never did anything properly." She sounded like she was cross with him, but then she started kissing the paper. I asked her about the scribbles on the other side. I'd seen the words *golden* and *heart* but Mum just frowned at them. She said: "I found it in his pocket at the hospital. When do you think he wrote it? What can it mean?"

I didn't reply. I hate it when people ask me two questions at once because I don't know which one to answer first. And, anyway, I didn't know the answer to either of them so I went back to my room.

Nessa

SHE LOOKED ACROSS the consulting room at Ruth, who was hunched in her seat, hands pressed to her face, and thought that if she didn't get her moving they'd be stuck there all day. She wanted to carry her out. It would be easy enough, she thought, to crouch beside her, slip one arm under the crease of her knees, the other under her armpits, and to heave herself up with her sister slumped against her belly.

Nessa had been described as strapping in her time. She didn't much like it, but she was glad of her sturdy thighs and muscular arms. In her twenties she had felt invincible. She could keep up with the men at sports, drink as much as them too. Now, in her mid-forties, her body had begun to soften, but she still carried in her muscles the belief that she could not be defeated. With her class of six-year-olds, she had only to march once around the room and they were silenced.

"Come on, up you get," she said to Ruth, tugging at her shoulder. She wished again that she could lift her past the chairs and carry her, like a victim from a burning building. But they had to shuffle instead, all the way along the corridor, Ruth twisting her hands into the fabric of her dress. Outside, the sun was hot and bright, lancing off the cars in the car park. She saw Rich on a bench, staring slack-faced ahead, and she pushed Ruth toward him.

"I'll fetch the car," she said. Her scalp throbbed in the heat as she strode across the car park. She swept her hair from her neck and pulled it into a tight ponytail that tugged at her brow. All day she had been thinking, *I'm not having it*, and she thought it again now. She wasn't sure exactly what it was she wasn't having: Dr. Ahmed had made it perfectly clear there was nothing to be done. There was no point in running marathons or jumping from planes to raise money for a miracle cure. Rich was going to die, and no amount of chemotherapy or weeping from Ruth would make any difference.

Rich was one of Nessa's oldest friends. She had met him at teaching college and in those days they'd hitch halfway across the country together to see a band they liked or spend whole days cooking elaborate meals. They'd tripped on magic mushrooms and danced on the tables of strange pubs where they never seemed to call time at the bar. They were often assumed to be a couple back then, but Nessa preferred female lovers on the whole, or men she didn't know or expect to see again, and Rich liked sweeter and wispier types, who got on Nessa's nerves. She'd felt like a genius when, in the summer after they graduated, she introduced him to her little sister. At that time Ruth was living at Black Coombe Cottage, claiming to be working things through with their mother, and saving up for a deposit on a house of her own. Nessa knew that "working things through" involved listening to long stories about how useless their father was and how they'd be better off lonely than with a man like him. Nessa had felt it was her duty to get her out of there and Rich, she realized, was the perfect ally. He'd taught her, after all, that you could be angry with your parents but still savor every mouthful of a delicious meal, or you could wake in a black mood one morning and be singing in the sunshine by the end of the day. So she had found excuses to bring him to the cottage whenever Ruth was there. Together, they enticed her back into the world.

But now she had to face the fact of his death. Dr. Ahmed had predicted he had six months left to live. During that time, she had told them, they could expect to see a gradual deterioration in his strength, his mobility and cognitive function. She had used words that Nessa could not match with the man who danced and drank with her—seizures, confusion, incontinence. Ruth, she saw, was too shocked to retain the details of this grim list. It was up to Nessa, as usual, to make sensible plans in response.

She opened the door of the car and the heat surged out. The steering wheel was scorching on her palms. She thought of the way Angran had tried to muscle in on this appointment and she was glad she had put a stop to it.

"She'll glare at the doctors and mutter to herself," she had told Ruth. "Don't let her near the place."

Ruth had frowned and chewed at her nails. "But she's offered now and she'll be offended if I say no."

"So what?" Nessa countered. "This isn't about her, it's about Rich."

That would be her focus, Nessa resolved now: to make Rich the center of everything. Their mother would have to keep to the sidelines for once. She wiped her brow and started the engine. What she needed was a cold shower, the water hitting her hard, fresh and alert. That's what she wasn't having, she decided, as she backed out of the space:

sweat, dirt and clammy skin. And, once refreshed, she'd get to work on the house. She could see that Rich and Ruth were ready to collapse, so she planned to lay out a rug for them under the apple tree. While they were lying there, she'd go through their house like a dose of salts, putting on washes, mopping the floors, filling the freezer with healthy meals. If Rich had only months to live, she thought, he should be somewhere bright and shining with the windows wide open and the breeze blowing through.

She drew up beside them where they huddled together on a bench, Ruth with strands of her dark hair clinging to her cheeks. Nessa tooted her horn and they staggered to their feet. Then she tooted again. Not because she needed to, but because a sob had escaped unbidden from her mouth. She didn't want anyone to hear. Better, she felt, to make a hard and definitive sound, prove to them all that she would tackle this disaster face on.

Ollie

MY DAD DIED. Auntie Nessa thinks we should have a party to celebrate his life. She said the funeral was too formal and the scattering of the ashes too gloomy. She came by with some frozen pizza but we nearly burned it because she ended up crying on Mum's bed. I didn't like it. I wanted someone to ask me questions about the Premier League so I wouldn't have to hear the snot rattling in her nose. When she'd finished she said: "Oh, well, I needed that. There's nothing like a good cry."

I hate crying. It makes my head feel swollen and my skin feel fizzy. My dad used to beg me not to cry if we had guests. He'd take me off into another room. And if the guests were Other Grandma and Grandpa he'd bash his hand against his forehead and say: "Please, Ollie, not now!" He wanted me to stop the cries coming out of my mouth, but I never can. They just keep swelling up inside me and they sting at the back of my throat. Sometimes I bite the bedclothes or the sleeve of my jumper, but it doesn't really help.

Auntie Nessa didn't do any of that. She came downstairs and smiled at us, blowing her nose. She said we should dance on the beach for my dad's birthday, and order big platters of cheese. She said: "Come on, Ruth, you know that's what he would have wanted. This is the man who had a party once, just because he found two jars of olives at the back of the cupboard."

So Mum got out her notebook and started writing down plans. I told her I didn't want cheese at the party. I don't like the smell. It's like wet shoes that have been left in a bag overnight. Mum said, "What would you like, then?" but I didn't answer because I knew I'd get it wrong. Parties for dead people have to involve herons and things with special meanings that I don't understand. In the end she asked everyone what sort of party they wanted and wrote it down in a list. It said:

Ollie—no cheese.
Nessa—dancing on beach.
Other Grandma and Grandpa—meal in hotel, will pay.
Angran—no party. Too much fuss.

When it was done she laughed out loud. I asked her what was funny and she said: "Oh, God, Ollie, it's all so meaningful."

Mum's always going on about things being meaningful. One day, just before the funeral, Auntie Nessa broke a cup when she was making coffee for Angran. The cup said *World's Best Mum* on it, and Mum said, "Well, if that's not meaningful," and then she stood in the corner, laughing for ages with Auntie Nessa. When Angran came in they stopped. Auntie Nessa made her another cup of coffee in a mug that said *Keep Calm and Carry On*. I thought that one might be meaningful, too, but no one laughed or commented so I wasn't sure. I hate trying to work out special meanings. You can never be sure whether you've got them right or wrong.

I looked at the list of party ideas and said: "How are they meaningful, Mum?"

Mum said: "Well, they're like clues, aren't they? Each answer tells you something about what we're all like."

I ran into my room then. I was itchy under my fingernails and I had to grab at the edge of my mattress and press hard. My dad's puzzle will be like that. When I find the list of presents I'll have to work out the special meaning for each one. I won't be able to do it on my own. It won't be like an acrostic or a word ladder where the answers are clear and neat. Mum came into my room and said: "Oh, Ollie, you look like you're going to cry. It's OK you know, to let it all out."

I took off my socks and threw them in her face. I never want to cry about my dad. I want to finish the puzzle. I want to get all the answers right and know for certain what it means to be alive. Then I'll never need to cry again.

Gerald

RICH'S FATHER SAT on a patio chair and looked across the lawn at the newly pruned banksia rose. His ears were full of gurgles. He felt he was under water half the time with all the gulping and swirling in his head, all he heard was a booming series of vowels while people moved their mouths and flapped their lips at him. Tinnitus, the doctor had said. Not cancer. He'd have felt a damn fool if he'd got cancer at the same time as his son. Same symptoms, but his were just the result of old age. Nothing to worry about, one of those things. Gerald didn't tell the doctor there were voices in the gurgles, though. He didn't want to admit to the nonsense that came burbling up from the depths. Conjugations of cod-Latin verbs, nursery rhymes that no child would ever want to hear. The doctor gave him a nasal spray, said it would help with . . . What was it? With . . . The damn word wouldn't come.

"A question of indirect digestion," a voice in his ears said now. He swallowed hard, attempting to adjust the pressure. He was damned if he was going to use the spray anyway. He wasn't the sort of man who stuck things up his nose and wiggled them. *Congestion*. That was the word. The spray would help with *congestion*.

The hedge looked dull and stunted now that the flowers were gone. He turned to the table where Marjorie had placed a teapot and cup. No milk jug. She had brought the tray out, told him to sit and rest in the shade, and now she'd gone and left him stranded. He could fetch the milk himself, of course, but he didn't fancy the fuss she'd make if she saw him back on his feet or pouring from a milk jug that didn't match the pot.

"Top-notch hodge-podge," a voice said in his ears. Gerald didn't think he needed to rest. He'd be happier mowing the lawn or pulling up a few weeds. He didn't like the way the boy from the village hacked at the banksia. Used the shears like a . . . a damn . . . He tried to force the word into his mind, though he had been told often enough that it wouldn't help. *Just wait and it will come,* they said, but Gerald wasn't a waiting sort of man. He'd had a long stride in his day, and he'd used it: shoulders back, eyes front and forward without fear. So he clenched his fists now and butted up against the gap where the word should have been.

The phone rang in the house. He rose to his feet. It wasn't as easy as he'd expected. His left knee wavered and set him off course. He had to flail with his right hand like a damn fool and then Marjorie came warbling up beside him with the phone to her ear.

"I told you to sit down, Gerald. I've answered it already. It's Richard."

Machete. That was the word. The boy used the shears like a *machete.* The ribbons on the collar of Marjorie's blouse fluttered as she tripped back into the house, twittering into the phone. Still no milk jug. He lowered himself back into his seat. Damn fool idea of his to answer the phone anyway. He'd only have heard a stream of burbles and clicks. He swiveled in his chair and looked through the patio doors. Marjorie was standing by the bureau with her back to him, still talking. He saw the neat waves of her hair, almost geometric in their precision. Suddenly she leaned forward, grabbing at the bureau with her free hand. A spasm of indigestion, Gerald thought. He got those sometimes. Cucumbers set it off and . . . What was it? That damned purple stuff.

Marjorie edged along the bureau, grasping at the edges. She came to a chair and fell heavily onto the seat. *Beetroot*, Gerald thought, but he had no idea why the word had come to him. Something was wrong. Marjorie's face was white now, all of it, even her lips. The voices in his head fell silent. He pushed himself to his feet and stood before her as she reached her arms toward him. He heard her words clearly.

"He's just come back from the hospital, Gerald. There's nothing they can do."

Ollie

My dad used to eat breakfast with me. He used to drink strong coffee and test me on footballers' names. He liked the Italian ones best and he made his voice sound like an opera singer's when he pronounced them. *ChiellEEni, BaloTAYli.* Mum used to stay in bed until the taxi came to take me to school, but the other day she said: "It's been six weeks since he died. It's time to get into some new routines." She didn't ask me about footballers. She sat at the table rubbing her face and puffing out long breaths. She said she wanted to do everything that my dad did, but it wasn't the same. My dad never had to ask me if I had a special cup for my tea or whether I wanted to swap apples for satsumas for my breakfast fruit. My dad had it all written down in a list he could tick off. Weetabix on Mondays and Fridays, porridge every other Thursday. He only asked good questions that didn't make me feel stupid.

My dad died. My mum kept asking me all these breakfast questions and it made me clench my teeth. It wasn't that I didn't know the answers, it was that I had to look at her face when she asked because she was trying to chat. I don't like chat. You have to say things that people already know, like *It's pouring down out there.* You even have to lie.

When the taxi comes to take me to school in the morning, Jack from the farm is already in it, telling me things about his little sister. Mum says I should say *How lovely* or *Isn't she sweet?* She says that chatting isn't about what you say. It's about showing people you're friendly and making them feel nice. It doesn't make me feel nice. It makes me tired. I have to think really hard about whether people are lying and whether it matters or not. It's even harder to work out what will make them feel nice. My dad's football questions were much better. Even if I had to think hard for the answer, once I found it everything was neat and correct.

My dad died. That's not neat and I really wish it was.

Mum wanted to see the chart we'd made for my breakfasts. She started looking in the kitchen drawer. She pulled out some letters from the hospital and a sketch of a jacket she was going to make for Auntie Nessa. Then she took out something else and said: "Oh, Ollie, come and look at this." I knew it was the envelope I'd been looking for. She was holding it against her chest but I could see the doodles he'd drawn in the corners and the rip on one side where he had opened the card. I grabbed it from her so I could see all the presents and what their meanings were. It said:

Mum—Pink Vase
Dad—Boat Picture
Nessa—Necklace
Angran—Shawl

Underneath it said: *Something for the hospital staff? Candles?*

This was the start of the puzzle, but there weren't any

meanings written down. I could feel my heart beating fast and the skin getting fizzy at the back of my neck. I said: "What does a pink vase mean, Mum?" but she didn't answer my question.

She just reached her hand toward me and said: "You snatched it from me, Ollie. That's rude."

I stuffed the envelope under my shirt. I didn't want her to have it. If she started kissing it or asking stupid questions I'd never get the puzzle done. She said, "Hey, Ollie, what's wrong?" but I could hardly hear her voice over the rushing sound in my head. The envelope was scratching at my skin. It was crumpled up like a piece of dirty rubbish and I'd spoiled it already. I ran up to my room and yanked my mattress onto the floor. Then I threw myself down and pulled the covers over my head.

Marjorie

GERALD HAD EMPTIED out the drawers of his desk. Now he was rummaging through the bureau. Envelopes and papers were scattered at his feet. A spool of address stickers unfurled and sped across the floor. Marjorie went after it and tried to roll it up.

"Gerald, sit down, please!" She heard a pen crunch under his feet and hoped it wouldn't leak onto the carpet. The last thing she needed now was a dark mark on the floor, just where the women's committee from the church would see it when they came, as she knew they would, with flowers and cards of condolence. Or would they? Perhaps they would have to wait for Richard to die before they brought cards.

She knelt down and tried to gather the papers into a pile. Her hands were shaking and her mouth was dry. Sweet tea was the thing. She ought to be bringing a tray to the table, a biscuit on the saucer. She had bought some lovely tissues only yesterday, with gladioli on the box. She should be sliding them across the table toward him now as he sipped his tea. She should not be on her knees with a bundle of bank statements in her hands.

"That podgy fellow," Gerald said now. He rattled through the pages of an address book and tossed it aside.

"Knight-something with the ghastly wife. We should get on the phone to him." Gerald was a tall man, but in recent years had developed a stoop. It thrust his chin forward and loosened the skin around his jowls.

"Anthony Knight?" Marjorie said to him, sitting back on her heels. "Why on earth? Look, just let me get you a drink." She struggled to her feet and placed the papers on the desk. He swept them all back onto the floor.

"Where's the damn address book? It was here yesterday. Someone's hidden it."

Marjorie's vision began to speckle. She could see Gerald leaning on the bureau, rattling it, but puffs of stippled silver covered his face. If she fainted now, she thought, feeling for the wall with her hand, Gerald wouldn't even notice. There had been a time when he would have been the one urging her to sit down. He'd have brought the tea, patted her hands. Three little taps, he used to give her, their secret signal. *I'm here, we're in this together.* He'd tap her waist as they walked together into a party, or her knee under the table at a work dinner. Even at Ruth and Richard's house he'd give her those three little nudges as they sank into their dreadful sofa. They kept her smiling if Ruth offered her tea in a chipped mug or if Ollie started fretting. But now she could not imagine how she would ever smile again. And even if Gerald were to give his three little taps, what good would they do?

"I've remembered his name," Gerald said. "Anthony Knight. Top of his field, he is. He'll sort this out." He peered behind the bureau, crumpling papers underfoot as he shuffled around it.

"Anthony Knight's an accountant," Marjorie said. "I don't see how he can help."

"High up, isn't he, in the hospital trust? Knows who's who. If I could find his damn number I could get on to him now."

She had to leave him there. She was crying and she didn't want him to see her with her makeup smudged. If he'd sat with her, over tea and tissues, they could have comforted each other. But now tears were coursing down her face. She could taste the mix of face powder and salt as they leaked into her mouth.

She went to the bedroom and wiped it all away with a cotton pad. She looked faded when she'd finished. Her eyes, the same blue as Richard's, were bloodshot, and, without the makeup, they seemed to sink away into her brows. Her skin was thin, finely wrinkled, and her hair, with its chestnut tint, was too harsh against her temples. *Lifeless*, she thought, and the word jabbed at her. Would Richard seem faded the next time she saw him? Would his eyes cloud and his shoulders sag, as his father's had? There was a photograph of him on the dressing table. He had emailed it only recently and she had printed it out and put it into a frame. He stood between Ruth and Ollie, the sky pink behind him. *Celebrating the end of term*, he had written. *Six weeks of relaxing ahead.* She had written straight back. *Please bring Ollie to see us, darling. I'll speak to your father. Surely we can sort this out.* It seemed like months since she'd seen Ollie. There had been an uncomfortable altercation— one of those moments when she'd turned her attention away from Gerald and he'd lost his temper over something silly, Ollie stamping his foot and not saying thank you for a present.

"He doesn't mean to be naughty," she had said to Gerald afterward. "You know he's a sweet little boy." But Gerald, unable to remember the details of it by then, would only repeat his demand for an apology.

Now she looked into the picture at Richard's smiling face. She couldn't see the blue of his eyes, but she could bring it to mind easily. She used to love the way he blinked up at her from the bath when he was little. He'd dip his head into the water to gurgle, then rise up, chuckling, water streaming from his chin. All through his boyhood she had delighted in those blue eyes and she still felt a shock of pleasure when she saw them now. A shock that she had assumed she would enjoy until the end of her life.

Gerald came into the bedroom and began tugging at the wardrobe doors. "Have you packed, Marjorie? We ought to go."

"Go where? What are you looking for now?"

He began pulling his jackets from the hangers, thumping them onto the floor. "You've hidden the damn car keys! I'm not going to just take this, you know. I'm going down there. Talk to that doctor myself."

It was a two-hour drive to Richard's house. She quailed at the thought of Gerald crunching the gears on those narrow country lanes. She bent to gather the jackets in her arms.

"Gerald, you know you're not allowed to drive." He threw another jacket toward her. The sleeve grazed her cheek as it fell.

"Of course I can drive. I know where the brake is, and the . . . the damn . . . Oh, you know the word."

She stood up. She tried to replace the jackets in the wardrobe but the hangers twisted on their hooks, spinning away from her. Gerald began to tug at the chest of drawers. He fished out the handkerchiefs and dropped them into heaps. She folded them, and Gerald pulled out her tights and slips. She followed him around for the next hour, lifting things from the floor, placing them back in the drawer. Finally, at five, as if a switch had been flipped, he stopped. He poured himself a whiskey, and a gin and tonic for her, and placed them carefully on the patio table.

"Poor Marjie," he said. "Damn shock this."

She sat beside him and, in her mind, traced his path of destruction through the house. She had patted down the papers in the desk, tugged at the lapels of his jackets, put the socks back into pairs. But as she pushed each drawer closed and shut each cupboard door, she was aware of the mess behind them. The bank statements were curling at the edges, the jackets were creased at the arms. No one would be able to tell, but it was hard to swallow her gin and savor it, knowing it was so.

Ollie

I DIDN'T GO to school on the morning that I found the envelope. I heard the taxi coming for me and I knew Jack would be in the back seat with his shoelaces still undone. I didn't want to chat with him. I lay on the mattress on the floor, pressing my face into the sheets. When I got up Mum was in her bed with the curtains closed. I stood at her door and she said: "Go away, please." Then she said: "Oh, God, Ollie, I'm sorry. I've asked Angran to come over. She'll see to you soon."

Everyone hates me when I shout and pull the mattress off my bed. They think I'm stupid. Especially Grandpa. But even my dad hated me then. He'd close his eyes and say: "Don't start, Ollie, please."

I went downstairs and waited for Angran. I knew when she was coming because I could hear her muttering to herself as she walked up the path. When she arrived there was a smudge on her big black glasses. She said: "I'm worried about you, Ollie. Tell me what set off this silly fuss."

I told her it wasn't a silly fuss. I said: "I'm trying to work out some meanings, Angran. You got a shawl, didn't you? What do you think it means?"

She didn't answer. She wiped her glasses on the pocket

of her shorts and said it must have been a silly fuss because Mum was so upset.

I remember I had a nightmare about Angran, once. It was something to do with her glasses, slapped across her face like capital letters. When I told Mum about it, she said: "Don't worry, Ollie, I have nightmares about Angran too." Then she looked at Auntie Nessa and said: "And not only when I'm asleep."

They laughed about that for ages, but it wasn't funny. People don't have nightmares when they're awake. Mum said they do if they're scared all the time.

I'm not scared of Angran. I can ask her about any turn of phrase and she'll always tell me what it means. At the funeral she stopped people hugging me. When Other Grandma came running up to me, saying, *Ollie, you poor little thing*, Angran thrust her arm out to stop her. I like Other Grandma, but I didn't want to smell her perfume and I didn't want Grandpa to tell me to learn some manners and put up with it, so I was glad Angran did that. But I wasn't glad she was talking about silly fusses now. She put her glasses back on and the smudge was still there. She said: "And I don't see why I have to come traipsing over here whenever you need help. Don't you think you'd be better off at Black Coombe Cottage?"

I didn't like that question. I couldn't work out what the correct answer would be. So I went back to my room and kicked my mattress. The envelope was on the floor. The wrinkles were like ugly scratches over the writing and the worst one went zigzagging right across where it said *Angran—Shawl*.

I haven't seen any of those presents since he died. I saw them all before, because we had to pack them into boxes to send through the post. I walked with my dad to the post office and he had to keep stopping on the way to take big breaths. He kept leaning on his stick and wiping his forehead with the back of his hand. He said he'd run out of puff, but when we got to the shop he found some puff to laugh with Michael Wardle's old mother at the counter. He said: "What do you mean, no new puzzle books? I asked you for a daily delivery!" Mrs. Wardle smiled at me then. She lifted the glass screen and took the presents away. No one has mentioned them since. Maybe they didn't like them. Maybe they never stopped to think about the meanings because my dad died so soon after they were delivered.

I kept trying to smooth out the wrinkles in the envelope, but they wouldn't disappear. I thought I might never solve the puzzle. I thought as hard as I could about what it means to be alive, but the answers wouldn't fall into place.

Rich

IT WAS OBVIOUS to him that he should host a party. So
many people wanted to visit: Geoff and his kids from the
farm, people from the village, even old friends from school,
who drove miles down the motorway in the heat, their cars
tucked into the hedgerow along the lane, ticking as they
cooled. He set up a circle of chairs beneath the apple tree
and welcomed them. All day the sky was a bright hard
blue above them and the sun flashed on the glasses. Salads
wilted in the bowls and the melting Brie surged out from
its rind and dripped into the grass. He wondered if he was
expected to say something profound, or if he should take
each guest aside and elicit promises from them to look out
for Ollie and Ruth when he was gone. But he found that
people were happiest when he made jokes or offered them
morsels of cheese. They were reassured by normality and
so was he.

Now the last of the guests was gone and the rumble of
cars in the lane had receded. Lying back in his deck chair
he could hear the faint whisper of the river from across the
field, the insects humming in the hedge. The sky was paler
too, softening into a blush of pink above the trees.

He'd dreamed about the sky last night, a sunset, red and

sweet as a nectarine. It was a flying dream and he'd soared into the sweetness, loving the rush of air against his skin.

When he'd described it to Ruth, as they mixed the sangria for the party, she had pushed the jug of wine aside and put her hands over her face. "That's about dying," she said. "The sunset is the end of your life, and you are rushing toward it."

He pried her hands away from her cheeks, ran his thumbs across her eyebrows. "It might not be," he said. "Dreams can have more than one meaning, you know." He wanted to say that he didn't care what it meant, that he loved the way he tingled when he thought of it, and he wished she could feel that way too. But Ruth was never one to tingle. She was never one to throw herself down on the grass, arms spread wide, or leap into a swimming pool with a shriek. Rich knew that she found pleasure in other ways, in making beautiful things to brighten the house: the bedspread appliquéd with sunflowers, the paper pom-poms to hang from the ceilings, the shiny red curtains that glowed in the lamplight. She said it was a gift to herself to fill the rooms with color, to dispel the darkness of her childhood. Rich felt like it was a gift to him. He had grown up with polished tables and hoovered floors. Now he lived with mess and abundance. When his friends came visiting he felt blessed to live in this crazy house where he could welcome them all.

He settled his head against the cloth of the deck chair. The binoculars, slung over the frame, began to swing and tap against his shoulders. He decided he needed to thank Ruth in some way and he considered buying her a gift. He thought of embroidery threads or bolts of silk. The first time he met her, when she was living at Black Coombe

Cottage, she'd had her arms full of orange satin, great ruffles of it frothing around her face and tumbling to the floor. She was making a ball gown for a giantess in a children's play, she told him. She wanted the sleeves to look like pumpkins. He'd watched her hands riffling through the gathers of fabric, noticed her large veins and prominent knuckles. He thought perhaps he'd fallen in love with her hands first, the quick flick of her wrist as she pushed the needle through the cloth. If he gave her bolts of silk, he thought now, he'd have to tell her that he was thanking her for all those tiny stitches and the bold and wonderful creations they held together.

Through the open kitchen window he heard her talking to Ollie. "I can't possibly keep track of every puzzle book you own."

Ollie's Crocs squeaked on the lino as he shifted his feet around. "I don't want you to keep track of every one, Mum. I only need the one with the pencil taped to the front."

Rich thought it was likely that, despite the mess in the house, she actually did keep track of all Ollie's puzzle books. He could hear her walking through the rooms now and he knew it wouldn't be long before she found the one he wanted, drawing it out from behind a cushion or from under a stack of papers as if she had known it was there all along. He thought she should be thanked for this mysterious ability too.

"Come and join me," he called. "There's a gorgeous sunset out here!"

At his feet was an unopened greeting card from his colleagues at the school. He lifted it onto his lap, but found he didn't have the heart to read the messages of love inside. Tom, his classroom assistant, had brought it, blushing as he handed it over, and Rich thought he might have written one of his sweet rhyming ditties and slipped it inside. But he, Rich, was the one who should be sending out missives, he thought. What better use of his limited time than to let people know they were adored?

He thought of Ruth and the loving things he could say to her now. She needed to know that he had absolute confidence in her. He could hardly bear to consider the difficulties of her life ahead, but he was sure she would manage somehow. He had always admired her for the way she handled Ollie. She had understood his needs right from the beginning and never pushed him to conform.

"It's just how his brain's wired," she'd say. "If he can't see the world as we do, then we have to honor that."

For Rich it was more of a struggle. He had felt embarrassment at times, when Ollie shrieked in the street because a stone had got into his sock or when there were guests in the house and he wouldn't smile at any of them. There had been a terrible row with his father some months ago when Ollie refused to thank him for a gift of some pencils.

"But I never do coloring, Grandpa," he'd said, his voice clear and open. "So I won't ever use them."

"Just pretend you like them," Rich had whispered, but Ollie had flinched away from his breath in his ear.

"I hate lying!" He glared at Rich, snapped all the pencils in two and threw them to the ground. Gerald was furious. He had only just arrived at the house and was still pulling bags from the back of the car, while Marjorie, halfway up the garden path, exchanged kisses with Ruth. Gerald slammed the trunk and demanded an apology. He was still waiting for it now, and it seemed that even Rich's illness would not soften his resolve.

Rich wished he had known what to say that day. Ruth was always quick with her responses, explaining that they would never punish their child for something he could not control, that it was kindness and acceptance Ollie needed, and the pain and distress he suffered in meltdown was punishment enough.

But Rich had been speechless. He had watched Ollie scrabbling at the fabric of his trousers, had seen the quivering folds of skin on Gerald's neck as he shouted about discipline and manners, heard the thump of Angran's boots as she made her way toward them from the house. When he found his voice at last, it came out high and quavering: "Can't you waver, Dad, just once, from the rules of etiquette?"

The whole situation was a mess and Rich could not see how to resolve it. Gerald, he remembered, had cocked his head and put his hand up to his ear, as if he was flummoxed by Rich's response. Then Angran had arrived and coaxed Ollie away. It had seemed to Rich that Ollie and Gerald must always be kept apart: neither was capable of understanding the other. But now, as he watched the magpies cackling in the trees and the sky turning rosy before him, anything seemed possible.

"Come out here," he called again. "Let's do some puzzles together!"

Hope had come rushing over him at the party today. Rich had spotted Ollie standing silently at the kitchen door. His fists were wound into the seams of his T-shirt, pulling it taut against his back. For half an hour he scanned the guests, turning his face toward Michael Wardle whenever he laughed, frowning as he studied the huddled groups of adults, the scampering village kids. Ollie was a thin child with a long jaw. The planes of his face seemed stark, and impassive. But Rich realized, as he watched him, that he was gathering information. He might have no instinct for being with people and he took scarce pleasure in their company, but it was obvious that he was making an effort to understand. He was storing up his observations and somehow, in the future, he would put them to use.

The back door opened with a click and Rich turned to see Ollie, silhouetted against the light behind. Ruth was right, he thought. It was time to sort out this row over the pencils. He had never dared to tell her everything that Gerald had said that day, that he'd used that awful word, *defective*, but now, watching Ollie make his way toward him, puzzle book clutched to his chest, head lowered, like a charging bull's, he knew he must think as Ruth did: Ollie must never apologize for being his marvelous self.

"So, Dad," Ollie said, arriving, breathless beside him. "What does it mean to be alive?"

Ruth

THE PICNIC BASKET was heavy, crammed with boxes of salad, homemade pasties and a bottle of ginger beer that Ruth intended to lodge between two stones in the river. She lugged it to the hall and found Ollie and Rich at the foot of the stairs, each with a tangle of socks clutched to his chest. Ollie's jaw was set and Rich was flushed.

"Is that every pair in the house?" she asked.

"Of course not," Ollie replied. "They're only my socks. We're not bringing any of yours."

Rich shrugged and a single red sock flopped to the floor.

"It's either this," he said, bending to retrieve it, "or spend the whole morning in a fight, and you know . . ."

He let his voice trail off, but Ruth knew exactly how the sentence was going to end. He had taken a perverse pleasure in telling people, since his diagnosis, that life was too short. It was too short to worry about money, to clean the fridge and now to fight about socks. *Yours is short*, she wanted to say, *but mine's not*. She was the one who'd have to live through the aftermath, and it seemed that it wouldn't be grief alone she'd have to contend with. At this rate there'd be debt, a filthy fridge and now Ollie expecting to take bagfuls of socks each time he left the house. She thought of saying this, but she held out the basket instead and they piled the socks on top.

"Let's go," she said, leading the way down the garden to the back gate.

She had been planning this picnic for days. Once people knew that Rich was dying it seemed that the phone had never stopped ringing, the doorbell too. Couriers arrived with parcels and bouquets of flowers. Friends came and wept quietly in corners or held Rich in long hugs. Angran had told her to send them away. "You'll be no good to anyone if you exhaust yourself," she said. But Ruth wanted to take her cue from Rich. She saw how his eyes crinkled as each car drew up the lane. He went straight to the fridge to see if there was beer to offer, or lemonade. So she smiled, too, threw a bright cloth over the garden table and weighed it down with a jug of flowers. She ordered interesting crackers and strawberries with her online shop, polished the wineglasses so they sparkled in the sun.

"Good job," Nessa had said to her, more than once. She came to the house daily and she brought Rich's favorite music from his student days or old photographs where his face was smooth and eager, his curls a blur around his head. "Got to make the most of him while we can."

Ruth didn't see how she could make the most of Rich when there were so many people in the house: Michael Wardle, lying sprawled on the blanket under the apple tree, yelping out his irritating laugh; Geoff from the farm urging him on, or setting up the hose and spraying the kids. So many people came with their children. It was the summer holidays, and she knew they had no choice, but there always seemed to be some child needing biscuits, or help with the flush on the toilet, and poor Jack was forever asking why Ollie wouldn't come out of his room and play. She thought they were keeping her from Rich, all these people, arriving after breakfast and leaving maudlin and bleary-eyed as the sun went down.

Today, though, visitors arriving unannounced would find the front door locked and the garden deserted, while she and her family headed for the river. She shifted the basket from one arm to the other and fixed her eyes on the trees across the field. The air was thick with heat and the birds had fallen silent. There was only the murmur of the river and the vague rustle of the sunbaked grass at their feet. She knew, though, that nestled somewhere in the shade ahead was the picnic place, a green bank between twin oaks. There she would spread a blanket and they would lie down, just the three of them, dipping their toes into the shallows. So many summer afternoons had been spent at this place. They'd had arguments there when Ollie was little, whispered across the all-terrain buggy while he slept, sticky-faced and pouting under the trees. They'd had luxurious picnics with wine and tiny pastries for themselves and Weetabix for Ollie in the days when that was the only food he'd willingly eat. Once, when she was newly pregnant, they had sat down in the water together, fully clothed, clutching at each other and shaking with laughter. They had just been to visit Angran to tell her their news and Angran had frowned in response and folded her arms.

"Is this sensible?" she had demanded. "Are you sure you can cope?"

Rich had gaped at her. "Of course it's not sensible," he said. "That's not why we did it!" Then, as they made their way home, climbing the steep path toward The Ravages, he had started to laugh. "Who has a baby to be sensible? She didn't even congratulate us!"

Ruth, shivering a little as they came to the viewpoint, had smelled the wet moss and dank shadows of the waterfall and had begun to feel sick. "She only means that it's a lot of work," she'd said. "You know, the lack of sleep and the worry." She had listened to the hiss and spatter of the water on the rocks and remembered how when she and Nessa were small they used to hear their mother crying at night. There were days, too, when she lay for hours on her bed with one hand over her eyes.

"What if I don't cope?" she'd said to Rich, imagining her own small child standing thin and forlorn in a nightdress at her bedroom door.

Rich tugged her hand and led her down the steps toward the pool. "You're not living the life your mum did," he said. "You won't have to do this alone." They made their way downstream to the picnic place, and when they got there, he dipped his finger into the river mud and drew a line across her brow. She flinched away at first, but he held her still and traced dipping curves below her eyes. She giggled as she began to understand that he was drawing a pair of glasses. "Just because you look like your mum," he said, "it doesn't mean you can't have fun."

He had dragged her into the river then, and pulled her to her knees. She remembered the bolt of cold against her shins. She had screamed as the water slapped against her knickers.

"It'll hurt the baby, if you make me laugh too hard," she said. "My stomach muscles feel strained."

"My love," he said, "it's the best thing for it."

Now she had more peaceful plans in mind. She wanted to lie still with him and take it all in: birds flitting between the trees, an airplane rumbling overhead. Often, when Rich woke in the early hours, he said: "I just want to take it all in." This was their chance. She held out her hand to him as he stumbled toward her in the tussocky grass. He leaned in close and she felt the warmth of his body against her side, smelled the secret, familiar smell of him, soft, like sanded wood or warm wool. In the basket her phone rang.

"Who is it?" Ollie called to her.

"No idea. I'm going to ignore it."

"I thought it was rude to ignore people."

"Oh, life's too short to worry about that," she said, winking at Rich. A moment later his phone began to ring in his pocket. "Are you going to be rude too, Dad?"

Ruth knew he would find it impossible. He cared about manners, especially Ollie's. She had been hoping for weeks now that he would sort out the row with Gerald, but she suspected that he lacked conviction, believing that whatever had happened that day reflected badly on him.

Now he grimaced into the phone. "It's Angran," he said, passing it to her.

"Where are you?" Angran's voice clacked. "I've brought you a lettuce from my garden. I thought it was about time you had something fresh to eat. All these gatherings you've had, with those shop-bought quiches."

Ruth took up the trek toward the picnic place once more, the basket pinching into her arm. The lettuce, she thought, would have slugs curled on the bases of the leaves and clots of mud lodged stubbornly in the creases. "We're on our way to the river. Use the spare key and leave the lettuce in the fridge. I'll make a salad tomorrow."

"I've let myself in already and your fridge is full of silly food. I think I'll just join you out there."

Ruth swallowed. The heat of the sun pressed on the back of her neck. "We really need some family time, Mum. It's been so hectic."

"Well, I'm family, aren't I?"

She did not dare to press it further. At best it would result in Angran glaring at her when she next visited, eyes fierce and magnified behind the lenses of her black-framed glasses. At worst—well, Ruth preferred not to think about that. She had memories, from when she and Nessa were small, of Angran stalking off into the woods at night, leaving them alone in the house. It happened if they cried a lot, if Ruth wet the bed, or Nessa asked too many questions about their father. Ruth remembered creeping into Angran's bed while she was gone, shivering under the covers as she pictured her climbing the paths toward The Ravages, trying to guess if she was at the viewpoint, staring over the edge of the falls, or if she was staggering down the muddy steps toward the roiling water at the bottom. A boy had drowned there once, someone had told her at school. When Angran came back to the house, Ruth thought she smelled river mud on her shoes.

"You're going to the usual spot, I take it," Angran said now. "The picnic place?"

Ruth trudged on. Dry grass had given way to softer ground that sank beneath her feet. The basket knocked against her hip.

"Well?" Angran's voice rattled in her ear. "Are you

going to answer me? Is that where you are?" Behind her, Ollie called for a clean pair of socks. Ruth looked down and saw that there were scrolls of mud at the edges of her sandals. "If you don't want me with you, Ruth, you should just say," Angran went on. "I can tell when I'm not wanted, you know." Water was bubbling under her toes now, squelching at the balls of her feet. Puddles glinted in the grass ahead and insects quivered above them in hectic swirls.

"No!" Ruth urged. "No, really, of course we want you here. We'd love that. I'll see you in a bit."

She rang off and looked about her at the waterlogged field. This was not what she had been expecting and for a moment she could not locate the picnic place. But a few splashy steps onward revealed that it was submerged. There was no grassy bank in the shade, only a sheen of lapping water. "We can't stay here," she cried. "It's flooded!"

"I know," Ollie called. "I want clean socks. It's horrible!"

She saw now that a log had fallen into the water and the stream was dammed. The grassy bank was flooded but the riverbed beyond was almost dry, the water dribbling under the log in little sprits and gushes.

"Wow!" Rich said, coming to join her, his footsteps squelching in the grass. "Come and look at this, Ollie. We've got our own private paddling pool." He held out his arms to balance himself and waded in. Ruth held her breath. This could be the last time, she thought, that he would be strong enough for something like this. He was buoyed up by steroids now, but no one knew how long this would last. She knew she should join him. She should leave the basket in the grass, coax Ollie out of his socks and take him crashing through the water to his dad. But she could not draw her eyes from the log. It was black and pitted, gathering slime on the underside. It belonged to the dark world of nightmares, and the menace of it, shifting and jolting in the current, brought a prickle of heat across her temples.

Rich, she was quite sure, never dreamed of black logs and slime. Even with death at his shoulder, he dreamed of flying through a golden sky with his arms outstretched. *What is it that keeps me transfixed*, she thought, *rooted here when I could be dancing with him, flicking bright drops of water through the air?*

"Yoo-hoo! It's me." Angran's voice came ringing across the field. She was holding the lettuce aloft. Flecks of mud speckled her shins as she stomped across the saturated grass.

"Well, this is no good," she said, surveying the flooded field. "You should have found a dry spot in the shade." She thrust the lettuce into Ruth's basket, pushing the muddy stem into the tangle of socks. "Let's see what we can find."

Ruth followed her downstream to a stony beach where the air smelled dark and mushroomy. There was a dark scar of silt and dried-out mud on the pebbles where the river had shriveled away.

"Perfect," Angran said. "What have you brought to eat?"

Ruth looked into the basket at the lettuce, wilting in the heat, and at the socks smeared now with earth. "I don't know," she said. "I can't be bothered to think about it now."

"You're tired, that's why," Angran told her. "I expect you've been overdoing it. I was the same when you were little. Worked myself into the ground, I did, moving us to the cottage, sorting it all out, single-handed."

That was not how Ruth remembered it. She remembered the curtains still drawn in the house when they came home from school, the smell of wet washing left to molder in the twin tub. They had moved to the cottage when she was a baby, but for years afterward Angran was still working on the repairs. Every game with Nessa, every squabble too, had been punctuated by the sound of hammering and sawing, and it seemed that every job took months to complete. For more than a year there had been gaps in the bathroom floor where the boards had been pulled up to plumb in the shower. Ruth had shuddered whenever she crossed them, but if she complained to her mother she was given a lecture in reply. *You girls need to know that you don't need men for anything. That's why I'm doing this myself. They might look like fun, men, but they'll let you down in the end.* Ruth never told her that she crept out into the garden to pee at night, rather than brave those voids at her feet, the cobwebs quivering beneath them, a musty chill seeping from the shadows.

Now in the pool behind her she heard a splash and a giggle. She turned to see that Rich had somehow coaxed Ollie out of his socks and into the water. They were clapping out high fives and Rich was beaming. She thrust the basket at Angran.

"Take this," she said. "I'm going paddling with my son." She wobbled toward them along the edge of the shrunken river and saw that they were playing some elaborate game that involved standing on one leg and shouting numbers to the trees above. Shadows fluttered over their faces, water ruffled around them and lapped against their shins.

"Six!" Ollie cried.

"Nine," Rich replied.

"Twenty-seven?" Ruth called, as she unstrapped her sandals.

Rich and Ollie bent forward gasping with laughter. Even from her place on the bank she could see Rich's leg hairs under the water, each one strung with tiny bubbles. Ollie's feet were white, glinting with strands of rippled sunlight.

"Twenty-eight," she tried, and they guffawed again. "Twenty-nine! Thirty!" She was shouting and dancing on the stones for them now, and she knew that she had to hold this moment in her memory, let it guide her through the dark days ahead. This was her mission now, to laugh with Ollie as Rich did, to keep pulling him forward into life.

"Wait." Angran was behind her, her voice close against Ruth's neck. "There's something I need to discuss."

"Later," Ruth hissed, but Angran plucked at her elbow.

"I've had an idea. You should move back to Black Coombe Cottage with me."

Ruth turned toward her, still dancing, a laugh half out of her mouth. "What? All of us? There's not enough room and you wouldn't like all the parties."

"Don't be silly, not now. Afterward. Just you and Ollie. You could rent out your house. And I could look after you both."

"Try another number, Mum!" Ollie shouted. "Go on, try again."

But Ruth's voice had thickened in her throat. She saw the black log ahead of her, the heft of it, the sputters and dribbles of water leaking out beneath.

"Thirty-one," she said, but she knew Ollie could not hear. She stared down at the dry stones of the riverbed at her feet. She saw ripples in the shriveled strands of river weed. They looked as if they were searching for the flow of water that had once kept them alive.

Ollie

MY DAD DIED. I keep missing the taxi for school and I don't know how to answer when the teachers ask me why I've been away. I asked Mum why the mornings keep going wrong and she said: "We're just sad, Ollie, that's all." She looked out of the window at a magpie in the apple tree and she said: "One for sorrow. See?"

I like magpies. You can't be wrong about what sort of bird they are, because they're the only ones that are black and white. Sometimes Mum says my thinking is black and white. I know it's a turn of phrase, but I don't know what it means. I asked her what color her thinking was and she laughed. She said: "Oh, God, Ollie, these days mostly black."

I asked her what color my dad's was. She said: "Ooh, bright red." Then she changed her mind and said: "Maybe it was fresh and green." I don't answer questions unless I'm sure I'm going to be right, but Mum doesn't care. That's why she's rubbish at puzzles. I fetched my binoculars and focused them on the magpie. Mum started pulling out papers from the drawer by her bed. She told me she was looking for the letter my dad had started writing to me because it had something important on the back about golden skies. She said: "That's what color his thinking was, Ollie, it was gold. It made him feel blessed and he was glad to be alive."

My heart started beating really fast. I thought she was talking about the puzzle and what it meant to be alive. I said, "Let me see the letter. I need it too," and I stood really close to her while she rummaged through drawers. She said: "I'm sure we'll find it, Ollie. We just need to focus."

The phone rang then and I looked down at the binoculars in my hands. I wondered if she wanted me to use them to find the letter, to focus on the drawers so we could see what was inside. Then I realized that focus has two meanings. One for binoculars, and the other for thinking hard. It was a clue. My dad had given me the binoculars so I would focus on the puzzle.

I got the envelope out of my pocket. I wanted to write it down. I wanted to draw a big tick next to my name because I'd found the special meaning of my present. But Mum was making me speak to Other Grandma on the phone instead. Other Grandma said: "Hello, Ollie, why aren't you at school? Are you poorly?" I didn't answer her because there were two questions at once. She said: "Are you there, Ollie? Can you hear me?"

I saw that on the envelope it said *Pink Vase* next to Other Grandma's name. I remembered seeing that vase on the night we packed up the boxes. It was made of glass, all frilly at the edges, and someone had covered it with bubble wrap. I unwrapped it because I wanted it to fit more neatly into a smaller box. Now I wondered if it might have a double meaning, like the binoculars. I said: "What does it mean, Other Grandma?" but she didn't understand. I said:

"The present my dad gave you. I need to know what you've learned about being alive."

After that, Mum grabbed the phone and took it to her sewing room. I heard her apologizing as she walked away. She only likes it when I say, *How are you, Grandma? I'm fine, thank you.* But if I do that, I'll never find the answer to the puzzle and my thinking will never be gold.

I looked at the envelope again, ready to draw the big tick next to my name. But when I read down the list, I couldn't see my name anywhere. Across the landing I heard Mum say, "We're getting there, Marjorie, we're getting there," but I knew that I wasn't getting anywhere at all.

I picked up my binoculars and looked at the magpie. I saw that it wasn't black and white. There was a dirty gray smudge on its belly.

Rich

RUTH AND NESSA had put up a gazebo beside the apple tree and Rich lay stretched out in its shade. Beside him in the grass was a notebook, a plate of charcoal crackers and a wedge of blue cheese from a local farm. The flesh of this cheese, he reckoned, would feel muscular when he cut into it, vital and firm.

"Who's coming for a taste?" he called. Ruth and Nessa were in the kitchen. He could hear the thump of the cupboard doors, a sudden laugh. "Join me," he called again. "It's going to be amazing."

Ruth came to the back door and stood with her hands on her hips. "You've got work to do," she said. "That cheese is meant to be your reward."

"But maybe a little taste of it will inspire me. Especially if you brought out some cider, and you sat with me and—"

Ruth flicked her hands at him. "It's way too early for that. Get *on!*"

She had told him to write a letter to Ollie. Their son would need something, she said, to return to and consider, some fatherly lessons for life. Rich knew she was right and he wished he'd thought of it himself. He hoped he would compose something Ollie could treasure. Treasuring, after all, was what life should be about. He looked at the cheese on the plate before him, at the sepia-colored rind, textured like bark, and at a path of ants scurrying toward it. How eager they were and how he treasured this opportunity to witness that. It was a gift, he felt, to notice the glory in the world. If he could accomplish his plan to give presents to everyone he loved, maybe they would share it too. His mother, if he gave her a vase, could breathe the soft scents of her roses as she arranged the blooms. She might even stand back and marvel at the way the petals splayed toward the light. Ollie, with his binoculars, could encounter whole new worlds in the branches of the trees, shadows flutter-ing in the crown, fledglings fidgeting in their nests. There was so much to admire on this earth and he was compelled to share this discovery.

He had not felt like this when the cancer was first diag-nosed. The illness had begun as a snickering little buzz in his ear. He'd put it down to exhaustion at first, a long school term with a rowdy class. Then came the nausea. He had dry-retched and writhed with it, numb on one side of his face, fizzing on the other. What he felt then was terror, as black clouds barreled before his eyes.

"I don't like the look of this patch, here," one of the doc-tors had said, after his scan. Rich, shivering in his hospital gown, had clenched his teeth to stop himself retching again. He thought there was something alien inside him, a bullet fired by death, lodged in his flesh. He could imagine only a life of pain before him and he didn't want to live it. Now, though, the terror had receded. He knew it was still there, like an aching scar, or a shadow glimpsed from the corner of the eye, and he knew there was anger in it too, stabs of it, at the thought of Ollie desolate afterward, or Ruth waking in their bed alone. But what seemed more prominent, right now, was Nessa's off-key singing in the kitchen and the sun on the hedge, making tiny darts of silver on the cobwebs.

He sat up and placed his plate of cheese on a chair, tenderly brushing the ants away. Ruth and Ollie were walking down the garden together, Ruth with a stack of bunting in her arms, Ollie with the binoculars bouncing on his chest.

"It's too difficult to focus them, Mum," Ollie said. "And I want to see the magpies."

"Just experiment," Ruth told him. "Turn it one way, and if that doesn't work, turn it the other."

"I hate experimenting. Why don't you just make it right?"

He was wearing yellow shorts, too tight at the top of his thighs. One sock was pulled up to his knee, the other was slumped around his ankle. Rich could just make out a red railway track around his shin, where the elastic had clung too tightly. He pulled the notepad onto his lap. *Dear Ollie,* he wrote. *One day you will be a man.* He thought about how eccentric Ollie would be and wondered whether he would ever learn to use the binoculars. It seemed a shame that he only ever wanted to look at magpies. Down at the river there were kingfishers and herons and he was missing out. But that was the risk of giving presents, he thought. You never knew how they would be understood.

He was considering buying a necklace for Nessa even though he knew it was an odd choice. She had never been one for jewelry—it didn't match the dark jeans she favored, or the men's shirts she wore unbuttoned at the collar, but he was hoping that she would remember a time, early in their friendship, when she had seen this particular necklace and longed for it.

They had camped together at a music festival on a farm and had danced late into every night, sidling into the center of the crowds, grinning and whooping at strangers. On the last day, tired and sunburned, they found themselves wandering through the fields toward the grove dedicated to healing and well-being. They laughed at first at the trinkets on offer there, the dream catchers and crystals, the men with plaited beards offering shamanic journeys and aura realignment, but when Nessa was offered a half-price massage she agreed to give it a go. Rich waited for her, sitting on a hay bale in the shade, and when she returned she was transformed. Gone was the prancing Nessa who'd smirked at him and rolled her eyes as she ducked into the doorway of the yurt. Now she was still and quiet, blinking slowly as she surveyed the field. She stood behind him and cupped her hands around his shoulders.

"You've got to feel this," she said, her voice low. "It's like magic." He remembered the smell of her, woodsmoke from the stove in the yurt, and some sweet citric oil on her skin. He had never had a massage before, and she had probably never given one, but something was ignited in her and he was intrigued. She swiped her hand across his shoulders, then pressed with her thumbs on the hard muscles at either side of his neck. He felt a cramp at first and he wanted to duck away from her grasp, but soon the pain turned to something softer, shifting under his skin. He found himself thinking of his father's shoulders, the thrust of his chest and the tight disapproval lodged in his rigid stance. He let out a tiny gasp and tears sprang to his eyes. Nessa dropped her hands and stepped away.

"I don't know what I'm doing, do I?" she said. "I'm an idiot, sorry." She shuffled up beside him on the hay bale and rolled a cigarette. She told him she'd wept too, in the darkness of the yurt. "There was this hand-spun blanket in there, llama wool or something. I think it's going to shrink now because I've blubbed all over it."

She was trying to make him laugh, but Rich, feeling a kinship with her now, found himself telling her about his father, and how he himself never liked to stand too tall or straight lest this posture somehow engendered his father's attitudes. If it seemed like a strange thing to say she gave no sign of it—she'd understood immediately.

"My sister's the same," she said. "She won't ever cut her hair short in case she turns into our mum and starts hating every man on earth. I'm lucky. I don't take after our mum, not physically anyway. I just inherited the bit that doesn't take any crap." She was keeping him talking so that he wouldn't cry and he was glad of her kindness. "She'd make you laugh, my sister," she went on. "She thinks her body is programmed to turn her into a mad old bat. I reckon, if you both got decent massages, you could escape that feeling once and for all."

It was then that she had spotted the necklace. It was on a nearby stall, spread out on a red velvet cushion. The beads were fat and brown, polished to a shine, tapering around a silver pendant in the shape of a hand with its fingers splayed, filigree patterns cut into the palm.

"It says it all," she cried. "All the magic that massage can do."

They had both run out of money and no amount of bargaining on Nessa's part would persuade the girl in the stall to lower the price. In the months that followed, they had both searched for it in craft markets and hippie shops, but they had never come across it again. These days Nessa rarely offered massages and it seemed like years since he'd heard her wax lyrical about their benefits. He thought she'd laugh if he bought her the necklace now, but he hoped, too, that she'd remember her sense of wonder at the time, and the way their friendship had deepened. He fished his phone from his pocket and typed *hippie hand necklace* into the search bar. Ruth, stringing up bunting on the gazebo, turned to look at him over her shoulder.

"Don't forget that letter, love," she said. He beckoned her over. The necklace had come up instantly, the first result.

"Look at this. It's for Nessa."

Ruth knelt beside him and gasped. "But it's hideous! She won't want that!"

He leaned against her and told her about the festival, how Nessa had claimed afterward that she was going to give up teaching and learn massage instead.

"I remember!" Ruth's face lit up. "She took a course, didn't she, over the summer? Blimey, Rich, that was before we even met!"

The gazebo had the look of a festival tent now, strung with bunting. Nessa leaned out of the kitchen window. "Did I hear someone mention cider? Too early? Who says?"

She appeared moments later with a tray of rattling glasses. Her ponytail swung behind her as she walked toward them, her jeans shushing together at the thighs.

"Why didn't you finish that massage course?" Ruth asked her.

"What course?" she said, placing the tray on the grass. "You don't mean that flaky thing I did way back? What are you on about that for?" The cider fizzed and sparkled as she poured it. "Actually, it was pretty cool. I remember feeling really calm all the time." She gulped from her glass and shuddered as the cider went down. "But I couldn't stand the lentils they kept serving up for lunch."

Ruth laughed. "Were any of the students called Moonbeam?" she asked. Rich ordered the necklace. He listened to them working themselves up into hysteria, imitating the breathy voices of the tutors, describing their floaty scarves and handmade shoes. Something flared at the edge of his vision, a flicker of heat in his left eye. There was an answering flutter at the base of his spine.

"Are you OK?" Ruth asked, as he lowered himself onto the grass. He tried to smile at her. He wanted to work a little more on Ollie's letter, but there was a tightening in his neck now, a needle of pain. He lay down, felt himself dragged into sleep, his brow creasing the page before him.

Nessa

SHE OPENED HER back door and the warm air pushed against her skin. It was ten o'clock in the morning and already the paving stones were humming with heat. The earth around her patio plants looked baked, a ragged gap between the compost and the pot. She listened for voices in the gardens to either side of her, before unwinding the hose and fixing it to the tap. There had been a hosepipe ban for a week but Nessa had no intention of sticking to it. She turned on the water and let it stream into the patio herbs. Bubbles frothed at the edges of the pots. Drops glinted on the spiked leaves of her rosemary, winking naughtily in the sun.

She thought about bucket lists. She decided it was time for Rich to write one, and her job to make him follow it. She had spent the past week researching hospital beds and walkers, and how to apply for funding for specialist nurses to visit at home. Now she needed a break. It was too soon, anyway, to think of him staggering about or dribbling food down his chin and she didn't want to find herself sniveling about it in his presence. Better, she thought, to galvanize him into living the best life possible. She had heard him speculating with Tom and his boyfriend on the pleasures of satin sheets only last week. But it was no good letting him grin about it in his deck chair, she thought. Someone should make damn sure that he bought some. He'd been planning to sleep out in his hammock too, but she knew it wouldn't happen unless she chose a date and strung up the hammock herself. And if she didn't, another precious day of his life would be gone before he knew it, with the same old arguments over Ollie's socks at bedtime, the same stack of washing-up waiting for him in the morning.

She pulled the hose down the patio steps and aimed it into the shrubs along the borders. Rich had at least committed to a trip to his favorite beach today. He had always loved swimming in the sea and she was not going to let him miss out on that. She left the hose running in the center of the lawn, and returned to the house to scribble some ideas on a Post-it.

Sleep in satin sheets.
Hammock under the stars.
Swim in the sea.

There was a bottle of wine on the dresser. She eyed it, wondering if she had time to chill it before leaving for the beach and enough blocks in the freezer to keep it cold. It would mean lugging the cool box down the steps to the sand. She didn't reckon it was worth it without some gourmet food to accompany it, or the plastic wineglasses that Ruth kept for picnics. She piled up packets of crisps and biscuits, pausing every now and then to add to her list.

Eat a truffle.
Drive a Ferrari.

The last one she crossed out. Driving was out of the question now. Many things were: plane journeys, mind-altering drugs, scuba-diving probably. But he might like to be a Ferrari passenger. She thought she could put something out on Facebook, give it the whole sob story, and someone with a swanky car was bound to show up to take him for a spin. But perhaps a spin was not enough. He could be driven to a restaurant with truffles on the menu. Her mind ran on as she gathered some towels and stuffed them into a rucksack.

She was ready to leave within minutes, but it was a different story at Ruth's house. She had to pry Ollie away from his puzzle book and there was a fuss about how many socks he needed to take. Ruth kept them all waiting, piling up unnecessary items—first-aid kits, spare pens, flannels. As if every outing was a disaster waiting to happen, Nessa thought, a source of terror instead of a golden opportunity to celebrate the last months of Rich's life. She couldn't persuade Ruth to join them. She said Nessa needed time with Rich as much as she did and claimed to be looking forward to tidying up the house, while she had the chance.

It was five miles to the coast, the wooded valley opening out into farmland. Steep fields dipped into rocky gullies and clusters of stunted trees. Nessa drove fast along the lanes, spurs of wild rose and honeysuckle pattering against the windows. Ollie shifted on the back seat. She felt his breath, humid against her neck. "Auntie Nessa, I feel sick."

"Oh, not now," she said. "We're nearly there."

Rich turned in his seat and winked at him. "Do you remember that time when you were sick in your welly?" he said. "There was nowhere to pull over and it was the only thing on hand."

"I've never worn wellies since," Ollie replied. "I never will."

"Yeah, but it was pretty clever," Rich went on. "You filled it right to the top and you didn't spill a drop. Then Mum had to hold it all the way to the service station, and if she'd squeezed it even a tiny bit, it would have squirted into her lap." He turned to face the front again, pushing his curls from his forehead. Nessa saw him blink out of the window. "I feel like I've got to remember all those moments now," he said. "I want to gather them up, make sure nothing precious is forgotten."

They had reached the outskirts of the seaside town. It was bungalow country—huge plate-glass windows facing the horizon, pampas grass and palm trees in the gardens. The light was clear, silvery, glancing off the sea.

"Rich, your son's vomit in a welly is hardly a precious moment," Nessa said. "What about your first kiss, or the smell of freshly baked bread?" She swung into the car park and drew up before the rusty railing at the edge of the cliff. "And this! Isn't this wonderful?" She climbed out of the car and danced around it, pulling open the doors. "Did you know, Ollie, that this is the beach where your dad proposed to your mum? And once, when I was swimming, he hid my clothes and forgot where they were because he was drunk. We always have fun when we come here!"

The metal handrail on the cliff-side steps was almost too hot to grasp. They turned their faces to the sea, hoping for a breeze, but none came, and heat pounded off the cliff-face at their backs. Nessa was the first to arrive on the sand. She heaved off the rucksack, pulled off her clothes and trod them into a heap at her feet.

"Last one in's a rotten egg!" She ran whooping into the

sea. The waves came at her, crashes of cold that made her shriek and gasp. She pushed against the current and the chill of the water surged over her. She called to the others to join her as she swam out, but heard no response. When she turned to look, she saw Ollie standing limp on the sand by the rucksack, arms dangling, and Rich still making his way down the steps. He was hunched, both hands on the rail, peering down at his feet, like an old man.

She swam back in toward the shore. She cursed herself for not swimming fast enough. She had been so happy to see him out in the sunshine that she had forgotten about the wobble in his walk, the tremor in his left hand. Now, as she pelted back up the beach, she noticed how crowded it was, how she had to skirt around sun tents and piles of bags, dodge toddlers waddling before her with their buckets.

"You look scared," Ollie announced. "Was there a jellyfish?"

She rushed past him and clambered up the steps, sand stinging her feet.

"Hey, relax." Rich smiled at her. "I'm just nervous because the steps are uneven. I'll be fine in a sec." She saw a quiver in his arm as he clung to the railing. "Mind you," he said, "I don't think I'm up to playing volleyball, or swimming out to the point."

"What about sharks, Auntie Nessa?" Ollie called up. "Did you see a dorsal fin?"

Rich lowered his foot onto the next step and bent his head to whisper. "We went through this with him earlier. No sharks, no jellyfish, no U-boats or piranhas. He thinks there's something terrible coming for him, wherever we go."

"Was it a riptide, then?" Ollie said. "I can tell you what a riptide looks like. I googled it."

"Of course there really is something terrible coming," Rich added. "But we can't get him to talk about that."

At last he was down on the sand. Nessa gestured toward the sea. She saw him gaze toward the horizon, at the gulls as they swooped over the water, the liner, hazy in the distance. But it was the breaking waves she wanted him to see, the promise of the cold and the fizzing thrill of it.

"Come on," she urged, tugging at his hand, but he took a long, deep breath and did not move. Ollie began to whine about ice cream. He wanted vanilla, he said, and went into excruciating detail over the sauces he liked and the sprinkles he hated. He had to have one now, he whined, because he was hot.

"Of course you're hot!" Nessa ratcheted her voice up to teaching volume and pulled on Rich's arm. "You're both supposed to be cooling in the sea! That's the whole point!"

Rich laughed, but still he did not move. "Can't I have an ice cream?" he said, winking at Ollie. "Can't I have a cheese-flavored one? A Stilton ninety-nine with Wensleydale sauce?" Ollie roared with disgust. Nessa nearly stamped her foot. But she ran instead. She pounded down to the sea. When at last he followed she cried out with relief.

They swam out together slowly. Once he was buoyant in the water, all signs of his illness were gone and they turned, treading water, to gaze at the red cliff glowing in the sun, at Ollie sitting in the sand, unrolling his socks from his shins.

"This is the life," Rich said.

"Mission accomplished," she replied, and slapped her hand down on the water so a spray of silver drops rained down on their faces.

Later, when their skin was cool and tingling, when they'd finally had ice creams, and Rich had wiped between Ollie's toes with the flannel and helped him into his fourth pair of socks, they rested at last, lying back against their rucksacks with their legs stretched out before them. Ollie began to pile sand around Rich's feet. He tutted and scowled whenever Rich wiggled his toes.

"You're not allowed to worry about the future," Nessa told Rich. "You know you can trust me, don't you, to keep everything going?"

Rich scanned the horizon. "It'll keep on going anyway," he said. "That's the hardest thing, you know. Being the only one in this situation who really won't keep going."

Nessa swallowed. She watched Ollie shoveling sand onto to Rich's shins and she gestured weakly toward him. "But what about Ruth?" she said. "Don't you want to know that I'll look after her?"

"Not really," Rich said. "I don't think you'll need to."

Nessa was stung. This was not how the conversation was supposed to go. She had hoped Rich would turn to her at this point, clap out a high five, call her his right-hand man. But it was Ruth he was praising now.

"She's more than capable," he said. "She'll find her way through in the end."

Nessa looked away. He doesn't remember, she thought, how Ruth had been festering in Black Coombe Cottage when he first met her, how they'd had to drag her away from Angran's clutches. They had both decided, hadn't they, to apply for jobs in Devon schools, not just so they could have fun together, but because they worked so well as a team to keep Ruth from despair?

She watched Ollie smoothing the mound over Rich's feet, slapping at every crack in the sand. Something about the panic in his hands made her squirm. Her own hands were similar to Ruth's, veined and large-knuckled, but where Ruth's were deft and accurate, hers, as she looked down at them now, seemed uncouth. She spent too much time grabbing at people, she thought, yanking them about. Even on the beach today, she could not let Rich rest, but had tugged at him, then urged him into the sea.

Images came to her from the massage course she had taken all those years ago. There, her hands had moved more slowly over her patients. She had paused as she pressed the soft pads of her palms against their skin. And she had cried too, quite inexplicably, when she gave her first full-length treatment. She had sensed a loosening in the muscles of her patient and felt, for a moment, like a true expert as the knot beneath her fingers melted into something more tender. The tears had come a moment later and they would not stop. The tutors told her it was normal, hugged her and let her rest for the afternoon in a private room. But she could not return to face them the following day. She cut her losses and gave up on the course.

Now she stood up and began gathering the water bottles and rumpled towels.

"Home time," she announced. She found a pair of Ollie's socks slumped into sandy nests and tossed them at Rich's belly. He kicked in surprise and Ollie bellowed as his sand hill burst open.

"Auntie Nessa! You've wrecked it!"

"I'll wreck you in a minute. Come on, folks. Time to get moving."

She herded them up the steps and into the sweltering car.

Ruth was waiting at the front door when they returned to the house and she looked exhausted. Nessa peered past her into the hall, hoping to see everything tidy and bright at last, but the stack of empty envelopes and bills was still piled up on the table. Ruth's sewing box lay on its side beside it, a tangle of threads and cotton reels spilling onto the papers.

"Mum came by while you were out," Ruth said, rubbing her eyes.

"What did she want?"

"Lunch, I think. And she was still going on about moving us into Black Coombe Cottage when Rich is gone." Nessa went to grasp her arm but thought better of it, and shook her head instead. "I know, I know," Ruth said, "but it might be best for Ollie."

"If you move back into that stinking hole, I'll never speak to you again."

She turned away and looked back at Rich, who was coaxing Ollie out of the car. Steroids had given his face a ruddy tone and he looked like a jolly farmer in a children's book. He grinned at Ollie and dangled three pairs of sandy socks between his fingers.

"Well, that's one thing ticked off your bucket list," she called to him. "I'll have to get you moving on some more."

"Oh, I don't need a bucket list," Rich said, yawning. "All this is good enough for me."

She stalked back to her car before anyone saw how his words had hurt her. When she got home, she discovered she'd left the hose running all day. She thought she was seeing the garden through tears at first, the way it glistened in the dusk. Then she saw the hose snaking down the patio steps. She heard it too, the hiss and gurgle in the rubber tube as it flowed into the borders and rippled against the walls. The lawn was a pond and the grass lay flat and limp beneath the surface. She cried harder then. Not just for Rich, and her thwarted efforts to give him the best life possible, but for her garden too. She didn't know if by the end of the summer she would have the only green lawn on the street, or if it would be a churned-up mess of dead grass and clotted mud.

Ollie

WE WERE SUPPOSED to have a party for my dad after he died, but no one talks about that anymore. They only talk about all the days I've missed at school and whether Mum can manage on her own. Auntie Nessa keeps coming by and telling her to get help, but I need help, too, so I've been asking her about the puzzle.

My dad bought her a necklace. It had fat brown beads and a silver hand with patterns all over the palm. I remember winding the bubble wrap around it when we were packing the presents to send through the post. Round and round I wound it so the rustling noise drowned out their stupid conversation about his life being too short. It made a fat, crinkly package and I stuffed it into a nice big box.

I asked Auntie Nessa if she knew what a necklace meant and she said: "What? I don't know what you're on about." She was pulling the sheets off Mum's bed and a pair of sewing scissors thumped to the floor.

I said: "We're supposed to find out what it means to be alive, to learn it from my dad."

She threw a pillow onto the bed and started laughing. I hadn't asked a funny question and she didn't give a funny answer, but she kept on laughing anyway and saying she knew all about being alive. She said: "What you've got to do, Ollie, is grab life with both hands. Hold on tight to every special moment."

That was a perfect answer for a necklace with a silver hand on it. I ran to my room and wrote it down on the envelope. With a good answer like that, I thought, I'd be able to solve the rest of the puzzle at last.

But I didn't get a chance to think about it much, because Auntie Nessa came into my room. She said: "Oi, you, shoes on, now. We're getting out of the house, whether you like it or not."

Rich

"I'M GOING TO buy Angran a shawl," he said to Ruth, as they drove back from a radiotherapy appointment. They were heading for Black Coombe Cottage, where Angran had been looking after Ollie. She had asked them to buy bread and now, after a trip to the delicatessen in town, their shopping bags bulged with tubs of pâté, olives and slices of artisan cheese. How giddy they had been in the shop, staring down at the stoneware bowls of artichokes and tabbouleh, and how awed they had been by the beautiful shaven-headed Spanish woman at the counter. It was all so different from the musty-smelling village shop, with its tins of fruit and dog-eared greeting cards; afterward, in the throng of people and traffic in the street, they had laughed at themselves for being thrilled.

Now, as they turned off the valley road and took the grassy track to the cottage, Ruth tapped Rich's knee with her finger. "If you're still thinking of buying all those presents," she said, "you'd better get a move on." From his diary he fished out the envelope where he'd scribbled down his first ideas. He leaned it against his lap and added *Shawl* to the list, the letters wobbling as the car rattled over the pitted surface of the track.

"Don't worry," he said. "I'm working on it."

It was true, though, that he hadn't made as much progress with any of his plans as he'd hoped. There had been too many hospital appointments and blood tests, too many long phone calls with old friends and too many tired evenings when his jaw ached and his eyes seemed dry in their sockets. In a spirit of determination he had visited his parents, only two days ago, intending to tackle the argument over the pencils. He'd made the journey alone, by train, in the hope of speaking freely without stirring up Ollie's fury or inciting Ruth's if she discovered how spineless he had been.

"It's not insubordination when he screams like that," he had planned to say to Gerald. "He's had it by then. Think of it as man down." But when he arrived at the house, breathed in the old familiar smell of cut flowers and furniture polish, saw the ironed-in folds of his father's handkerchief as he dabbed his eyes, he quailed.

"Hay fever, you know," Gerald had said. "Dreadfully itchy eyes. There must be some new foreign crop in the fields because I've never had it before."

Now Ruth drew up outside the cottage. "Do you really think she'd like a shawl?" she said, helping him out of the passenger seat. They could hear Angran splitting logs in the garden. Each blow of the axe echoed against the rock, a hiccup in the air. "I can't see her wrapping herself up in it," she went on. "She doesn't sit still for long enough." They walked across the lawn. Ollie was sitting at the picnic table with a puzzle book while Angran worked. She caught sight of them, sank the axe into the chopping block and wiped her hands on the pockets of her shorts.

"You've got the bread? I've made soup. It'll be a useless

meal if you forgot." Ruth handed her the loaf. "White?" Angran scoffed. "It'll have to do."

She walked to the house. Ruth joined Ollie at the picnic table, and Rich followed her, shuffling himself along the bench so the table rocked and creaked.

"Angran was swearing when she made that soup," Ollie said. "I don't want to eat it."

"You'll have to have one mouthful," Ruth told him. "If you don't make an effort she'll think you're not grateful."

"But I'm not grateful. I've never liked Angran's soup."

Rich looked away, avoiding Ruth's eye. He wanted to say, *No one does,* and he wanted to hear the sudden bright spurt of her laughter. But Angran was already advancing toward them with a tray of steaming bowls, and he knew that if she heard Ruth's laugh she would falter. He could imagine already the way her mouth would droop, her shoulders curving inward to form a protective shadow around her heart. He understood that Ruth and Nessa were compelled to make jokes about her, that it was a kind of defense against the frowns and criticisms, but he was aware that his own life was limited now: he didn't want to contaminate it with unkindness. He rose to his feet as she approached and held out his hands for the tray.

"Don't be silly," she said. "I can manage on my own."

She set the bowls before them and from the rising steam came the composty tang of old wooden spoons.

"Mmm, thanks, Mum," Ruth said. She lifted her spoon and widened her eyes at Ollie, but his hands were clasped between his knees. Rich looked into his bowl and saw islands of oil floating on the surface, slices of onion drifting among them, charred at the edges and trailing brown strings in their wake. The kind thing to do, he thought, would be to eat this soup, but he couldn't face it. If his life was limited, so, too, were the number of meals he had left to enjoy. He didn't want to waste them on burned stuff, and he didn't want Ruth to do that, or Angran either.

"I'll fetch the salt," he said, rising from the table. He was thinking of the olives they had bought, the smoked mackerel pâté and artichoke hearts to be saved for tomorrow. He thought of the way the flavors would burgeon on his tongue, of the soft slide of the pâté against his palate. If he laid all this on the table now, with a round of melba toast made from the last of the loaf, surely he'd be bringing them happiness to share. They could sit longer in the evening sun, he reckoned, listening to the birdsong spring up in the woods, watching the roses, pale against the tangled hedge, grow luminous in the dusk.

"Why are you taking your bowl?" Angran called as he made his way to the kitchen. He tipped the soup into the sink, shuddering as the onions turned slowly around the plughole. Ruth followed him in.

"What's going on? You're not feeling sick?" She spotted the steam rising from the sink. "My God, you threw it away! You know she hates wasting food." She began prodding at the onion slices and he saw that she was genuinely afraid, her breath coming in flutters, eyes darting to the window. It always pained him to see this. His own mother had not been perfect, too anxious to keep him clean, or quiet when Gerald was at home, but he had always felt sure of her kindness and her soft, yielding presence. To have lived with this fear was unimaginable to him, and he could not believe that Angran intended it. When thought of Ruth's future without him, he wished there was something he could do to free her from the stranglehold of this history.

"Don't you think the artichokes will cheer her up?" he said, cutting into the loaf. "All she wants is for everything to be all right."

Ruth dried her hands and began rubbing at her face. "Yes, but it *has* to be all right," she said, and she started on the complaint he knew almost by heart, that she and Nessa were not allowed to cry as children, that any sign of upset sent Angran running off to The Ravages in the night. "It never occurred to her to comfort us," she went on. "I don't think she knows how."

Rich knew there was something he could tell her to refute this view, but he had never dared. If he revealed that she had come running the day that Gerald had started bawling at Ollie, that she had stood between them and coaxed Ollie back into the house, Ruth would discover that he'd failed to rescue Ollie from that argument himself. So he'd never told her about the gentle tones of Angran's voice as she ushered Ollie away, or that just for a moment it had looked as if Angran put her arm around Ollie's shoulders. He knew it couldn't be true, that Ollie would never have tolerated her touch, but in his memory there was a real sense that Ollie had accepted the embrace, as if there were an invisible shawl around them both.

He toasted the bread and then worked a knife through the center of each slice.

"Oh, melba toast," Ruth said. "You're the best, Rich. Ollie's going to love it." But Rich could not look at the soft, split-open insides. His belly churned and he couldn't tell if it was a wave of sadness and remorse, or just the usual nausea that washed over him every day. He shoved them hastily under the grill.

Ollie clapped his hands when they brought the wafers to the table.

"Can I have the curliest bits? Is there hummus, Dad, to dip it in?" He reached for the shopping bag and rooted through it, holding each tub above his head like a trophy as he drew them out.

Angran glared. "The expense," she said, frowning. "And the waste, when I'd already provided an adequate meal." She turned her attention to the toast. "And now there'll be nothing for my breakfast in the morning. Why can't you look ahead?"

Ruth began to apologize, but Rich interrupted her. "I don't like to look ahead, Angran," he said, setting the jar of pâté on her plate, dipping a curl of toast into it and angling it toward her. "It's kind of painful for me, these days."

She turned away. She spent some time wiping her glasses on her T-shirt, scrubbing at them. When she was finished she sighed, lifted the toast from the jar and pushed it into her mouth.

Later, when all the pots were scraped clean and they were dabbing at crumbs with their fingertips, Angran offered to bring out coffee. Rich leaned his head on Ruth's shoulder.

"You see," he said, watching her go. "We're forgiven."

Ruth put up her hand to stroke his hair. "I still can't understand why you think she'd like a shawl."

He couldn't explain why he had hit upon this gift for her. He didn't want to remind anyone of the row with Gerald. Besides, there were other reasons behind it, too. Sometimes he felt lonely. The end of his life was hurtling toward him and there was so much he wanted to enjoy: Ollie's rare laughter, the heat of Ruth's hand against his scalp. But sometimes it felt as if no one could share it with him. They were caught on the barbs of their own long lives ahead of them, and Angran, with her sharp elbows, was at the center of it all. She needed tenderness, he thought, and he sensed that a soft shawl in muted colors might be comforting for her. If she would only snuggle into the sweetness of life, all that love, trapped inside her, could flow out.

"Oh, I don't know," he said, reaching his arm around Ruth's waist, feeling her hot and nervy against him. "I thought a shawl would be like a hug or something. And everyone needs a hug from time to time."

Ollie looked toward him, scowling. "I don't. I hate hugs."

"She'll think you mean she's an old granny," Ruth said.

Ollie looked up at the house where Angran's boots were ringing on the flagged kitchen floor. "Well, she is old," he said. "And she's a granny. She's mine."

Angran

A CROW WAS cawing in the woods. The sound of it made her tired. It made her think of the days, way back, when she first moved to the cottage and the only voices she heard were those of her whining children and the goading of the crows. Now, standing at her kitchen door, picking specks of muesli from her teeth, she wished there were robins in her garden instead, cocking their heads at her and blinking their bright eyes. She didn't like the way crows fidgeted. She was quite sure that this one would be hunched somewhere in the woods, shuffling sideways and ducking its beak beneath its wing; she was glad she couldn't see it.

She looked out toward the trees and listened for voices on the paths. Ruth, Nessa and Ollie would be arriving soon and they'd promised to bring lunch. Rich's parents were visiting for the day and Ruth had suggested they should spend some time alone with him. Angran thought that really it was an excuse for Ruth to avoid them, that she was hoping for some refuge at Black Coombe Cottage. But if this place was to be a sanctuary, she thought, they should hold off for an hour or two, at least until the crow had ceased its pestering and the sun had risen above the rock and flooded the garden with light.

It had been her life's work to make this cottage into a haven. She had inherited it from an ancient aunt at a time when she was desperate for stability. No one expected her to move in: the walls were running with water and the garden was a tangle of brambles right up to the rock. For Angran it was her salvation. She had been living with John in a house they shared with three other friends, and for a year or two she had loved the life of parties and late-night sing-alongs after the pubs had closed. With just one child, it had been easy enough to move the ashtrays and empty wine bottles out of reach, to laugh, even, at Nessa's chubby hands on a box of matches, but with two children it was a strain. John pressed his fingers to his eyes sometimes, or cursed, especially if they cried in the early mornings or if Angran begged him not to practice his guitar when they needed to nap.

"I'm going traveling," he told her one day. "I'm going to busk my way around the world. Come if you like. Our kids can run free."

She had fled to the cottage instead. At first she'd thought that if she made it beautiful there—a log fire crackling in the hearth, no cot shoved up against the bed, no strings of drying nappies above their heads—he would return. There had been a wrought-iron garden gate in those days, and she found herself listening for the rattle of it against the stone pillars. On the day she received a card from Australia, she unscrewed the gate from its hinges, carried it to the edge of the woods and used it to weigh down the lid of her compost heap.

"Don't think about that," she said to herself now. "Irrelevant."

She rubbed at the goose pimples on her arms. She had begun to shiver, listening to the crows in the woods. There were more of them now, squabbling and scolding as they thrashed about in the canopy. The source of their ire, she saw, was a buzzard wheeling high above the rock. They made jabbing little flights toward it, beating their ragged wings against the sky. The buzzard's cry was high and plaintive, like a baby's.

"Sledgehammer," she said, and began to march across the lawn to the shed. A plan was taking shape in her mind. It was no good worrying about the garden, and whether it would be sunny when the family arrived. There were other ways to welcome them.

She took the sledgehammer to her spare room, and began bashing at the alcove wall. She was going to make a connecting door between this room and the one behind. That way, when Ruth and Ollie moved in, and when Ollie cried in the night, Ruth could reach him easily. It was unbearable, the thought of him calling for Rich and pummeling his mattress in the dark, but Angran wanted Ruth to know that she was prepared for it. It would be soothing for Ruth, she was sure, if she arrived today to find her mother laboring away on her behalf, dust in the air, muscles straining at the sleeves of her T-shirt.

Each time she struck the wall, her wrists jolted with the kickback and an ache thrummed along the sinews of her arms. But she did not allow herself to pause. Over and over she pounded until cracks began to snake across the plaster and grit rattled to the floor. No child, she thought, should suffer for the loss of a father on her watch. It had been bad enough when Ruth and Nessa were little, seeing them yearn for a man who was never coming back. Often, the sight of them standing in their limp little nighties was too much for her. She never meant to leave them on their own, but she was afraid that she would start whimpering herself. She ran out of the house so they wouldn't have to witness it. She was down the garden in what seemed like two strides and over the broken wall. Nessa came howling after her more often than not, while Ruth stood on the lawn with her thumb in her mouth. Angran never let them follow her. She had to keep them safe. The paths were slippery. Too easy for their feet to snag on the roots of the trees, to slip on the mud and rocks. They didn't know where the precipices were. But she did. She had stood by them often enough, raging about John while the wind roared overhead in the trees.

Later, when she was back in bed, the sheets streaked with mud, they'd come to find her.

"Where did you go, Mummy? Did you go to The Ravages?"

"I didn't go anywhere," she told them. She didn't want them to know how close she had brought herself to the crashing water, how she'd had to clench her fists and force herself home; she tried to reassure them. "I wanted some fresh air, that's all. But I was here all along."

Now, as the wall began to split beneath her hammer, she hoped she would have a second chance with Ollie. This connecting door was her promise to him that he would never cry alone. She urged herself onward as her shoulders burned and dust clouded in her face.

Downstairs the latch clattered on the front door.

"What the hell?" Nessa called, as she and Ollie came

clumping up the stairs. "That'd better not be a supporting wall or the whole place is going to come down."

"Of course it's not. I know what I'm doing."

Ollie stepped into the room and recoiled. "Your hair is hideous!"

She put her hand to her scalp and felt the dust there, thick and matted in the heat. "It's only stuff from the walls. I'm making a door for when you move in with your mum."

"I don't want to move in." He poked with his toe at the grit on the floorboards. "I'll get my socks dirty."

Angran saw that Nessa was smirking. "What?" she snapped.

"You're mad! You haven't even asked Ruth if she wants to come." She beckoned Ollie away and Angran heard her shouting on the stairs. "She thinks you're moving in, Ruth. You'd better talk to her before she starts on a five-story extension."

Angran turned and swung the hammer at the gash in the wall. Her arms were trembling, aching now, in the fold of her elbow, but she couldn't think what else to do. She could hear Ruth and Nessa laughing in the kitchen below and each blow of the hammer seemed to set off more sniggering. She knew they wouldn't share the joke: they never had. All too often she would glance up from a meal to see them shaking with suppressed laughter, Nessa with her cheeks mottled, Ruth leaking tears at the corners of her eyes. She couldn't imagine what might be so funny. She had never been the sort of mother who disapproved of swear words or elbows on the table. True, there had been fierce arguments when they were teenagers—she had smashed almost every jug and vase in the house—but she had granted her daughters freedom, too. She had let them write poems directly onto the walls of their bedrooms, make dresses from the sitting-room curtains. Anything to keep them from the misery of her own repressed childhood. But they had never thanked her for that, or for any of the efforts she made to keep unhappiness at bay.

From the foot of the stairs she heard Ruth calling her for lunch.

"Not hungry!" she yelled, and struck the wall again.

"Can you stop the banging, then?" Ruth went on. "All the noise—it's one of those days when Ollie gets jumpy."

"No, it's NOT!" Ollie's voice echoed along the passageway. Angran swung the hammer once more and this time she broke through, skidding on the debris at her feet as she lurched toward the jagged hole.

"Please, Mum, it's so loud!"

"Well, it's bound to be, isn't it? This is a huge undertaking." She squinted through the gap in the wall. Glimpsed from this new angle, the room behind looked still and posed, as if no one had ever truly lived there.

"Mum, you do know, don't you," Ruth called up, "that I've never said I want to move in?" Down in the kitchen something clattered, a chair kicked over perhaps, skidding across the stone floor. Then there were footsteps in the passageway, and Ollie came shrieking to the foot of the stairs.

"Why are you shouting? Shut up!" The front door slammed. "Shall I go after him?" Nessa cried.

Angran heard Ruth groan. "No, I will. Look, Mum, I can't have this discussion now."

Angran kicked the rubble at her feet. She didn't see the point in having the discussion at all. There wasn't time. Better for Ruth to start looking into letting agents and packing up the house. She'd be in no fit state to do all that when Rich was gone. But she knew that no one else would agree. She let the hammer fall to the floor and picked her way to the bed. Dust had settled over the coverlet, accentuating the creases as if it were sharply shadowed. She lay down. All she wanted was to gather her children around her and save them from pain. But now, hearing Ruth's cries in the garden, Ollie's too, she couldn't see how she would ever make them understand.

She woke an hour later, when a vehicle drew up outside the house. She went to the window and saw Marjorie standing at the car door, watching over Rich as he clambered out. Through the sheen of the windscreen she could just make out Gerald in the passenger seat, the glow of his pink forehead, the oval of his open mouth.

"What if he wakes up?" Marjorie said, her voice clear in the well of the driveway. "He'll be frightened if he doesn't know where he is."

Rich staggered a little and grasped at the roof of the car. "He won't, Mum. He's flat out. Come on, you haven't seen Ollie for ages. Tell me if you think he's grown."

"He'd better not wake up," Angran muttered. "Or he'll have me to answer to."

She went down to the kitchen and swilled out her mouth beneath the tap. What sort of person, she thought, uses a word like *defective* to describe a child like Ollie? And what sort of father does not defend his son, but stands there with hands dangling at his sides, talking about *wavering*? She filled the kettle and watched Rich and Marjorie make their way across the lawn to the others, who were gathered at the picnic table. She couldn't tell if Rich was supporting Marjorie as she wobbled in her heels on the grass, or if she was steadying him: there was a lurch to his gait that had not been there two days ago. They were calling to Ollie, trying to get him to look up from his puzzle book, and their voices reverberated against the rock. Angran noticed a tremor in Marjorie's cooing cry, as if she were holding back tears.

"Poor woman," she said to herself. "Being kept from her grandson." Here at last was her chance. No one would doubt her love for her family if she sorted out this mess once and for all. She loaded a tea tray and marched across the garden, dust puffing from the legs of her shorts.

"Well," she said, clapping the tray onto the picnic table so that the tea slopped into the sugar bowl. "Time for a frank discussion, don't you think?"

Her question went ignored. Ollie yelped as the cups clacked together on the tray and leaped away from the table, teeth bared.

"My ears, Angran. You've hurt my ears." He bolted across the lawn, clenching his fists, bashing them against the sides of his head. Rich staggered toward him.

"Don't crowd him," Ruth cried, but Nessa was up now, holding Rich by the arm to steady him. "I told you he was sensitive today," Ruth said, rising to her feet.

"Don't blame me," Angran called after her, "I'm doing this for him!"

She found herself alone with Marjorie and busied herself with the tea things, lifting the lid of the pot and peering into the murky pool inside. The crows were back. There were three of them now, strutting about on the roof, thrusting their heads forward as they cawed.

"Your roses are very lovely," Marjorie ventured. "Do they last well in a vase?"

"I wouldn't know," Angran replied. She had run out of love. All day she had been pushing help and kindness at her family, but every offer had been thwarted. Now she was spent. Marjorie fussed with a little bow at the collar of her blouse and Angran narrowed her eyes. She didn't like the way she was sneaking behind Gerald's back to be here. Clearly the woman had not attempted to sort out this row herself, or confront Gerald about the terrible things he'd said to Ollie. Who was to know, in that case, that she didn't secretly agree with him? Angran wanted her gone—off the property—and not to return until she had apologized, she and her husband both. "I don't cut my roses just to make things pretty for the house," she said. "I think it's wasteful."

Marjorie drew back. "Really? I thought it encouraged more blooms."

"But think of the cut ones, dying and shriveling up," Angran replied. Then she shivered again. She had noticed that her voice was much louder than Marjorie's, but it came back to her, echoing from the rock, puny and forlorn.

Ollie

MY DAD DIED. Auntie Nessa told me we have to grab life with both hands and then we went for a walk. When we came back it was Angran who was grabbing things. She emptied our shelves and took everything to Black Coombe Cottage. So now we live there and Angran drives me to school instead of the taxi. I don't have to listen to Jack anymore, I have to listen to Angran instead. She swears if we meet any cars in the lane and she makes the other drivers reverse into the gateways. Mum's always in bed when I get home. Angran says I have to stay downstairs and give her some peace and quiet, but Mum calls me into her room anyway. She says: "Oh, Ollie, what have I done?"

Sometimes she says that to Auntie Nessa and she says: "You've made your bed, and now you've got to lie in it." I think that's a stupid turn of phrase to use on my mum because she lies in her bed all the time anyway.

Everything's changed, but if I complain, Auntie Nessa says: "No need to moan at me, young man. I'm trying to make things better."

It makes my head fizz when she says that and I have to press my hands to my ears. Only my dad could make things better. If we got invited to a party everyone would cheer when he arrived. Geoff would be the loudest and he'd say: "Now you're here, Rich, this party just got better."

He's dead now. No one can make it better.

I'm working hard on the puzzle. Grandpa phoned and I asked him about the boat picture. He just said what he always does now. He said: "Nothing prepares you to see your own son dead."

Grandpa never used to phone. He stopped after I snapped those pencils. I don't know why he's started phoning again, but when I talk to him he always says the same thing: "Nothing prepares you to see your own son dead."

I think it might be a clue, but I can't work out what it means. I just keep thinking of the night we packed up all the presents. The picture had thick and crusty paint on top of the waves, and I remember how it slid so neatly into the box that I'd selected for it. My dad was going to send it off in a bigger box, but I could see that the one he'd chosen for the candles was exactly the right size. Seeing it fit so perfectly gave me the same neat feeling that I get when I finish a sudoku. I loved it and I wanted to feel it again.

I wrote down Grandpa's answer, *Nothing prepares you*, on my envelope last night, but it didn't get me any further with the puzzle. My pen kept snagging on the creases in the paper. Sometimes if I stare at a killer sudoku the solution just comes to me like magic. I lay on my bed and stared at the envelope, but no magic happened. I felt a bit sick.

Rich

FOR HIS FATHER, he decided on a painting of a boat. It was a delight for him now, choosing the gifts, thinking of the moment when people would open them and understand that they were loved. Ruth was worried that a boat would be too sad. She knew that Rich used to cry when Gerald was at sea. He used to ask why he and Mummy couldn't join him on the big gray ship, helping with the cooking and the making of the beds. And she knew, too, that Gerald had been disappointed that Rich did not join the Navy after school, but chose to go to teaching college instead.

"I don't mind if things are sad," Rich said, as he scrolled through an online gallery of nautical art. Every day there were moments that made him ache at the back of his throat: his colleague Tom visiting, now that the term had started, bringing a stack of cards from the class of ten-year-olds he had taught last year; Ollie fumbling with his schoolbag in the mornings, reluctant to leave, Rich guessed, in case he returned to find his father gone. Rich quailed at these moments, but there was a sweetness to them, too, a rush of gratitude for the love that had wrought them.

"But your dad might mind," Ruth said, coming to stand

beside his chair. "You don't want to compromise his stiff upper lip."

Rich paused on a painting of a galleon in a storm. Clouds shadowed the horizon and the waves were topped with froth. "Well, I am going to die, you know," he said. "He's bound to feel something."

All the same, Rich wondered if he should choose a picture of a calmer sea. He considered a sunset, ripples shining red and gold, and he remembered the glorious sensation in his dream that he was soaring away from every petty concern. Better that for Gerald, he thought, than raging waters.

He looked again at the galleon in the storm. The prow was dipping into the gulf between the waves, and for a moment he felt it, the sensation of the deck tipping beneath him. He tried to look away, but the room lurched as he swung his head. The floor had become an escalator, sliding steeply downward, blurred. He grabbed at Ruth and found himself calling for Ollie.

"Where is he? Where has he gone?"

Ruth put her hands to his face. "He's upstairs, in bed, Rich. What's going on?"

He could not bear the touch of her palm on his cheek, the heat of it, the pressure on his jaw.

"Rich," she whispered, a quiver in her breath. "Something's wrong. Do we need to get you to the hospital?"

He pushed her away. Her hand slipped from his face and he felt the air move over his skin. He sat for a moment, panting, as the room fell still. His fists were clenched. He loosened them and stared down at the tiny hairs glinting on his knuckles.

"I'm fine," he said, though his tongue felt stiff in his mouth. "I just need to lie down."

Ruth guided him to bed and placed a cool wet cloth across his brow. He thought again of the galleon on the squally sea. He remembered hiding in his parents' wardrobe during a thunderstorm. Gerald's uniform, hanging dark and stiff, had scraped against his face and the buttons on the cuffs were cold. But his father's hands were warm when he came to find him.

"But a storm could drown you, Daddy," Rich had said, his mouth against his father's belly. "What about hundred-foot waves?"

"I'm man enough for that," Gerald had replied. "And one day, you will be too." Well, now they were weathering a different sort of storm and manliness was not the answer. Gerald had not been proud of Rich for hiding from the thunder, but he had come to find him anyway. Rich wanted him to remember that, and to remember, too, how he pulled him from the darkness into his arms.

Gerald

IT WAS BAD enough, Gerald thought, hearing these distant voices all day long and half the night, these voices that sounded as if they were bubbling up from the bottom of some dark lagoon, without having blots on the periphery of his vision. For half an hour now, as he took tea on the patio, brown blobs had been drifting by, swelling and shrinking as they passed. Probably a sign of something bad. One of those damned things in the brain, a . . . What was it?

A voice burbled in his left ear. "Annual apparitions of organisms." He struck the side of his head with his palm, trying to bash it out. The blobs, he thought, were like an invasion. An army with an inexhaustible supply of re-inforcements. *Aneurysm*. That was the word. He was having an *aneurysm* in his brain. He hoped it would get on with its job. You weren't supposed to outlive your children.

Marjorie came onto the patio. She was a yellow blur in her summer dress. "Richard's just emailed," she said, waving her hand as a brown blob rolled past. "I've printed out a photo. Put on your glasses or you won't see a thing."

He didn't bother and he was glad of it. He could just

make out Richard leaning on Ruth's arm, like a drunkard. That was the last thing he wanted to see, his own son wobbling about like he'd never found his sea legs. He didn't need glasses to see that one of Richard's shoulders was higher than the other and that his face was puffed up and red. A sound came out of Gerald's mouth. It was a whimper, the sound of a dog at the vet, and he hoped that Marjorie hadn't heard.

"I know, darling," she said, placing her hand on his arm.

She didn't know, Gerald thought. It was all right for her to make a sound like that. It was expected from the women. He did it and he looked a damn fool. The voices surged in his ears: "Hobble-de-hoy, hobble-de-hoy."

"But he looks happy, doesn't he?" Marjorie said. "Apparently we'll be receiving some parcels soon, but he wouldn't say what will be in them." She waved her arms about again, whirling them through the brown blobs. "Shall I bring you some tea? You look . . ."

The burbles in his ears drowned out the rest of her words. He thought there was something about flying spiders, but the chances were he'd misheard. Either that or he was going gaga.

When she was gone, he steeled himself and looked at the photo with his glasses on. Ruth was grasping Richard's left arm. Her dress was too bright and her hair unkempt. Ollie was on his right, a wide gap between them. His face, as ever, was sour, eyes cast down. At least Richard had never been like that. Eager, he'd been, playing racing games or hide-and-seek. Too eager, really, too quick to cry. Result was he'd turned into one of those liberal types. Too lenient, especially with that boy of his. Perhaps it was just as well he hadn't followed in his father's footsteps to the naval college at Dartmouth: might have flunked it if he had.

Gerald wondered who had taken the photo. Must have been the ill-tempered mother-in-law in the shorts. She seemed to crop up at every visit, with her dirty nails and her . . . her damn . . . The word was gone and he hoped it wouldn't return. Didn't want to think about the woman anyway. Bad enough he'd have to face her and those bohemians at the funeral. Didn't want to face anyone. He'd rather be gaga, an old man blubbing at the graveside, thinking it was his father in the coffin, shot down in the war.

"Oh, Gerald, let me get you a hanky," Marjorie said, as she returned to the patio with a tea tray to set beside him on the wrought-iron table.

"No need," he said, but there was a wobble in his voice.

He pictured himself in a nursing home, tartan blanket over his knees, a nurse with a solid bosom and an upside-down watch, wiping dribbles of gruel from his chin. He knew Marjorie had been looking at homes on the internet. He wasn't a fool. He'd heard her whispering about it with Richard, too. Still, it was better to sit in a home than to sit in a church with that scruffy family wailing in the pews. They would wail at the funeral, he was sure of it, or throw themselves onto the coffin. They were just the type. Doolally, the lot of them.

"Down into the ditch," said a voice. Gerald tried to bat it away. If he had to hear a voice at all he wanted it to be Richard's, even if he did speak with his mouth full half the time.

One of the blobs flew past. Now, though, with his glasses

on, he saw that it wasn't a blob. More of a tangle. His focus sharpened and he realized it was an insect. The air was speckled with them. Floppy great things whose name wouldn't come to him. A swarm of . . . The white walls of the house were flecked all over. Hundreds of them drifting by, silent as the gap in his mind where the word should have been. With their translucent wings and their dangling legs they looked like parachutes in a stealth landing. A new voice came through, this one full of static, like a command over a radio. "Keep the landing party moving. Reinforcements on the way." *Crane flies.* That was their name. Damn daddy longlegs. He knew where they were coming from too. Those fool artists on the far side of the lane. Bohemians they were. They'd never kept control of their lawns and now there was an invasion. He stood up. Time to have words. Fed up with their rusty old van in the lane and their orange front door.

The static in his ears crackled again. Richard's voice came through. "Try to be more wobbly." He couldn't mistake it. He heard the low tones, the soft laugh behind it. He stopped walking and cupped his hands to his ears to hear it again.

"More wobbly. Just wobble and waver." He'd been longing to hear Richard's voice for days, but he should have known his mind would mangle it to poppycock, a preposterous command to an army of flies.

"But why should we be wobbly?" Gerald said. "And how do we do it?"

"Do what?" Marjorie said. She had followed him across the patio and was pawing at his sleeve. "What are you doing out of your chair?"

"Shush, woman!"

Richard's voice was fading, breaking up in the static of the radio. "Can't you even waver?"

Gerald was standing at the edge of the lawn, but he had no idea why. A fly brushed against his brow. He batted it away, and it was soft as a cobweb, offering no resistance to his hand.

"We'll be finished with that lot, won't we?" he said, as Marjorie helped him into his chair. "When it's over, you know. We won't need to see them again."

Marjorie blinked at him. "Who, Gerald? You don't mean Ruth, do you? And Ollie?"

"I jolly well do. The boy's defective and you know it." The words were coming easily now, no gaps, no pops or bubbles in his ears. "Defective," he said again, pleased with the word. "You'll have to put me in a home if you want to go charging down there to their filthy house and their—"

"Oh, Gerald, don't start on that again, please." She poured a cup of tea. "We have to keep seeing them," she said, more faintly now, the cup rattling on the saucer as she passed it to him. "They're our link to our son. How could we not?"

"Defective," he said, but the word had lost its pleasure now that Marjorie was in tears. He couldn't remember why he was saying it anyway.

He sipped his tea, longing to hear Richard's voice again as he watched a flimsy little crane fly waver through the air.

Ollie

My dad died. Mum invited Other Grandma to visit us and I woke up early that day. I was excited about the puzzle. I was going to ask her about the vase, but I thought I could ask her about the boat picture too. She might have talked to Grandpa about it and he might have said something more than *Nothing prepares you to see your own son dead.* If he did, then I'd get two new answers to the puzzle by the end of the day.

But in the morning it all went wrong. I ran up to Other Grandma and I said, "Is your vase very beautiful, Other Grandma?" but Mum laughed. She said I had to give Other Grandma a chance to arrive. It was a stupid thing to say. She had already arrived. She was standing right there in the kitchen. After that, every time I tried to ask her something, Angran talked over me. I went itchy under my fingernails. I started to shout. I thought Angran was spoiling the puzzle, that I'd never find out what it means to be alive.

Mum took me up to my room. She said: "Please, Ollie, not now, or it could be the last time I see Marjorie." At first I thought she meant that Other Grandma would drive away because I was shouting so loudly, so I stayed in my room, gripping at the mattress to keep myself quiet. But later, when Other Grandma was gone, Mum went running out of the house. Then I thought she meant something worse. She was crying and Angran went chasing after her. I was too scared to think of what it might mean, but I knew it made me feel sick. I went downstairs and there was mess everywhere. I saw a bag of flour split open on the floor. I saw the bin in the middle of the room with squashed tins and boxes piled up beside it. I said, "Why is this here?" but there wasn't anyone to answer. My belly started shaking and my skin went hot. Rain splattered on the window. A scream was swelling in my chest and I didn't want it to come.

Rich

HE WOKE FROM another dream about flying and found there were tears on his cheeks. He wiped them away and lay for a while, listening to the faint murmur of the river and Ruth, snoring gently beside him. She would claim, if he woke her, that she'd been wide awake, that she'd hardly slept a wink since his diagnosis. Tears came again, hot and sore at the corners of his eyes, as he considered that she really would struggle to sleep when he was gone.

It was horrible. All those words she used for tired now—"whacked out," "knackered" and "wired"—they would take on a darker aspect in the future, with the force of grief behind them. And Ollie, he'd be horrendous on no sleep. Rich pictured his bared teeth, strung with saliva, the crackle in the fabric as he clawed at the knees of his trousers. Gerald had asked once if there wasn't some sort of medication that would make him behave. Rich had shrugged and laughed so he didn't have to answer, but there had been moments when he, too, had secretly wished for such a thing. No therapies had ever been offered by the pediatricians or the school—Ollie was deemed to be managing too well to warrant it—and it was true that he held fast to a stiff and careful composure in the classroom. The carapace only ever cracked at home. Sometimes he screamed himself hoarse, or clenched his fists so tightly that his fingers were stiff and swollen the next day. There was a look to him in meltdown, his skin mottled and the lines between his nose and mouth stretched taut. It was not a child's face Rich saw then, but something glimpsed in a nightmare, and it horrified him that he could find his own son so grotesque. It was at these times that he wished for some kind of medicine that would magically solve it all. He wanted his boy to be plump-faced and innocent again, and he longed for an easier life, too, with a child who could simply behave.

He was crying again, his breath shuddering. Ruth jolted awake.

"What is it, Rich, what's wrong?" She grasped at his shoulder and her breath was hot and sour across his face.

"I'm not sure," he said. "I don't know where to start." He didn't even want to. There were too many terrible things to say: that he had got things wrong with Ollie and there was no chance now of putting them right; that he was afraid for him and for Ruth, too; that the pounding of his blood in his aching skull sounded ominous, like marching boots.

"Come on, Rich." Ruth was stroking him now, her hands warm on his chest. "You'll feel better if you tell me." He didn't agree. If he spoke now, he thought, there'd be a deluge, and he didn't know what horrors might be unleashed.

Ruth rolled onto her back and lay staring up at the ceiling. "Do you ever feel like giving up?" she said. "You know, just throwing in the towel and saying, 'Look, it's death we're dealing with here, what's the point in trying to cope?'"

Through the open window came the smell of the jasmine she had planted on the patio below. She had filled all their pots with night-scented plants soon after he was diagnosed. "Insomnia," she had said, "should have some compensations." He breathed in the scented air. If he could not tell her of his horrors, he thought, perhaps he could speak of this, how such a simple act had gladdened him. And he could tell her, too, that he didn't believe she'd ever give up. After all, when Ollie was tiny, she was the one who had walked up and down with him at night, had jiggled him and sung to him through his colicky screams when everyone else had advised her to leave him in his cot to cry it out. He could point out how successfully she'd managed their finances after she'd given up work, how she'd made the brilliant decision, early in Ollie's life, to keep him away from any sort of gaming on a screen, finding him puzzles instead to occupy his thirsty little mind.

"Ruth," he said, finding his voice, at last. "You don't have to *try* to cope. You just do. You always have."

She sat up and pressed her fingertips to her eyes. "That's not true." She sighed. "You're the one who's kept me going the whole time."

"No, I haven't," he said, shuffling closer to her on the bed. "I couldn't have managed anything without your backup."

She took her hands from her eyes and looked down at him. "You're the support," she said.

"No, you are."

"It's you." She laughed and turned to stroke the hair from his brow. "We could keep this going all night."

Rich closed his eyes. There was a sting behind them now, a crackle of heat beneath the lids. He supposed it was the crying that had caused it. "Happy to," he said, resting his head against her thigh. "And all of tomorrow if you want."

She laughed again. "Well, why not? It's not like we've got anything better to do. You know, like pick up that vase you ordered for your mum, get that leak sorted under the sink, cook dinner and all that."

Now, as her hand moved over his forehead, his bones seemed to buzz in response and the heat swelled behind his cheekbones. "What vase do you mean?" he asked. He had a vague image in his mind of pink glass, fluted at the edges, but he couldn't think why he'd be buying such a thing.

Ruth shook her head at him, still stroking his hair. "You're slurring your words," she said. "You need to get some rest." He knew he would not sleep, not with the cramping in his tongue now, the pulsing in his gums. But he decided not to tell her. Better if she believed he was drifting off, that together they were breathing in the jasmine, basking in the whisper of the river through the trees.

Marjorie

SHE STOOD AT the fridge with a packet of steak in her hand. She couldn't face frying it for Gerald's lunch. It was the thought of him sawing away with the steak knife. It would squeak on the plate and there would be flecks of gravy on his shirt by the end of the meal. Chicken would be safer.

The steak was soft in her hands, cool in the plastic packaging. She wondered if Richard would like it, if some good red meat would bolster him, put some strength into his blood. She could take it to him now. There were green beans in the fridge, and new potatoes. If she left now, she'd be with him before tea. She imagined leaving this minute, walking across to the car, starting it, just driving, then arriving, running across the lawn to his back door. Running! Perhaps she would open her arms ready to embrace him. She used to run to him like that in the garden when he was tiny, and she had loved the way he reached for her then, palms open, fingers splayed.

If only she could run across his lawn today. She would ignore the mess of blankets and mismatched chairs by the apple tree, the broken fence and the unpainted smear of render beneath the kitchen window. They wouldn't matter because Richard would be there—his smile, the blue of his eyes.

Gerald appeared at the kitchen door. "Steak and chips," he said. "Is that what's on the menu today?"

There would be no driving down today and no running across a lawn to her son. Not with Gerald in the picture. "I haven't decided. What would you like, darling?"

She opened the freezer. She had an urge to press her forehead to the inside of the door, but she did not do it. She slipped the steak into a gap, watched it flop against the rigid packets inside. She could tell he hadn't heard her. He was squinting into the freezer, seemingly baffled by what he saw inside. What he needed, she knew, was certainty.

Time for your nap. Now your bath. Now your pajamas. No question and no doubt. That was how he'd run his life for himself. He knew all the rules, the correct tie for every occasion, the time of day for every sort of alcoholic drink. He was like a handbook for manners. Maybe that was why she'd married him. She'd always loved a handbook. There'd been one at her day school with pictures of smiling girls with hockey sticks. It told you how to fold your gym slip, how many clips to wear in your hair. It was so easy to get everything right, and such fun to get it just a tiny bit wrong, to stand in assembly knowing you had parted your hair to the side instead of the center and watch Mrs. Wilson's eyes bulge when you were spotted. But there was no handbook to tell her if it was wrong to consider putting your husband in a nursing home, just when his son was going to die. Now she had to make her decisions alone.

She took Gerald's arm and led him to the dining room. She thought of this room as a private place now. It wasn't suitable for visitors anymore. The bureau drawers were broken where Gerald had shoved them too hard. There was a rip in the curtain, cup rings on the table. Gerald used to be so careful to use their pretty ceramic coasters, but lately he couldn't quite manage to balance the saucer in the center. That was why there were tea stains on the carpet. Sometimes her arms ached from scrubbing at them. But it had to be done. Even when she was weak with the thought of Richard and his swollen face, distorted now around his left eye. Even when her head ached from lying awake in the night, listening to Gerald shuffling about downstairs.

"Lunchtime, is it?" Gerald said now. "Is that why we're in here?"

"No. It's just a bit quieter, and there's something I'd like to discuss."

The laptop was open. An advert was running on a side section of the screen. It showed a gray-haired lady in a stair-lift, ascending a stately flight of stairs. Beside the advert was the email Marjorie was composing to the manager of Cedar Park Nursing Home. She closed the screen as she passed.

"Now then," she said, easing Gerald into a dining chair, "I've been thinking that we need to visit Richard more often. Do you think the journey would tire you out?"

She sat down beside him and he gave her three little taps on her knee. "Perhaps I should ask if it's too tiring for you," he said.

He smelled faintly of lemon soap. He had always smelled of it, even as a young man, leaning in toward her on the station platform. He wouldn't smell like that if he lived at Cedar Park. She took his hand. "But if we do go visiting regularly," she pushed on, "you'll have to forget all about that business with Ollie."

He snatched his hand away. "I've said I want an apology and I stand by what I said."

"But now Richard is . . ." Marjorie began, but her courage failed her. Gerald was rising to his feet. She saw his leg quiver and he steadied himself with his fists on the table.

"What's that doing here?" he roared.

"What's what, darling?"

"That . . . that damn . . ." His voice faded, but his legs had found their stride. He was on his way to the bureau and she saw what he'd spotted. She had thought the Cedar Park brochure was out of sight there, beneath the Marks & Spencer catalogue, but perhaps she had glanced toward it involuntarily when he started raising his voice. Now he was holding both booklets above his head.

"Put them down, please, Gerald. Be careful."

He looked as if he was shaking with rage. "We don't need the damn things."

He dropped them onto the table. The Marks catalogue clattered, spine first, into a coaster and smashed it apart. Shards of pottery skidded over the edge of the table. The brochure skimmed after it and slapped to the floor.

"Please, Gerald," Marjorie said. His arms were still raised and she found herself cowering. "Sit down, please."

He blinked at her. Pages flapped against the carpet.

"Is it lunchtime?" he said at last, lowering his arms. "Is that why we're in here?"

She heard the broken coaster grind into the carpet beneath his feet as he made his way toward a chair. There were long scratches on the polish of the table, a dent where the catalogue had struck. Soon the whole house would look like this: the pictures off-kilter on the wall, potpourri bowls overturned. She'd have to forgo fresh flowers before long.

"Sit down," she said to Gerald. "I'll get it all cleared up."

In the kitchen she gathered the dustpan and brush, the cloths and polish from the cupboard under the sink. As she rose to her feet her vision speckled and her knees swayed. She stood for a moment with her head bowed, steadying herself with her hand on the drainer.

The trouble with that brochure, she thought, was that there were no residents in the photographs of the rooms. Sunlight flooded through Georgian windows, fell across the empty armchairs, glinted on the wineglasses set out on polished tables. When she visited, it had been teeming. The air was thick with the sour breath of all the people there. She saw a woman grasping at the arms of her easy chair, her gnarled fingers kneading the fabric, like a cat's paws. The man beside her kept gulping, and another wept with his head bowed. There was the usual murmur of conversation you might hear in a theater foyer or crowded café, but it was punctuated every now and then by squawks and sudden moans. The manager explained that four residents had their birthdays that week, and there were more visitors than usual, but Marjorie couldn't shake the feeling that she'd be thrusting Gerald into a crowd and he'd be jostled and swayed, swept away from her, blinking, tugging at his tie.

"Have you any other family?" Denise, the manager, had asked. She had a soft voice and a slow, rocking walk. At their first meeting she'd lifted the hem of her trousers to reveal the metal struts of an artificial leg. "I'd much rather be nursing than managing," she had said, "but it's against health and safety. This way, though, I'm still in the field I love." It was this that had swayed Marjorie. Cedar Park was noisier and smellier than some of the other homes she'd visited, but Marjorie liked the kind way Denise spoke to residents; she knew them all by name. She liked the kind way Denise spoke to her too. "Any children?" she asked.

"Well, a son. And it's important for me to be with him now."

Denise took Marjorie's hand. "I know you feel guilty about this," she said, "but you mustn't forget the benefits. You'll have more time for your son now. Your relationship will blossom in the next few years."

Now Marjorie poured herself a glass of water and took tiny sips. She gathered her cleaning things and went to the dining room, offering Gerald her kindest smile. He blinked at her.

"I thought I heard Richard's voice," he said. "Is he here?" His eyes were bright. She couldn't tell if they were shining with hope or with tears and she looked away. She lowered herself to her knees and began to sweep the shards of broken coaster. She pushed the brush against the carpet, over and over, until the fibers stood up, a forest of peaks.

Ollie

I DON'T KNOW how long I screamed in the empty house, but I made myself stop when Auntie Nessa arrived. She said: "This place is a mess! What's been going on?"

I didn't know the answer so I didn't reply. Auntie Nessa looked at me and said: "What's wrong, Ollie? Why are you gritting your teeth?" I wanted to ask her where Mum had gone and why Angran's breath went all fluttery when she ran after her. Auntie Nessa said: "Well, don't just stand there. You can at least help tidy up."

Just then the latch clacked on the kitchen door. Mum walked in and her clothes were all wet. Angran was behind her, glaring and jerking her head so her glasses kept catching the light. I said, "Where have you been?" but no one heard because they were all talking at once. I saw the drips gathering on the hem of Mum's dress. They splatted to the floor, the sound high and sharp as an itch in my ears. I couldn't make sense of what everyone was saying and they wouldn't explain when I asked them. I thought I might scream. I thought I might kick the cans piled up next to the bin, send them clattering across the floor. But then Mum held up her hand as if she wanted to shut us all up.

She said: "Rich is the one who died, you know. I'm completely alive."

After that it went quiet. I looked at Mum. She was taking off her dress. She was naked and shivering and there was a puddle at her feet. She had said she was *completely alive*. It was time, I thought, to find the answer to the puzzle. I pulled the envelope out of my pocket and waved it over my head. I said: "Who's going to help me?"

Mum was already on her way to the bathroom. Auntie Nessa had gone to the back door. I saw her push it open and leap out onto the lawn. So I chose Angran to get me started. I followed her to the sitting room and she knelt down at the hearth. I thought about the shawl my dad had given her. Mum had said shawls were for old grannies and it made my dad laugh. I'd rolled it up tight when we packed up the parcels. I'd made it fit into the smallest box we had. Now I looked at Angran, who was picking up her little axe. I said: "Can we find out, Angran, what it means to be alive?"

Angran stood a log on its end and clapped the blade into the top. She said: "You want advice, do you? Well, I can tell you one thing. Don't do what Ruth and Nessa do and dwell on all the bad things in the past. We'd be happier if we just forgot it all."

The axe was stuck in the log. She bashed it against the hearth, over and over, until my ears went tight in my head. I said: "But that's not in the puzzle, Angran. That's not why my dad gave you a shawl."

The log split in two. I saw the splintery center, dangerous to touch. Angran turned to me and frowned. She said: "I never got a shawl from your dad. I don't know what you're talking about."

Rich

RUTH HAD LAID out the gifts on the kitchen table and placed a suitable cardboard box beside each one. She instructed Rich to write the addresses on each of them and called Ollie to the table.

"This is going to be fun," she told him, piling up old copies of the Cheese Wheel catalogue. "We're going to decorate these boxes. And it's just the three of us, working together. Proper family time."

Rich knew that Ruth had always loved family time—picnics by the river, trips to the museum, biscuit-baking competitions where they used every bowl and utensil in the kitchen, their teeth furred by the end of it from all the sugar they had consumed.

Ollie looked into a gluepot and recoiled. "Stinks," he said. "Why do we have to have the Cheese Wheel catalogue? I don't like cheese."

Rich laughed. "I promise you there's no real cheese," he said. "Only pictures. Though I wish there was," he added, riffling through the pages. "This blue one here looks delectable." He smacked his lips and Ollie recoiled again.

"Stop it," Ruth said. "Or you'll put him off completely."

It was probably too late. Ollie was pushing the catalogues across the table, his lips drawn up to his nose in disgust. But Rich wanted to make him laugh. There was an ache in his jaw, a throbbing in his gums against his teeth. If Ollie laughed now, his face bright and focused, he could ignore the pain, keep from hunching into it. He opened his arms wide as Ollie shoved the catalogues toward him.

"Gimme cheese," he growled, in a greedy monster's voice, and began sweeping the pile toward his chest. Half of them slid to the floor so he lowered himself down and spread them over his body. "Cheese," he cried again. "Bury me in cheese!"

Ollie did not look at him. Rich made gurgling noises and rubbed the catalogues on his belly, but Ollie just frowned, prodding at the tray of scented candles. "These are stinky too. Who are they even for?" He picked up the box beside them and inspected the address. "The hospital staff? You don't know their names."

"I know their names," Rich called from the floor. "There's Dr. Emmental, Nurse Brie and assistant radiologist Mrs. Cave-aged Cheddar."

Ollie glowered at him. "Those are names of cheeses."

He knew he had gone too far. Ruth was smiling down at him, but he could see her eyes darting toward Ollie, even as she laughed, alert to the curling of his fingers, the clenching of his teeth. He pushed the catalogues from his belly and sat up. The room swayed. Table legs quivered before him, too many table legs, seven at least, and Ollie's feet, shuffling in and out of his Crocs, looked enormous, swollen, like rising dough.

"Scissors," he said, though he wasn't sure why. There was something he was supposed to be doing. Pasting pictures onto parcels perhaps or making Ollie laugh. What he wanted to do was listen to Ruth, snipping away with her scissors. He loved that sound, just as he loved the fusty smell of her sewing box and the creak of the wicker lid. He had spent many evenings dozing on the sofa, exhausted after work, while she laid out patterns on the floor. The shining sunflower quilt she had made for their bedroom had been a reminder, always, that summer would come and the long school holiday would revive him. On sunny days, the way the satin petals reflected a buttercup glow onto the ceiling never ceased to delight him. But it was not his own delight he should be attending to now, he realized: it was Ollie's. So he heaved himself to his feet and held on to the table as an eddy of nausea swirled through him.

Ollie was peering at the painting of the galleon. He was holding his hands above it, measuring it in spans. Then he reached for the box beside the scented candles and measured that too. "Look at this, Dad." He lifted the picture between the flat of his palms and lowered it into the box. "It's perfect," he cried, as the picture slid slowly down inside. "Completely neat."

Now Ollie was smiling and Rich seized the moment. He held up his palm for a high five.

"Wait!" Ruth said, over the sound of their clapping hands. "That's not the right package."

But Ollie was reaching for the smallest box on the table. He was eyeing the shawl and holding the box against it.

"I reckon it'll fit," Rich said. "We just need to fold it up tight."

"Neatly, though," Ollie instructed, as Rich swung the shawl from the table. "It's got to be perfect and neat."

Together they rolled it up and squashed it into the box.

They taped down the lid and Ollie patted each side, marveling that all the space inside was filled.

"What next?" Rich asked, but Ruth put her hands to her head. "Those are the wrong boxes. I can't keep track!"

Rich just wanted to dance about with Ollie. He was loving the light in his eyes, his quick, darting fingers as he measured out the next box, which was addressed to Angran.

"Let's not worry," Rich said to Ruth. "Life's too short to worry."

Ruth stared at him, her fingers still pressed to her temples. "Your life is short," she said. "But what about mine? I'm the one who has to undo this muddle you've made."

Rich pulled her into his arms. "Just go with the flow," he said. "It'll all work out in the end. It always does."

But she was biting her nails now and the flow was gone. "Everything's so simple to you. You never see the undercurrent."

It wasn't true. He saw undercurrents all the time: sighs of disapproval from Angran, twitches in Ollie's fingers that warned of a meltdown. He just didn't always dread them as Ruth did. He watched Ollie bundling the bubble wrap into a ball. He was still smiling to himself, but he was stuffing it into a box with unnecessary force. Undercurrents, Rich thought, were mostly miserable things. It didn't make Ruth happy to notice them. It made her scared. She pulled away from him, saying she was tired, and sorry that she had spoiled his fun. He followed her to the foot of the stairs.

"I just don't see how you manage it," she said, holding on to the banisters with both hands and hauling herself up. "How can you be so positive all the time?" She paused on the landing. "You will sort out the boxes, won't you? Make sure the addresses get moved to the right gifts?"

"Of course." He nodded, hand on his aching jaw. "And I'll get them sent off in the morning too."

He returned to Ollie and found him taping down the last box. "All packed up?" he said. "All of them clean and neat?"

Ollie nodded. "I want to do a sudoku now."

Half the catalogues were scattered over the floor. The other half were crumpled on the table, with jagged cuts across the pages. There was a ringing in his ears, a throbbing in his neck. Ruth had asked him to finish something, but he couldn't remember what it was. He knew they had planned to glue pictures of cheese onto the parcels, so people would know they came from him. He guessed that was the task. He worked on it slowly, while Ollie completed his puzzle. The sun was setting, and Rich saw a bar of orange light fall across Ollie's book, gilding the white page and the black grid.

Angran

SHE WAS CHISELING at the edges of the knocked-through doorway when the postman rang the bell. He stood on the doorstep as he handed over the parcel.

"Excess to pay, I'm afraid."

She went in search of change. The package felt rough against her hands, tacky in places. Disks of paper were stuck to it, curling at the edges. The address label was written in Rich's lazy, wide hand. "What's he doing posting things, when I could just go around and collect?"

"Pardon?" The postman peered into the dark hall.

"I didn't speak." She pushed the money into his hand and shut the door.

There was no note in the parcel, just a vase inside, chipped on the rim.

"Typical," Angran said. "Not even properly packed."

She held the vase up to the light. It was a delicate piece in pale pink glass, the top fluted and frilled, but Angran had no affection for vases. This one wasn't even to her taste. It needed a doily and an occasional table polished to a sheen. When she tried it on her mantelshelf, a thick beam swirled with wood grain, it looked like a fairy dancing on a turd.

"What's it in aid of?" she said next. She supposed Rich knew about the vases and jugs she had smashed in the past: it was too much to hope that Ruth and Nessa had kept that part of their childhood to themselves. Was he trying to tell her something, get her to put something right?

"No need," she said. "I've always done my best for my children."

She searched for the chip of glass among the packaging, and wondered how much this broken vase had cost him. He'd have used his credit card, she thought, reveling, no doubt, that he wouldn't be around to pay it off. It was all about fun for him, sending gifts through the post and not caring if they were broken, throwing parties, using up all the bread to make ridiculous toast. Luckily for Ruth, An-gran was standing by, ready to pick up the pieces later.

"Men," she said, crushing the empty box beneath her booted foot. "Useless, the lot of them." She took the vase to her kitchen cupboard.

"Better out of sight," she said. And better not mentioned to Rich or Ruth. She didn't want to have to make some silly pretense at being grateful. She looked about her at the kitchen, the scrubbed table, shelves lined with jars of nuts and pulses, the sagging leather armchair in the corner, with the army blanket tossed across the seat. It was a handsome room, she thought, proof of who she was: prac-tical and self-sufficient. The vase was a frilly nonsense. She pushed it to the back of the shelf and shut the cupboard door.

Gerald

HE LOOKED OUT of the kitchen window and saw the red post van nosing down the lane and Marjorie fluttering out to meet it. He turned on the taps. The water swirled around the plug, surging up frills of . . . of . . . He couldn't find the word. Round things. Popping. He watched Marjorie duck her head to the window of the van. Even the postman knew about Richard. Marjorie had told everyone. She had a way of bending forward to whisper the latest news, but he thought she might as well shout it at the top of her voice seeing as there wasn't a soul she wouldn't tell.

Bubbles. They were frothing at the edges of the sink and spats of water were prickling his belly through his shirt. He couldn't think why the taps were on. *Hose,* he thought. *Water the lawn.* But they had a boy to do that for them now. Someone else who knew every last detail of Richard's health, no doubt. He'd seen these people peering around Marjorie's stooping back as she whispered to them, eyeing him with ill-mannered curiosity. Perhaps they expected some kind of display. A wobble in his legs, a quivering chin. They'd be . . . not sorry, not sad, they'd be . . . He couldn't remember what it was they'd be and he didn't like this damp patch spreading across the front of his shirt.

Like a child. A mucky pup. How did it get there? *Disappointed.* That's what they'd be.

Marjorie came in with some parcels under her arm.

"Richard's sent us something. Presents, I think. Isn't that strange? We should be sending things to him. Do you think he'd like some new pajamas? Or some hankies, maybe?"

She was twittering away and it set the voices going in his head. "Hanky-panky, Widow Twankey."

"Marjorie, the taps," he said. "There's a hosepipe ban, you know."

She turned them off and, for a moment, there was a blessed silence in his head. But seconds later she was rustling bubble wrap and skimming boxes across the table. He saw her pull out something brown, a piece of jewelry, and it made her gasp. She rushed out of the room with her fist pressed to her mouth. In the mess of packaging before him he saw a tray of candles. They were like night-lights, the sort to be burned by the bed in a saucer full of water. But there was something wrong. Maybe it was the color of them, sickly peach and insipid mauve. Or maybe it was the smell. He peered at the labels on the plastic wrapping. *Ginger to Contemplate. Lavender to Relax.*

The voices gurgled in his ears. "A randomized study of the pantheon of tendencies."

Something was certainly wrong. This gift made no sense at all. Nothing did. The candles smelled like his grandmother's handbag. His shirt was wet. The grass on the lawn was yellow and Richard was going to die.

Marjorie

SHE CARRIED THE necklace to the bedroom. The wooden beads were rough against her palm. She sat on the edge of her bed and let the tears fall. The silver pendant swung between her fingers. It wasn't real silver. She couldn't say what it was. So big, so strange: a hand with filigree patterns cut into the palm. It looked like a museum piece, the tribal jewels of a warrior princess.

She laid it out on the bedspread. It was coarse and savage against the pattern of sprigged roses. It would be worse against her blouse, each bead a dark counterpart to the tiny pearl buttons on the collar. Gerald came to the door. There was a wet patch spreading across his shirt. He nodded at her, then peered down at the necklace.

"Well, you can't be seen out in that," he said.

She dabbed at her eyes with her handkerchief. "But Richard—" She couldn't finish her sentence. When Richard was a child, he drew pictures of her, with bright crayoned dresses and enormous hands, each finger splayed wide, snaking to the edge of the paper. The bright colors and curling corners were too messy for display in the kitchen. But she loved them anyway, sensing that they were the missives of filial love, expressed the only way he knew how, and she tacked them up in the utility room. They were like his joyful splashes in the bath that caught her in the eye, or his hugs that left jammy prints on her apron. Perhaps this messy old necklace was the same. He was sending her a message of love that had somehow misfired.

She lifted it from the bed. The beads clacked together and the pendant twirled.

"You'd look like a damn bohemian," Gerald said. She stood up. She would have to treasure it. That would be the right thing to do. She looked about for somewhere to place it. The beads were too rough for the polished wood of her bedside table, too dark for the lace cloth before her mirror. She pushed it under her pillow. Gerald blinked at her.

"It's not a . . . a damn . . ." His hands began to flutter in frustration. She held them between her own for a moment, then led him out of the room.

"A damn *billet-doux*," he said, as she guided him down to the kitchen for a cup of hot, sweet tea.

Nessa

SHE CAME HOME late from Ruth's house, and found the parcel in her recycling box. She laughed out loud when she saw the collage of cheese on the wrapping. Rich had been scheming, she knew, to send gifts to people he loved, and she'd seen him scribbling ideas on a tatty old envelope, but she never thought he'd get around to making it happen.

She ran a knife around the edges of the box. It had been tightly sealed with tape and when she broke through it sprang open. A roll of green and gray knitted wool swelled out, like a rising loaf. She frowned. She didn't know what sort of gift she'd been expecting, but it certainly wasn't a shawl, a floppy, tasseled thing in the colors of a shady garden. Not something that prickled against her skin as she pulled it around her shoulders, that held her arms still, crossed over her chest, like a nun's.

She let it fall to the floor and walked away. A shawl was a winter gift, she thought, as she pushed open her patio doors. It was a gift for long dark nights, curled up by an open fire. When had she ever curled up by an open fire? She'd rather be dancing to keep warm, drinking whiskey and laughing out loud. But perhaps not this winter. Not if

Rich was dying. Not if he was blind, incontinent, too confused to laugh about anything.

She blinked back tears and opened her arms to let the night air cool her skin. Her lawn was in shadow ahead of her. She squinted at it through the dusk, trying to conjure green from the darkness, instead of the matted brown mess she knew was really there. She'd have to cherish the shawl, she thought, even if she couldn't bring herself to look at it yet. She'd have to draw it around her shoulders one day. But first, she thought, wiping her eyes, she'd have to give Rich a talking-to. She'd tap his chest with her finger. *Oi, you, what were you thinking? You could have bought me a bottle of gin!*

Rich

HE WOKE UP at dawn and shuffled to the edge of the bed. Ruth didn't stir. She always slept deeply at this time, when there was a chill in the air and the sky was dusky over the river. Rich, though, was at his most wakeful. He rummaged in the heap of clothes on the floor, sniffing at the T-shirts to find a clean one. There was a brassy taste in his mouth, like he was sucking a coin.

He wondered if his gifts had been delivered. He had an appointment at Outpatients later that day, and he wanted to go around shaking people's hands when he got there, making sure they'd each received a candle, that they understood how grateful he was. He'd wear his loudest Hawaiian shirt, he decided, the one with the pineapples on the sleeves, because the nurses liked to rib him about his clothes. They claimed to need sunglasses when they took his blood.

He fumbled into his shorts, his fingers numb and unresponsive with the buttons. Ruth lay still behind him, her lips slack against the pillow, a white smudge of spittle at the corner of her mouth. He hadn't yet decided on a gift for her. Bolts of cloth, he thought, might leave her with a feeling of obligation, that she had to create something special, a memorial perhaps, when really all he wished was for her to delight in the colors. A scarf for her hair or a dress seemed too plain. He wanted something magical and hopeful, secretive, even, a message perhaps that only she could understand. All their conversations in the small hours, with the smell of the jasmine at the window, the warmth of their bodies on the sheets—he wished he'd recorded them, could present them to her now. Then she would know, he was certain, just how much her love had sustained him. His greatest fear for her was not that she would collapse or fail when he was gone, but that she would believe she had. There was bound to be mess and misery ahead, and he wished there was something he could say now, so that she would not assume it was all her fault.

He made his way onto the landing, steadying himself with his hand on the wall. Inspiration would come to him soon, he was sure of it, but for now he had to concentrate on hobbling down the stairs and out to the garden.

Since his diagnosis, it had become a ritual for him to rise at dawn and stand barefoot beneath the apple tree. He liked to listen to the birds and feel the cool, complex patterns of the grass beneath his feet. The sky was not yet blue at this time; above the house it was pale and peachy. There was gold somewhere, he thought, and he was standing in the glow of it. The swallows dipped and curled in it, the leaf tips glinted with it, and with each breath, he pulled it deep into his being.

This was the gift he'd like to offer to Ruth. This precious glow and how it made him marvel at the world. The glow made him smile when Ollie scowled at him; it made him laugh when Angran jerked her head in disapproval. It made everything seem magical so that when he wanted drinks or strawberries for his guests there always seemed to be enough in the house.

"It feels like there's an angel watching over me," he'd said once, attempting to explain this golden pleasure of being alive. Ruth had laughed, kissed the top of his head.

"I'm your angel," she said. "I ordered the strawberries with the online shop."

How he loved Ruth's laugh. Sometimes her face was dark, frowning with worry, but her laugh was a flare of warmth. She had the glow in her too, but all too often she resisted it. Everyone did. Ruth turned it into a joke. Angran prickled at it. Nessa made it a quarry. She chased it at high speed, sleeves rolled up, hair flying out behind her, though it was there for the taking all along.

He turned his face once more toward the luminous sky. He wished they were all there with him, the people he loved. He wished his father was beside him, blinking up at the robin on the chimney stack. He still didn't know what to say to him about Ollie. *Cut him some slack, Dad, he's doing his best. You don't need an apology, you need a laugh.* It didn't really matter. The chances were, Gerald wouldn't understand, or would forget the conversation five minutes later. What mattered was that he should say something soon. On the roof, the robin lifted his beak and let fly a series of bubbling trills. Rich couldn't wait to see Gerald and Ollie together again. He couldn't care less if Ollie screeched, or Gerald wobbled his neck in disapproval. He no longer wished to deny them that experience, or withhold from them the chance to find their own way through.

He rooted around in his pockets and found a crumpled sheet of paper and a stub of pencil. *Sky the color of apricots*, he wrote. On the other side was the letter he'd started writing to Ollie. He would finish it later, he decided, once he'd made some notes for Ruth. *I've seen your eyes,* he added, sucking at his teeth to shift the taste of tarnished spoons in his mouth, *soft in the blush of the setting sun.* This seemed like nonsense when he read it back. Ruth would not understand it, not enough to know that he meant it as a gift to her. *Open your arms to the flow of the dawn. Heart full of golden sky.* His jaw was aching and his skin felt heavy on his face. Words swelled and bled together as he wrote them and the pencil slipped out of his hand.

"I'll buy a Dictaphone," he said to himself. But what he heard was a roar, a great buzzing in his head that set his flesh shuddering. The lawn had turned to sponge beneath his feet, undulating like a water bed. But when it rose to meet his face it was rock and struck him hard across his skull.

He did not suffer the slow decline the doctors had predicted. There was no gradual loss of balance, sight or hearing, just a sudden blow that morning. Ruth found him flailing on the lawn, bellowing and choking in pain.

There was no return to calm. Only sedation. Coma.

Ollie

MY DAD DIED. It happened when I wasn't there. I saw it starting from the kitchen window. He was lying in the garden and I saw his jaw swivel under his skin. I saw his mouth open and close and a juddering sound came out of his throat, like an engine. That was him dying. They carried him away on a stretcher and his arms were up above his face. His fingers were bent, like he was clawing at a curtain. Mum tried to hold his scrabbling hands. She said: "It's all right, Rich. It's all right, Rich."

It wasn't all right. He died. The lights from the ambulance flashed against the house. I heard the engine, burbling on and on. Then I heard my dad make that noise. It was like a motor, but it was also like a cow. I didn't know a human could make that sound. I didn't know my dad could open his mouth like that, all on one side with the other cheek stretched tight.

My dad died. I'll never have golden thinking, like he did. I'll never understand meaning or find the answers falling into place. The puzzle went wrong because Angran told me she never got a shawl. She found another log to split and bashed it on the hearth until my ears began to squeal. I had to yell to make myself heard. I said: "He did send you a shawl, Angran. It was green and gray and we sent it in a tiny box."

She said: "I don't know what you're talking about. Stop shouting and making a silly fuss."

Then I remembered. The tiny box I used for the shawl was supposed to have Auntie Nessa's necklace inside. The shawl must have gone to Auntie Nessa instead. I said: "Angran. I need to know what present you got from my dad." When she said it was a vase I screamed.

I ran up to my room. There were chairs piled up on the landing and they rattled as I passed. I pulled the mattress off my bed. I pushed my chest of drawers onto its side. I ripped up the envelope and stuffed the pieces into my sock. They went right down inside, past the arch of my foot, and they scratched at my skin like a hundred loose threads. Mum was calling me from the bathroom and I ran in and shouted at her. I said: "I'm stupid. I'm stupid. I'll never find out what it means to be alive."

She looked up at me from the bath. Her face was wet and water was running over her shoulders from her hair. She said: "I can tell you what it means, Ollie."

But when she told me I started screaming again. She said being alive was about loving my dad. She said we had to love him more and more, even if it made us sadder and sadder every day. I couldn't look at her face. Her wet hair was clinging to her skull and it made her head look flat and narrow. My dad's head looked like that on the hospital bed. I said, "No. That's not what it means," and I went to the window and shoved at it hard to make it open. Mum said, "Don't, Ollie, it's cold," but I took off my sock and shook it out over the sill. My dad died. I watched the scraps of paper fly about in the wind.

Ruth

As a general rule, Ruth had clear skin, but sometimes, if she had not been sleeping well, or when she was stressed, a single red spot would appear on her chin. All through the day she would feel it aching and she'd picture it shining, like a warning light, from her face.

This happened on the day that Rich died. Every visitor to the bedside kissed her as they left. Each one, she was quite sure, had to dodge their lips away from the spot. As she drew back from their embrace she checked their face for signs of disgust. Then, once they had gone, she wanted to chase after them, hold their hands and apologize for weighting her blemishes with more meaning than their dying friend. But it was always too late. Another visitor would arrive, there would be more kisses and more cringing once they had gone.

All the while, Rich lay on the bed, head lolling, upper lip lifted into a hare's snarl where the oxygen tube pushed against it. It was hot in the room and Ruth had taken off his hospital gown. His bare chest heaved and his breath groaned in the tube. The room, with its stream of visitors, began to smell of stale breath, spilled coffee and overflowing bins. There was always someone, it seemed, to observe that it felt like one of Rich's parties, that surely he would sit up at any moment and offer them some cheese. There was always someone tripping over a chair leg or a heap of bags, someone phoning for directions to the hospital, or asking her, as if she were an expert, if he was in pain or if he knew they were all there. Her standard reply was, *I'm sure he can feel our love*, but she had no idea if it was true. She had no idea if anything she said or felt was true. Rich's breaths groaned on, as if driven by the motor in the oxygen supply. His cheeks were slack and his hands, when she lifted them into her own, flopped against her palms, his skin dry and feverish. Everything, it seemed, had been stripped of truth and meaning.

Earlier, at dawn, before visiting hours, she had ducked under the oxygen tube and lain down beside him on the bed. She pressed her hips against his legs, ran her fingers through his chest hair and tried to offer him a meaningful farewell.

"I'll look after Ollie," she had said. "I might even make him laugh." She had talked of their happy times together, the parties and things she had sewn for him—the sunflower quilt and the cushions made to look like cheeses. "Remember how I thought you were shy when Nessa first brought you to meet me?" she said. "You hardly looked at my face that day, just stared at my fingers as I tacked out the sleeves for that giantess's dress. Can you feel my hands on you now, Rich? I'll keep stroking you just in case." She went on whispering to him—about the day Ollie was born, how they had both cried when they brought him home because they didn't know what to do with him next. She reminded him of the first time they tasted an apple from their tree, the tart green shock of it on their tongues.

When they had fed one to Ollie, as a toddler, he had howled and spat his mouthful into Rich's coffee. When she ran out of stories she rested her head against his chest.

"You can go now, Rich," she said. "It's OK. Don't worry about us. We're ready."

She thought she felt a softening in his muscles, a sinking away. But she might have been searching for meaning where there was none. What better than to believe that he was not beyond reach? But even if he'd heard her, the rhythm of his breath did not change. He kept dragging the oxygen into his chest and it seemed to her that each breath was meaningless. He was feeding his blood with oxygen, but to what end?

"You must be so tired," people said, but tiredness had lost its meaning too.

"I'm all right. Getting by on adrenaline."

How that seemed to please them. She'd seen them eyeing her as they stood around the bed. They suspected her, she was certain, of wanting to wail and draw their attention away from Rich to her own exhaustion and terror. And maybe she did. It might have been the most meaningful utterance she could make. All the darkness that was in her, the childhood fears, would billow out in a choking cloud. She imagined the oxygen in Rich's bloodstream, silvery and pale. In hers there was something dark, and if she didn't hide it from his friends it would swallow them all.

And threading through every interaction was the most humiliating lie of all: that she had shared something meaningful with each person who squeezed her hand and kissed her, when really she was afraid that the spot on her chin had brushed against their cheeks.

Angran

SHE BROUGHT A bowl of early apples to Rich's bedside, picked that morning from her garden. They were fresh and crisp with the smell of autumn on their skins, but no one seemed to want one. Not Ruth, sitting at the head of the bed with her arms draped across Rich's shoulder, not Nessa on a plastic chair, holding Rich's swollen hand to her cheek, or Ollie shifting from foot to foot at the window, Crocs squeaking against the floor. There was nowhere for Angran to place the bowl so she leaned against the wall, clasping it to her chest.

She wished Ruth had called her earlier. She would willingly have risen at dawn and sat beside her at the hospital, taking her role as the wise elder. She could have sent half the visitors away, set limits on people pawing at Ruth and sniveling on her shoulder. Two men had come into the room now and had been introduced to her as Alan and Tom, but she couldn't have cared less who they were. What bothered her was that Ruth had given up her chair for the older one, was handing a tissue to the younger.

"Wrong way around," Angran muttered to herself. "They should be attending to her."

Ollie turned from the window as she spoke. "I want to go home now," he said. His voice was flat and loud.

Ruth looked up from her embrace with this Tom person and Angran saw panic in her eyes. She thrust the bowl of apples toward her. "Have one of these, darling. I bet you haven't eaten all day."

Ollie's voice came louder. "Mum! I said I want to go home."

Ruth pulled away from Tom and began rummaging through her bag. "Let me think, Ollie. I need to think of somewhere you can go."

"Home, Mum. I said I want to go home."

Angran tried holding her apples out to him. "At least have one of these first. You need something healthy at a time like this." She offered the bowl to Alan and Tom, but they shook their heads, barely able to draw their eyes from Rich's face.

"I'll have one," Nessa said, standing up, scraping the metal legs of the chair across the floor. She took the biggest, bit into it and spoke with her mouth full. "You should take Ollie home," she said. "He'll be happiest with you."

Angran felt her knees weaken. "But Ruth needs me." She looked pointedly at Alan, who was clutching at Ruth's sleeve, tears streaming down his face. "I can't abandon her at a time like this."

"Ollie needs you too," Nessa said. "Come on, Mum, this is the best solution possible."

It didn't feel like the best, ushering Ollie out of the door, leaving all those people there, sharing their tears and their tissues, linking their arms. She stopped halfway up the corridor. Ollie was ahead of her, fists clenched at his sides. She turned back toward the room where Rich lay dying.

There were people in there saying their last goodbyes. They were kissing Rich's hands, stroking his hair. She had done nothing of the kind.

Ollie called to her from the end of the corridor. She looked down at the unwanted apples in the bowl, picturing for a moment the pottery smashing on the floor. "I have to do what's best," she said.

Ollie bashed at the exit button on the security door. "Angran, stop talking to yourself and take me home!" He was pale and she could see his legs quivering.

"I'm coming," she told him. "We'll go home and forget all this now. That's the best we can do."

Nessa

SHE SPAT A mouthful of apple into the bin. "There was a maggot in it. Gross." She chucked the rest of it away, stood up and rubbed her face. "I need some air. Can I get anything? Coffee? Ice lollies?"

She was shaking. She hadn't smoked in years, but she was planning to sidle up to some other glum visitor in the car park and cadge a cigarette. Anything to feel the liquid rush in her blood. Anything for a moment of silence as she exhaled. She remembered how she could step outside herself when there was smoke in her lungs, could consider her words before she spoke. So far, at Rich's bedside, she had wailed, sobbed and dripped snot onto his elbow. She had laughed at his fat hands and the mole in his armpit, spilled tea on Ruth and trodden hard on someone's toe. Now she needed to leave the room and return calmer, a more loving sister to the widow-to-be.

Ruth was bidding her goodbyes to Rich's classroom assistant and his boyfriend. She turned to Nessa when they'd gone. "Don't go," she said. "Don't leave me on my own."

Nessa gaped. "But I thought I was making a tit of myself here."

"Oh, God, no, I'm the tit in this room," Ruth replied, prodding at something on her chin with her fingers.

"We're a pair of tits, then." It was supposed to be a joke, but neither of them felt like laughing and they stood, staring at the floor, listening to the long rasp of Rich's breath in the oxygen mask.

After a while, Ruth put her hand to her neck, and winced. "I think I need a massage. My shoulders are actually hurting."

Nessa looked down at her hands. "I'm not sure I can remember how," she said, but Ruth was already settling herself in the plastic chair, beckoning Nessa over. Nessa took a deep breath. She remembered this instruction at least, that every massage should begin this way, with a moment of silence and a breath drawn from the depths of the belly. She placed her hands on Ruth's neck and breathed again.

It was better than a cigarette, that long, deep breath. And the whisper of her palms moving over Ruth's skin was better than the silence she'd sought in the exhaling of smoke. It was a similar sound, she thought, to the shawl shifting over her own shoulders only two nights before.

She worked slowly, eyes closed, as she pressed into the muscles, seeking the soft layer of tissue beneath. There was an urgency in the heat of Ruth's skin and she saw that it was her job to ease it. She wondered if this was what Rich had wanted for her when he gave her the shawl. Perhaps he knew that she would be yearning for this silence, this moment of peace.

She let her hands drop to her sides.

Ruth turned in the chair. "What is it, Ness?"

She could not speak. Her nose was hot and tears were swelling beneath her eyelids.

"Oh, my sister!" Ruth said. She stood up and pulled Nessa into her arms. "You've known him longer than I have. This is awful for you."

They held each other wordlessly while Rich's breaths groaned behind them. Ruth stroked Nessa's hair as her sobs began to ebb. It occurred to Nessa that massage might be good for Rich too. She wasn't convinced he could hear all his visitors and their choked farewells, but if she could hold his feet, push into his muscles and his skin, she might feel some connection with him. Just the thought of it made her palms tingle. Her hands felt full and she wanted to open them wide, like an offering.

Gerald

THEY ARRIVED AT the hospital and Gerald's legs were stiff from the two-hour journey in the car. The cracks and burbles in his head were loud, stirred up by the rattle and rush along the motorway, and the sunshine blaring in at them all the way. He wasn't hearing voices, though, not discernible ones, at any rate. It was like a crowd in his head, surging in and out of his consciousness as he lifted each foot and felt the pain shudder through his hips.

He held on to Marjorie's arm as they walked across the lobby, and he heard her speak to him. Or felt it, more like, a breath on his cheek, a high vibration near his shoulder. He had no idea what she had said. Nothing to say anyway. Not with their son dying in a room somewhere here. Dead already, really. Unconscious. Brain dead. Coma. No problem with word retrieval today. At least, not those words. The words he had no wish to retrieve. But trying to tell Marjorie that he had forgotten his damn hanky when they were halfway down the road had been a trial.

He stopped. No hanky. Better square his shoulders. Face it like a man. Marjorie tugged at his arm.

"Oh, Gerald," her voice came through to him, "we must try to be . . ." and then it was lost again in the jumble of sounds and pain as he pushed his legs forward. Ahead of him, someone was hanging a picture on the corridor wall. It was a rather fine painting, a ship in a storm, and he wished he could stop, forget about his dying son, and admire instead the cresting waves and foaming sea. As a boy, Rich used to cry about storms, and Gerald would give him pep talks, telling him no storm would get the better of him and his crew. But there was a storm coming now all right, a great raging one, gathering force as he urged his legs forward into the room, to Richard on the bed. He saw his bare chest, his head lolling, his arms limp against the sheet.

"Sit down, Gerald, sit down here." The voice came faintly through the crashing waves and he saw the oxygen tube and a pocket of urine hanging from the side of the bed.

"Thank you, thank you, how kind," he said—or, at least, he thought he did, as the chair was pushed up behind him, but he didn't know who he had spoken to and the words were swept away in the roaring wind. But the thing was to be polite. To sit straight and unflinching. Richard's chest rose and fell. His head looked narrow, flattened somehow, against the pillow. Everyone but Marjorie had left the room. He'd heard the word "privacy" from somewhere, and "peace and quiet," but there was no peace from this roiling in his head, from Marjorie's sobbing. Her fingers were tight on his arm and he could feel the shake in her body, see fat teardrops landing on the sheets.

"Talk to him, Gerald," she sobbed. "He might be able to hear."

He looked into Richard's face, saw his mottled cheeks, the creases on his eyelids. This was not the face of a dreamer, a man stirred by the murmurings around him. It was an empty face, lips squashed out of shape by the oxygen mask, all expression sunken away. *Come back, come back at once!* These were the only words that came to him and he hoped to God he had not spoken them aloud. The storm raged in his ears and the voices returned. The damn voices.

"Try to be more wobbly." This was Richard's voice and it was nonsense, but he wanted to hear it anyway. He wanted to forgive him every nonsense thing he'd ever done. Those candles, the stinking ones he'd sent through the post—Gerald felt a surge of longing for them now. He wished he was sitting before the flames, watching them wobble and waver before him. But the candles weren't here, not in this hospital room where he was holding Richard's hand. "More wobbly, more wobbly," said the voice, swirling through white water. Gerald slumped against the bed. Richard's hand was heavy, and Gerald held it to his face to hide the tears.

Marjorie

SHE DID NOT draw attention to Gerald's tears. She moved around the bed, pulling the sheet straight where it had bunched against Richard's chest. She was wearing the necklace, hidden under the collar of her blouse. The beads were warm against her neck and the silver hand tapped at her heart as she leaned over to wipe a crust of dribble from the corner of his mouth.

She had been afraid she wouldn't know what to do— that Gerald would start swearing at the doctors, or that she would faint and require medical attention. But all that happened was that she cried the moment she saw him. She was luckier than Gerald in that respect, she thought. There was no shame in her shedding tears. It had been the sight of Richard's forehead that set her off. His brow was too prominent with his curls damp and crushed against the pillow. All the laughter lines at his eyes had sagged away and he looked old and exposed. The shock of it rose up in her, a buoy bursting the surface of the water, and her tears came, hot and gushing. Afterward she felt clear-headed. The shock was gone and in its place came a flood of warmth and kindness. She wondered if Gerald felt a change in himself, now that he had wept too.

Richard's breath rasped in the oxygen tube.

"It's all right, darling," she said to him, resting her palm on his sternum, just where the silver hand was resting on hers. "You can breathe more gently." The rasping died away, and his breaths seemed to slow. She did not remove her hand. In the years since he'd left home, their only physical contact had been brief embraces in greeting and farewell. Now, the heat in his skin felt like a blessing. She felt holy as she leaned into him, listening to the shushing of the sheets as his chest rose and fell, but she was not thinking about God, or where Richard might be going: it came to her, like a revelation, that she must be with him when he died.

There was a tap on the door and Ruth peeped around. "We'll come back in a moment," she whispered, but Marjorie beckoned her in. Nessa shuffled behind her and she saw that their faces were wan.

"When did you last eat?" Marjorie asked. They exchanged astonished glances and they spoke together.

"That maggoty apple."

"My appetite is gone."

Something slipped to the floor from the chair beside her. It was a black vest, powdery at the armpit. She retrieved it and folded it into a square. She noticed that Ruth's lips were dry and Nessa's eyes shrunken and sore.

"Let me get you something from the café," she said to them, stowing the vest in the bedside cupboard. She had booked a hotel for the night, certain that she'd be exhausted after the drive to the hospital and the shock of seeing Richard so close to death. Now exhaustion had never mattered less. She beckoned the girls closer and reached for their hands. "I'm going to give Gerald a sleeping pill," she whispered. "Then I'm coming right back here." They stared at her. For a moment she thought they didn't want her to return, that they would tell her to take a sleeping pill herself, to lie still and sensible on the hotel bed. But then Ruth began to sob.

"Oh, Marjorie, thank you so much," she said, and Marjorie saw that they needed a mother here as much as Richard did, that she would be a comfort for them, too.

Ruth

IT WAS CLOSE to midnight when Rich began to weaken. The oxygen mask was still clamped to his face but he seemed to lap at it now, like a sleeping baby with the nipple. Ruth lay spooned against him, her arm stretched over his chest. Everyone but Marjorie and Nessa had gone home. Marjorie sat by his head and Nessa was at his feet with her palms cupped around his heels. They had turned out the overhead light and the room was lit by the bedside lamp and the dim display of buttons set into the wall. The motor in the oxygen tube hummed. They listened to his breath and leaned in with every swell of air. Each swell was smaller than the last, waves ebbing to the shore.

Soon he sighed and no breath came to follow it.

"He's gone," Nessa whispered, and Marjorie dipped her head. Ruth began to tremble. She reached for Marjorie's hand and clung to it. She didn't know how long she stayed there, pressing herself into Rich's motionless body, shaking to stanch the tide of grief. But in the next moment Rich's shoulders lurched. He sputtered on a gulp of air, snorted, and began heaving out the rhythm of breath once more.

Ruth began to laugh. She didn't mean to but all the anguish that was pushing at her throat came bursting out in an unseemly guffaw. She dropped Marjorie's hand and sat up, fist to her mouth, but there was no hope of stopping, not with Nessa cackling now, bent double and gasping for air. It was just like crying, the way the laughter came shuddering up through their bellies, sobbing out of their mouths; they shook with it, not daring to look at Marjorie, who was silent and still at the head of the bed.

Ruth was the first to recover, panting and flushed. "I'm sorry, Marjorie," she said, when she could muster a voice. "You must think we're awful."

Marjorie did not reply. She began patting down the rumples on the pillow.

"It's not funny, we know that," Nessa added, her voice small.

Still Marjorie bowed her head. She put her hands to Rich's chest and watched it rise and fall. "Oh, I don't know," she said at last. She raised her eyes and Ruth saw a gleam in them, a tiny sparkle of mirth. "I thought he could be teasing us just now. Staying cheeky to the very end." She laughed then, but it was only the gentlest of titters. It was more of a smile really, guileless and kind, and Ruth saw that they were forgiven. She lay down and shuffled herself into Rich's side. All day, she thought, she had been walking into a headwind, fighting the force of the sorrow to come. Now, as her shoulders slackened against the bed, she let it flow over her. She heard Nessa sigh, saw her cup her hands to Rich's feet again. Marjorie offered an answering sigh, and they turned their focus to him once more.

It was not long before his breath began to dwindle. Ruth saw the color drain from his face. Every freckle and blemish stood out for a beat, then paled. She thought she felt a buzzing in his skin. It seemed to circle, to travel through Marjorie and Nessa, and ripple back up to her. It was a thread, drawing them in toward his heart. Each time it brushed across her she felt a rush of love for him, but each brush was weaker, an echo of itself.

"We're here, Rich," she whispered to him. "We're watching over you." She felt as if they were an ark, the three of them, a vessel, cradling the interval between each breath. All that mattered now was being there, hearing every lap and puff of air.

Part 2

Ruth

IN THE WEEK after Rich died, nothing made sense. Ruth would find herself halfway across the field to the picnic place, her feet in mismatched wellingtons, and she wouldn't know how she'd got there. Or she'd be pegging Ollie's socks onto the airer feeling quite sure she had never put on a wash or even emptied the machine when it was done. She couldn't recall the order of things. When had she registered the death? She remembered the baby screaming in the office next door and the too-sweet perfume worn by the registrar, but she had no idea if it had happened after the meeting with the vicar or before. She didn't even know if she'd got dressed for either of them. It was perfectly possible that she'd discussed the hymns and eulogies in her dressing gown, or shuffled into the register office in her slippers. She didn't care if she had, but she wished she could remember.

Nothing made sense, but the people around her talked as if it did. Michael Wardle, stifling his laugh for once, had stood at the window and remarked that these rain-sodden days reflected their mood. Geoff's wife, Liz, bringing a casserole from the farm, said that Rich had taken the sunshine with him when he went. *If only*, Ruth thought. If only the loss of the bright skies and the pulsing summer heat were all she had to bear. If only she could think that Rich was somewhere in the sun, hair glinting, face turned toward the light. But she could only think of him in the mortuary, cold and lonely in an icy drawer, and she could not forgive herself for leaving him there on his own. Other times she could only think of where he was not. Not warm beside her in the bed. Not clattering plates in the kitchen. Not grinning at Ollie or hunting for his car keys, swearing and tossing paper from the hall table in his search.

She was bewildered by everything. Memories came to her vivid and sharp. Rich grinning over the atlas with a four-year-old Ollie, testing him on capital cities. The smell of his hair after a shower. The way he tapped at his front teeth with his fingernail when he was thinking. Angran told her not to dwell on these things, that she was torturing herself by dredging them up all the time. Nessa kept putting her hands on Ruth's shoulders, pressing down with her palms. They both made decisions on her behalf.

We'll have Liz's casserole for tea.

This is the perfect photo of Rich for the order of service.

You need a bath, Ruth, would you like me to get it running?

Then they'd compliment her as if she'd made the decisions herself.

Well, at least you're able to feed us all.

Such a good job you've done, finding photos for the funeral.

Lovely to see you looking clean. Well done, you.

Sometimes she came to with a jolt. Then panic prickled in her chest. "Where's Ollie? Is he all right?"

He always was all right. He'd be in his room, looking through his binoculars, or hunched over a book of sudoku.

"How's it going, Ollie?"

"Fine."

He wouldn't look her in the eyes but she could see that his cheeks were slack. How could he be fine? His dad was dead. She thought of Rich on the hospital bed, after the nurse had laid him flat. They had all left the room while the bed was lowered and the pillows removed, and when they returned, Rich had seemed smaller. His chest, still and silent, had lost its power. His head looked narrow, his features thinned. Sometimes when Ruth pictured this she felt the blood drain from her face. Other times she brought it to mind and found only a numb kind of silence in response. It was a test. She thought of his freckles, sharp against his pale skin, the snarl of his lip where the oxygen tube had pushed against it, and if it brought tears, all the horror in her heart made sense. If nothing came, she was mad.

It was clear that nothing came to Ollie. She said: "You don't have to be brave. No one minds if you're upset."

He shrugged. "I know, Mum. I'm not stupid."

He rarely said anything more. She almost wished he'd start grabbing at his knees, pulling his mattress from the bed. But she dreaded that too. She didn't think she'd cope, alone in the house with Ollie, his teeth gritted, his screams jagged in his throat. She'd coped before, of course, but she'd always known that Rich would be there in the end, if only to listen to the tale of it afterward, to give her shoulders a squeeze.

"You did your best," he'd say. "What else can we possibly do?"

She wasn't doing her best now. Much as she would have

liked to hold Ollie in her arms, or hear him talk lovingly of his father, she was, in truth, too grateful for his reticence. She left him in his room too long, didn't make him eat or go to bed. "Ollie will keep me going," she had said to Rich. "I'll focus on his needs." But she hadn't done that yet. It was too great a task when nothing made sense.

Angran

SHE DECIDED TO walk to the funeral, up through the woods
and down the track to the village, with the rainwater gurgling in the ditches. It had rained steadily since the night
Rich died, and now, as she crossed the fields toward the
church, the hedges were dark with it, the twigs blackened
and gleaming. Drought-withered grass lay in clumps
along the footpaths and she wondered if it would be rude
to arrive with mud clagging the soles of her boots.

"Too bad if it is," she said. "As if mud matters at a time
like this."

It irritated her that the funeral was taking place in a
church. She had brought up her girls to shun religion, to
scorn insipid talk of the soul and the eternal. Down-to-
earth was how she thought of herself, so far down that she
had her hands in it most days; it rimmed her fingernails
and dirtied her knees.

"Pandering," she said to herself. "That's what it is. Pandering to Gerald and Marjorie, and they don't deserve it."

The vicar, she was convinced, would be an obsequious
man, who spoke with his head cocked and his hands clasped
earnestly before him. She didn't see why he should get to

pronounce upon the enormity of death. She doubted he'd ever met Rich, and she couldn't imagine that he had any real understanding of the trials of life. "Try bringing up two sniveling girls on your own in a house with no bathroom. Then tell me that God understands us like a father."

The church was ahead of her now, across the last field, and she squinted through her rain-speckled glasses at the red stone tower and the wet branches of an ancient yew. The lanes of the village were lined with cars, sheened with water and tipped at odd angles where they had pulled tight into the verges. There were people gathered at the lych gate, hunched under umbrellas, and more sheltering under the yew and at the church porch.

"Poor Ruth," she said. "They'll all be wanting to speak to her. She'll be overwhelmed." She quickened her pace, ready to be on hand to chivvy them away. There had been so much talk of love in the past two weeks, among all the people who had arrived unbidden at Ruth's house with their tears and their hothouse flowers; so much talk of sympathy and keeping her in their thoughts, but really, Angran thought, none of them had Ruth's best interests at heart. They wouldn't keep turning up if they did, expecting her to give out hugs and cups of tea. Angran had never seen Ruth so exhausted, so gray around her eyes, so dry-lipped and shrunken. Once the funeral was over, she was going to send Ruth to bed. She couldn't ban Nessa, but she'd keep everyone else away. Family only, she would tell them, and she'd make sure Nessa didn't start trying to pull Ruth to her feet. What Angran wanted was the three of them together, squashed up and cozy, Ollie lying at their feet with a sudoku while the rain tapped at the window.

That was all she'd ever wanted really, her girls gathered around her, safe and snug in the home she'd made for them. She'd never wanted the tears, the broken crockery, or their secret little flutters of laughter behind their hands.

"Don't think about that now," she told herself, as the church bell began to toll. "Irrelevant."

And yet only yesterday there had been laughter in Ruth's kitchen, which had stopped the moment she'd entered. It was Nessa who had smashed crockery this time, a cup with some words on it she was eager to hide. *World's Best*—Angran couldn't imagine what on earth could have been so funny, or why Nessa didn't explain as she poured coffee into a fresh cup.

She climbed the stile into the far side of the churchyard and spotted Ollie edging away from Ruth and Nessa so that he was alone on the path. He did not acknowledge her as she approached. He stood watching the huddles of mourners shuffling by. His wet hair lay flat against his forehead.

"Aren't you going in?" she said.

"Stupid question, Angran."

She was surprised when he answered. He had been mostly silent since the death, wandering the house with the binoculars hanging on his chest.

There was a bottleneck of people at the porch, shaking out umbrellas, peering around each other in search of space in the pews.

"Well, you'd better go," she said. "It's getting full."

"Someone might hug me."

"Don't be silly. You just tell them not to."

To demonstrate, she thrust out her arm at a woman

who was approaching them now, peeking out from her umbrella.

"Don't touch him," Angran said. "He needs his personal space."

The woman drew back, clutched at her husband's arm. It was Marjorie, Angran realized, and Gerald's face was rigid with startled outrage.

"Good riddance," she said to herself, as they tottered toward the church door. "No good them coming over all sweet when they've never apologized for what they said." Rain trickled under her collar as she watched them make their way through the crowd.

"What are you saying, Angran?" Ollie asked.

"Nothing," she told him. "Come with me." She marched him to the church door and parted the crowds for him. "Make way," she cried. "Chief mourner coming through."

She ushered him to the vestibule and, when she got there, Nessa pulled her into an embrace that smelled of wet cotton. "Mum, Rich always said you're so great with Ollie," she said, as people filed past in their rain-streaked coats. "So good of you to step in now."

Angran pulled away. "I need to step in with Ruth too. Where is she?"

But Nessa didn't answer. She was bustling Ollie away to a pew at the front, where Ruth was sitting, crowded into the corner, shoulders quivering.

"Wait," Angran called. "I'm coming!" Her voice was drowned by the organ as it rumbled into a processional. She found herself running down the central aisle, boots thumping on the carpet. She arrived at Ruth's pew just as Nessa slid into the last place.

"What about me?" she cried.

Nessa put her finger to her lips. "There's more space farther back," she hissed, "with Alan and Tom."

"Who the hell are Alan and Tom?" Angran asked, as the organ music began to swell. "You should make room for me here, at the front." She bent her knees and began shoving her hips into Nessa's thighs, hoping to expand the three inches of polished wood she had spotted at the end of the pew. All along the row people shuffled and shifted, but hardly any more space appeared.

"You met them at the hospital," Nessa whispered. "You'd better go to them now. They're really nice."

The pipes of the organ shuddered as the chords grew mightier. Angran thought back to Rich's bedside and remembered the couple she'd seen there. Alan was the older man, sniveling and making a performance of blowing his nose. Ruth had kissed him. She'd been all over him, as if he were at the center of her life, while Angran had been made to leave, untouched, without saying goodbye to Rich. He and Tom, she thought, would remember all this. Now they would witness her banishment once more, from this pew, from her place at her daughter's side.

"I know when I'm not wanted," she muttered. She marched back up the aisle and found herself confronted by the coffin. The leading pallbearers startled. The coffin lurched on their shoulders and Angran stood before them, arms flapping, while the organ soared.

"Are you all right?" someone asked, from a pew beside her. It was Alan, of course, and she flinched.

"Be quiet!" she spat. "I'm trying to keep out of the way." She stepped aside and dropped to her knees, pressing herself against the edge of the pew. The coffin rocked and swayed above her head. She saw the pallbearers' shoes, speckled with rain, tottering and twisting as they staggered to right themselves and make their way past. Nessa slid out of her seat and advanced toward her, bent double.

"Mum! What do you think you're doing? Get up!" She pushed her hands into Angran's armpits.

"Don't make a fuss," Angran hissed, squirming away from her.

"You're the one making the fuss. You're in the way."

"Oh, you always think I'm in the way. You'd rather I wasn't here at all."

She pulled away and began crawling to the back of the church. Her knees scraped against the carpet and she could smell the garage-sale mustiness of the hassocks. The thunder of the organ diminished at last and the vicar's voice boomed through the microphone.

"Let us pray." The scuffling of feet reverberated through the church. "Father," he began, "you know our hearts and share our sorrows."

Angran, as she dragged herself on, thought of her night visits to The Ravages. She was quite sure that no one had ever known her heart, much less shared her sorrows. Her hands slapped against the carpet and her boots rasped behind her. Nessa pursued her, legs bent, shoulders hunched.

"When we are angry at the loss we have sustained," the vicar intoned, "when we long for words of comfort, but find them hard to hear . . ."

"Why did you have to follow me?" Angran said, over her shoulder, to Nessa. "Leave me alone." She had reached the tiled floor of the vestibule now and she twisted herself to sit with her legs outstretched before her, facing the altar.

". . . let us turn our grief to truer living," the vicar continued, "our affliction to firmer hope." Angran wondered where this hope the vicar was invoking was supposed to come from, and how he could get away with spouting such rubbish. The chill of the stone tiles crept along her legs.

"I'm trying to help," Nessa said. She had her head in her hands and tears splashed out between her fingers.

Angran shivered.

"Rich is gone," Nessa wept. "We're all suffering the loss here." The congregation raised their heads and, in a rush of breath and echoes, said *Amen* as one.

Nessa

SHE ARRIVED AT Ruth's house with three boxes of pizza and a carrier bag bulging with detergents and dishcloths. Ollie opened the door, but did not step aside to let her pass.

"I'm solving a puzzle," he said, "so I can find out what it means to be alive." Papers were scattered behind him on the hall floor: household bills, curled till receipts, scuffed shopping lists spotted with grease.

"Looks like you're making a mess to me," Nessa said.

Ruth appeared from the kitchen. "Don't worry about the mess, Ollie," she said, rubbing her face. "It's great you're out of your room today." He returned to his papers and Nessa saw him squint at an envelope and let it spin to the floor. She strode past him and dropped the pizza boxes on the kitchen table.

"Well, I need to borrow your mum for a bit," she told him. "I need a serious talk with her." She saw a look of worry pass over Ruth's face. "What were you thinking," she continued, beckoning Ruth into the kitchen, "letting Angran take charge with the scattering of the ashes?"

Ruth went to the sink and gripped the edge of it, blinking out at the gray sky. "I had to, Ness. She got herself into

a right state at the funeral. I had to make up for it somehow."

"No, you didn't."

They had scattered the ashes a fortnight after the funeral and Angran had chosen The Ravages, of all places, to
do it. She'd led them up the muddy path from Black
Coombe Cottage. The hiss of the waterfall, heard from her
garden, swelled toward them as they climbed the hill, until
the full-bodied rush of it filled their ears. Ten days later,
Nessa was still furious.

"This isn't Rich's place," she had whispered to Ruth at
the time, as they huddled around the picnic tables at the
viewpoint. "We should be in your garden, or at the beach."
Ruth tried to tell her they were reclaiming The Ravages,
overlaying the fearful memories with good ones of Rich.
What good memories? Nessa had thought. *Where were the
Hawaiian shirts? Why weren't they dancing like he did, arms
opened wide as if to embrace the sky?* A heron had risen from
the dripping trees and flapped lazily downstream. Nessa
pointed it out, hoping they'd all lift their eyes from the
mud, but Ollie was the only one to respond, tracking it
with his binoculars, while Angran and Ruth stared toward
the foaming water.

"You and The bloody Ravages," she said now, clattering
the baking trays out of the cupboard. "You're obsessed
with the place."

"Don't!" Ruth cried. "I can't cope with this now." She
ran from the room. Ollie followed her up the stairs, calling
something about an envelope as he went. Nessa shoved the
pizzas into the oven and kicked the door shut. If Ruth was
retreating to her bed, she thought, she'd have to be taken

right back out of it. She had never forgiven Angran for hiding in her bed when they were children, hair in a tangle, hand to her eyes, and she was not about to let Ruth go that way.

She started to climb the stairs. She could see partly into Ruth's room, the rumpled covers and the bedside table cluttered with cups and screwed-up tissues. She saw Ollie come scrambling out from under the bed with a ball of paper in his hand.

"Oh!" Ruth cried, as he smoothed it out and handed it to her. She held it to her face and kissed it. "When do you think he wrote it?" she said. "What can it mean?" Ollie did not reply. He pushed past Nessa on the landing and ran to his room. "But we should talk about Dad," Ruth called after him, flapping the paper in her hands. "Let's read it all again."

Something about the way Ruth reached her arms to Ollie, but did not rise from her pillows, filled Nessa with rage. Ruth was rummaging under her covers now, pulling out a pack of Tylenol. Nessa saw the spasm of her throat as she gulped one down. Fury surged in her belly and tightened her jaw. She had been holding down her temper for days. Now she was in the grip of it, her blood pounding in her ears, legs rigid as she stood at Ruth's door.

She knew that anger was part of the grieving process, but she was pretty sure you were supposed to be angry with the person who died. Nessa was enraged with everyone else.

"Get up," she said to Ruth, through gritted teeth. "Just get the fuck out of bed." Ruth looked up, startled. "If you want Ollie to talk about Rich so much, go after him! Don't just sit there. Make the effort. Go on!"

"But—" Ruth stammered, "I can't. I mean, it might not be the best . . ."

A tiny spark of remorse flickered in Nessa's heart at the sound of the quiver in Ruth's voice, but she couldn't bring herself to heed it. She stepped forward and pulled the duvet from Ruth's legs. A plate thudded to the floor, spilling crusts of toast. The mess of them on Ruth's favorite rag rug struck her suddenly as funny. She'd come to cook for Ruth and tidy the house, and now it was more filthy than ever. This seemed so hilarious that she clutched at herself, gasping for air.

It wasn't a pleasant laugh. It had none of the joy that came from sharing a joke with Rich, or the relief that shuddered through her when she laughed with Ruth about Angran. This was a bitter laugh, aching in her belly, harsh in her mouth. She fell back onto the bed, clawing at the duvet and twisting it to her chest.

She was not aware of the change from laughter to tears, or of the moment when Ruth crept out of the bedroom and left her alone, rubbing her wet face against the sheets. She did not know how long she lay there afterward, when the sobbing had subsided. She wanted to sleep. She wanted darkness to descend and she wanted to wake in her own bed, with a fresh new day ahead of her. But she opened her eyes instead to the grainy darkness of dusk and the smell of pizza beginning to burn. Down in the kitchen she heard the clatter of plates and Ollie's voice, high in complaint. She could not bring herself to go downstairs and join them. Not with her eyes sore and swollen. Not when she had assured Rich that she was capable and strong, but had failed at the first hurdle.

Across the rumpled folds of duvet she saw the paper

Ruth had been holding to her heart. She reached for it and switched on the bedside light.

> *Dear Ollie,*
>   *One day you will be a man and I'm so sad I won't see that.*

It made her smile when she saw that the letter was not finished. It made her think of their teaching-college days, how he rarely completed his lesson plans but approached his classes with haphazard confidence. "I'll be all right once I'm in the flow of it," he'd say. "I'll work it out as I go along."

She wondered if he'd made a similar excuse when he abandoned the letter. *He'll know what I mean by the time he's read this far.*

Rich had always believed that spontaneity would see him through, that things would work out for the best. Was this the way to live? Nessa wondered. Was this the way to die? Was his trust so great that he had left it to life itself to find the perfect ending to this letter? She folded the paper, slid it into her back pocket and went downstairs.

"Hey, you two," she called across the hall. "I've had an idea." They were hunched at the kitchen table, teeth crunching on the singed crusts. Ollie's mouth was smudged at the corners with tomato sauce. "We should have a party," she said, reaching for a slice of pizza. The letter crinkled in her pocket as she lowered herself into the chair. "A joyful one, for his birthday. Music, dancing, a great big platter of cheese." She grinned at them both. "Isn't that a brilliant idea?"

Ruth

RICH HAD BEEN dead for six weeks and Ruth still awoke to the ache of it. She had expected the heavy pangs of loss and bewilderment that came with grief, but not the physical pain. Some days her shoulders were so rigid they felt bruised. This morning there were cramps in her arms. The tendons in her neck felt taut, so that she could not turn her head. She did not want to turn her head anyway, not toward the empty pillows or the cold, flat sheets beside her.

Downstairs in the kitchen she could hear Ollie riffling through the cutlery drawer. She should have been up earlier, on hand to help him find the specific knife or spoon his breakfast required. She should not have been lying still for the last half hour, wondering what had happened to Rich's unfinished letter to Ollie. She could only half remember what he'd written on the back of it, about the color of the sky. She pictured his writing. *Open your arms to the flow of the dawn. Heart full of golden sky.* She was certain he was trying to tell her something, but she couldn't guess at what he meant.

Now she sighed and pushed her feet to the floor. Her

movements felt stiff and unnatural. *What if I can't do this?* she thought.

What if the effort of getting downstairs leaves me shaking, dry-mouthed, unable to speak? She remembered Angran, when they were children, standing at the kitchen door, forehead against the jamb. Ruth and Nessa would be squabbling over the last of the milk and if they appealed to her to intervene she would close her eyes and let her mouth fall slack. Ruth buried her head for a moment in Rich's dressing gown, breathed in the smell of his skin and stale deodorant. Then she wrapped herself in it and forced herself down the stairs.

She found Ollie at the sink, washing his hands.

"Time to get into some new routines," she said.

He did not look up at her. "I'm having three pieces of toast, Mum, one with honey, two with jam. A cup of tea with one sugar, Mum, and then a satsuma."

This was his longest utterance since Rich had died. She supposed she should be glad, even if it told her nothing of how he felt. She reached for the kettle and he pushed her hand away.

"No, Mum," he said. "I'm on my second toast. Tea comes after the third."

They got into a tussle, both of their fists around the handle while the water sloshed toward the lip.

"You can't fight over a kettle, Ollie. Imagine if it was hot!"

"It's not hot, stupid," he said, and yanked it away.

"Ollie! It's for my cup of tea, not yours!"

His mouth fell open. "Oh."

She saw that the buttons of his school shirt were mismatched and the fabric bulged at his chest. He did not pass her the kettle, but replaced it on the cradle and went back to his seat. She watched him scraping his knife rhythmically over his toast, attempting to ensure total coverage of butter. There were some apples in the fruit bowl, spotted and pale.

"How about one of these for breakfast?" she said. "The last ones from Angran's garden."

He glared at her. "It's Thursday," he said. "I don't have apples on Thursdays, Mum." A crumb had caught on the bulge in his shirt and a stain of red jam was spreading over the fabric. She didn't dare tell him. He might be glad to be more respectable for school, but equally, he could decide she was criticizing him and throw his toast onto the floor. Easier to pretend she hadn't noticed. So many things she had to pretend not to notice. The buildup of grease around the cooker, the smell of her unwashed sheets, saved because she didn't want to rinse out the last scents of Rich. She'd been ignoring any post that arrived addressed to him, the dialogue box that appeared when she opened her laptop, asking if she wished to log into his account or her own, all of Angran's hints about packing up her stuff and moving to Black Coombe Cottage.

"So it's satsumas on Thursdays," she said now. "When do you have apples?"

He glared at her again. "It's only satsumas on Thursdays if I'm having toast, Mum," he said. "On a porridge Thursday I have raisins."

"Did Dad remember all this?" Ruth asked.

"He made a chart to remind him, Mum. But I know it off by heart."

"Clever boy."

Her love for him came in pangs, a rush in her blood that

made her smile or gather her arms across her chest to stop herself hugging him. At these moments, she felt she knew him as a mother should, as if there was something flowing between them, the ghost of the umbilical cord holding them close. But there were other times when his face was so closed and unresponsive that she did not know how to offer him warmth.

"I'm going to find that chart," she said now. "Then I can get it right for you too."

She opened the drawer in the table and rummaged through the papers, crumbs and rubber bands. She saw Rich's handwriting on an envelope, *Angran—Shawl, Nessa—Necklace.* The fat certainty of the capitals and the sloppy curl of the *g* were so much part of his character she almost heard his voice forming the words on the page. She gasped with a stab of longing, but Ollie lunged at her and snatched the envelope from her hands.

"Wait, Ollie," she cried, but he grasped it to his chest.

"It's mine."

"But I need to see."

She could tell he couldn't hear what she was saying. He was intent now on stuffing the paper between the mismatched buttons of his shirt, and his breathing was fast and loud.

"Hey, Ollie, what's the matter?" she said, but he darted away and ran to his room, banging against the table as he left. She heard the thud of feet overhead, the slam of his door, the thump of the mattress being pulled from his bed.

She sat down and put her forehead against the table. The school taxi would be here soon. It would wait only three minutes if Ollie wasn't at the door. She knew he wouldn't be.

The wood beneath her brow smelled of rancid butter. The grain blurred before her eyes. She imagined herself rising from the chair, going to Ollie's room. She knew it was possible, and she felt a spark in her brain, an impulse, but it died before her limbs could respond. If she went to him, she thought, she'd have to speak softly, the words unhurried. Any edge of strain in her voice and he'd accuse her of shouting. There were times when he seemed oblivious to the kindness in her voice, or her motherly warmth. But he never missed her stress, and he seemed to take it as an insult. She didn't think she was up to it. Not with the twists of grief in her gut, not with Ollie screeching out his own misery with his sheets stuffed into his mouth.

The taxi came sloshing through the puddles in the lane. She heard the squawk of the handbrake and Jack's high voice calling from the car. The driver tooted the horn, once, then twice, and then a third, last-chance warning. She did not lift her head from the table.

Marjorie

HER HANDS SHOOK on the steering wheel as she drove away from Cedar Park. She'd left Gerald there, pushing the knot of his tie toward his Adam's apple, blinking at the woman in the opposite chair. She was strange-looking, Marjorie thought, with that mass of jet curls piled at her crown. It must have been a wig. Did she put it on herself, she wondered, or did one of the healthcare assistants place it there each morning? Perhaps she believed it made her look young, despite her sagging jaw and her wet, milky eyes. Old women needed pale colors around their faces, Marjorie believed. Ash blond or white, and light-pastel scarves to hide the floppy neck. She'd considered going to buy herself something like that this morning. Gerald had never enjoyed shopping and it would be a kindness to go without him.

"You should treat yourself," Denise had said, when she took her to sign the last of the forms in her office that morning. "You've worked so hard to keep Gerald going. You know you deserve it."

Marjorie didn't think she deserved it. Not after she'd seen Gerald's face as he lowered himself into that ugly winged chair. She saw him press his lips together. He'd worn the same expression at the funeral. He'd given her those three little taps on her knee as they settled into the pew, but there was no conviction in them. His lips had been a thin line, his eyes too still in their sockets as he stared ahead, avoiding the coffin. She'd passed him a hanky and he'd pushed it away.

She drove home from Cedar Park and went straight to the dining room. She stood on a chair and unhooked the curtains from the rail. They were heavy in her arms and she staggered a little as she stepped down. Without the curtains the light was stark, showing up the cup rings on the table. The comfort in the room had gone.

She had decided to take Gerald to Cedar Park for respite days after he'd attacked the curtains with a fork.

"It's only one day a week," Denise had said. "It will seem like nothing to him, but let me tell you, your life will be transformed."

Marjorie couldn't imagine that. Not with the weight of grief on her. She fingered the folds of fabric in search of the gash he had made. If she couldn't transform her life, she could at least transform her dining room, make it fit for the eyes of guests. Not that she wanted guests. So many kind people had called on her, brought her cards and flowers and promises of days out, but none of them knew what it was like to lose a son. Nor did they know the exact timbre of Richard's laugh, the way he shrugged sometimes before he spoke. And she had tried to hide the extent of Gerald's failing from them too. It wasn't so bad if they noticed the falter in his speech, but she was embarrassed by the way his temper flared, strange words leaping from lips, loud and improper.

She let the curtain fall to the floor. *Ollie*, she thought.

Now is my chance to talk to Ruth properly, to find out how he is. She went to the phone and called her, but she hardly got a chance to speak before Ollie came on to the phone.

"Shouldn't you be at school?" she asked him. "Are you poorly?"

She couldn't get any sense out of him. Half the time he was silent, the rest he was shouting so loudly that his voice crackled in the speaker. He wanted to know about the necklace Richard had given her. She put her hand to her throat and felt the bulk of the ugly beads beneath the collar of her blouse. She had come to feel a strange kind of love for this gift, though she was always careful to keep it hidden at her throat. She didn't see how she could explain this to Ollie.

"Speak up, Other Grandma." His voice jabbed into her ear. "What have you learned about being alive?"

"I don't know," she said, and she must have upset him because there was a crash as if the phone had been dropped. Then there was Ruth's voice, tired, apologizing.

"It would be lovely if you could visit us soon," Ruth said. "Do you think if I sat down with Gerald and—"

Marjorie found herself interrupting. "I could drive down alone, you know, if that would be easier." She thought of Gerald, sitting in that awful chair. Tears pricked at her eyes. "Actually, Ruth, I think I'd better go. Do excuse me."

She knew that Gerald would be trying to keep himself upright in that chair. That he would be tugging at his tie, trying to hide the way his chin quivered whenever he thought of Richard. Marjorie hadn't even told Denise that Richard had died. There had never been an appropriate time. There had been so many forms to sign. A consent for something, then contact information for emergencies. There had been so many rooms to see, so many people—

care assistants, a cook, a local historian with pink streaks in her hair, hoping to collect stories from the residents. What if she was asking Gerald about his family now? What if he was calling for Richard, like he did last night?

"Nothing prepares you," he said, every night, "to see your own son dead."

It was so intensely private, the way his voice quavered as he spoke and his fingers grasped at the sheets. She should never have left him exposed there at Cedar Park.

She phoned Denise to explain. "Ah," Denise said. "Perhaps we should rethink the whole plan."

"You mean I should come for him now, and bring him home?"

She couldn't wait to get into the car. What a relief it would be, she thought, to have him in the passenger seat on the way home, fiddling with the clips on the glove compartment, tutting if she was late to change gear. This morning, over breakfast, he'd smiled at her, wide enough for her to see the glint of his gold molar. He'd said: "Bloody good grub, Marjorie, damn bloody good."

It couldn't have been the first time she'd heard him swear, not after fifty years of marriage, but it came as such a shock that she laughed. How light and bubbling that laugh had been. She had forgotten there could be brightness in her blood after so many weeks of grief. He laughed back at her. It didn't last long. Just a few gasps that passed between them, but now she wanted more. She said to Denise: "I'm so terribly sorry. I should have told you before. I'll come now." She wondered why she had not taken his hand when he called in the night.

"Stay put for now," Denise said. "I'll talk to the man himself."

Marjorie replaced the phone in the cradle. She looked at the cup rings, the broken drawers on the bureau. She sank down beside the curtains. *What have I done?* she said to herself, and lifted them into her arms. *Please,* she murmured into the folds, and it felt like a prayer. *Please tell me how to go on.* The curtains were heavy and they smelled of dust. She gathered the fabric to her chest and rocked it like a baby. *Please,* she said. *Please, bring him back.*

Gerald

HE WAS THINKING about antimacassars. There were frilled white antimacassars over the back of every chair in the Garden Room. He thought they were pointless, seeing as most of the men didn't even have hair to put Macassar oil on. The women didn't either, apart from the one who looked foreign to him. She had piles of the stuff, heaped on her head like a coiffured . . . a coiffured . . . The word failed him. He thought she looked like some coiffured dog, with her foreign hair and the bright red beads at her neck, her jowls hanging down. She was rattling her cup against her saucer. He wished she would just drink the damn tea, instead of rattling like that, and he hated her hair, the way it overspilled the edge of the antimacassar.

Antimacassars. The word had come to him so easily, unbidden, and he didn't even want it. He wanted Richard. A photo of him would do. Better than the framed photos on the walls here, of errand boys on bicycles and the coronation of the Queen. Marjorie had said there was a lovely view from the . . . the . . . The words *French farce* came to him, then *French arse*, and he gripped the wooden armrests on his chair, hoping that he hadn't spoken aloud. The burbling started up in his ears, a sucking pressure that made him want to bash his palm against his temples. *French art, French tart.* He looked toward the French windows, but there was no view to be admired. The glass was steamed up and a man in front of them was yanking at the handles. "I'll be late," the man said, over and over, his voice hoarse. "I need to get out. Somebody open the door."

Gerald sat back with his head against the antimacassar. A woman came limping over to him. She was young, perfumed, and she knew his name.

"I'm Denise, the manager here," she said. "You met me this morning, remember?"

He tried to square his shoulders, but he couldn't. There was a curve to the back of the chair, and he could feel the antimacassar slipping down behind him. He said: "Yes, yes, naturally I do."

She patted his hand. "Well, that's great, Gerald, it really is."

The man at the French windows pounded his fist against the glass.

"Now I need a quiet word with you," the woman said. "Are you up to a walk in the garden?"

The burbling swirled in his head as he rose to his feet. He followed her to the garden, where the gravel crunched with every step. She asked if he'd been a keen gardener in his time, then said something he couldn't catch about thirst and rain, or it might have been hearses and pain. He wanted to tell her that Richard was not a keen gardener. Their place was a mess, weeds along the edges of the fence, brown patches and scuffs on the lawn, but he couldn't find the courage to speak up. He didn't want to burble. Except that "burble" wasn't the right word. He thought of "Bible," "bubble," "blab," and he pressed his fists to his temples.

He wished he'd been prepared. Someone could have told him how hard it would be to lose a son. But perhaps they could not. There were no words for this gnawing in his chest. For the way other people's smiles and voices, their footsteps on the gravel, seemed so far away, so small and irrelevant. He would not have believed that it would be this hard to keep his back straight, his face still and his hands steady while his blood churned with the force of this loss.

The woman stopped. She reached up to pull his fists away from his head. "I can see it's a struggle," she said to him, and he brought his hands down to his sides. He'd have to keep them there from now on. He didn't like this habit people had taken up these days, touching each other when they'd hardly made acquaintance. He quickened his pace and she followed, her footsteps uneven behind him. He could hear her talking but couldn't make much sense of it. Something about bereavement. That it wasn't a good time to start a plan of respite. He wanted to tell her there was no respite from bereavement, not even for a second. He would have done, except there was this cacophony in his head. Besides, it wasn't the sort of thing one said to a stranger. There was a bank of rhododendrons ahead. The leaves were dark, the shadows black in the depths. Something clicked in his head and her voice came through clearly.

"So if you'd prefer, Gerald, we could give up for a while."

He stopped. He wondered why he was walking with his hands so stiffly at his sides. "Give up?" he said. "No one got anywhere by giving up, you know."

She put her hand on his elbow and turned him away from the rhododendrons. He saw a set of French windows ahead, and a man in the room behind them, face against the glass.

"Well, if you're quite sure," she said. The leaves dripped in the bushes along the path. She led him past the French windows and over a checkered patio. "We'll stick to your plan of weekly visits, then. How brave you are."

She brought him to a room with frilled white antimacassars on the chairs. A woman with hair like a poodle's rested her jowls on her chest and snored. A man stood at the French windows and rattled the handle. These weren't his people. They knew nothing of Richard and what it was like to lose him. Who did? Ruth? The woman in the shorts? He was glad he wasn't in a room with them. He thought of Ollie at the funeral, his face pale and sullen, and a shock of something like fear twisted through his chest. *No one prepares you*, he thought, *for the loss of your son*. For the other losses that follow. That boy, when he saw him, had grown. His jaw had lengthened and misery was sharp on his face. Of course it was. The boy was bereaved. But hadn't he, Gerald, caused that misery once?

"I need a phone," he said. "My grandson—"

"You need quiet," the manager said. "This room here's the best place for you today."

"The phone," he said. He wished he had one of those mobiles. There was one at home. He'd have to start keeping it in his pocket with his hanky. Keep the boy's number with him and give him some guidance every day. Without a father, Ollie would need the advice of a man.

"Nothing prepares you," he'd say, "to see your own son dead."

No, he wouldn't say that. Damn crackpot thing to say to

a child. And if the bubbling in his ears kept up he wouldn't hear anything back.

"Do you want a paper, Gerald?" the nurse woman asked him. "The *Mail*? The *Telegraph*? The trolley will be along soon." He lowered himself into a chair, reached behind his neck for the antimacassar and threw it to the floor.

Ruth

NESSA STOOD AT the foot of Ruth's bed with her hands on her hips.

"Why aren't you out of bed?" she asked. "It's a lovely day. You should be out in the fresh air."

It was a Sunday morning. The curtains were still drawn and the light in the room seemed grubby, tinged with dust and shadows. Ruth looked down at the quilt bunched around her knees, the satin sunflowers turned to rumples of orange and yellow. She wasn't sure why she wasn't out of bed. Perhaps it was because she couldn't bear to spread out the quilt, see the flowers glowing in the sun, when Rich was not here to marvel at them. Or it could have been the dream she'd had, so vivid and intense she had woken up shaking. Across the landing Ollie sat on his bed and stared at her, a crumpled envelope in his hand. She closed her eyes. "I've had a letter from the school," she said to Nessa. "I haven't dared open it. Will you?"

"No," Nessa replied. "You've got to read it yourself. Do it now and face up to it."

It was all right for Nessa, Ruth thought. Her mind was clear and her energy never seemed to dwindle. Ruth didn't think she had bad dreams either, not recurring ones that left her breathless and afraid to sleep.

"It'll be an attendance letter," Nessa said. "How many days has he missed now?"

"I don't know. Twelve? Maybe more."

She couldn't stop thinking of the dream. There had been dead rats swirling in the river at the picnic place. The black log she had seen at the picnic with Ollie and Rich was damming the water, wet and bloated, like a limb with gangrene.

"Christ, Ruth," Nessa said now. "You're lucky he's not at secondary school. They'd be taking you to court by now!"

The bodies of the rats were swollen, their fur slick and viscous. The current pulled them under the water, spun them back to the surface and thudded them into the log with a sound like the pounding of a headache or a jumping heart.

"I'm so tired," she said to Nessa. "Won't you just sit with me and help me work out what my dream means?"

"It doesn't mean anything. I don't hold with that crap." She yanked at the quilt. Ruth's legs prickled into goose-bumps as the cold hit them, and they quivered as she pushed her feet to the floor. She hated that quiver. It was part of the dream, standing on the bank, watching the rats. It was part of her childhood, standing in the garden at Black Coombe Cottage when Angran disappeared into the woods. "There," Nessa said, steering her toward the bathroom. "I knew you could do it. You just need to put the effort in."

She stood in the shower wishing she could cry. Tears had come often in the first weeks after Rich died. Too often, she had thought, at times. She'd take her hands away from her sore wet cheeks and find Ollie before her, holding out a tissue at arm's length. But lately the tears seemed to have shriveled away. She longed for the release they brought her, but her eyes were unyielding, knotted in their sockets.

She wanted to explain to Nessa that she had been putting the effort in from the moment she woke. She had been calling for Rich in her dream and she'd had to choke back the cry as she woke so that Ollie wouldn't hear it. The effort left her reeling, but it didn't stop there. Five minutes later, Ollie had come to her, thrusting a sock at her chest, and she had forced herself to smile in the hope of soothing him. There was a thread loose in the heel, he said, and he couldn't stand it. His voice jabbed at her as he described the itching at length, the grinding into his skin. She'd wanted to flick her hand at him: *For God's sake, Ollie, what does it matter?* Most parents would have said something similar—and they'd have forgiven themselves for their irritation, trusting that their child would survive. But Ruth had no such trust in Ollie's survival. Not when he was grieving. And not when he could barely distinguish between irritation and anger, and could not be comforted by conciliatory cuddles that would otherwise reassure him he was loved. And not when, for him, every itch was as urgent as a wound. If she told him it didn't matter, she'd be telling him, in fact, that it didn't matter who he was. So she had put in the effort and snipped off the thread with a smile. It would have looked like nothing to a bystander, but now she was exhausted.

She stepped out of the shower and stood for a moment

shivering in her bathrobe. She could hear Ollie talking to Nessa in her room.

"We're supposed to find out what it means to be alive, to learn it from my dad."

Ruth had heard him saying something similar before, to Marjorie perhaps, or Gerald on one of his many phone calls to the house. She was glad he hadn't embarked on it with her. She might find herself telling him that life was about dreaming of dead rats and forgetting how to cry. She moved across the landing and saw Nessa with her arms full of bedclothes. She was laughing into Ollie's serious face.

"What you've got to do, Ollie, is grab life with both hands," she said. "Hold on tight to every special moment."

What special moments? Ruth wanted to say. But she thought she saw something joyous in Ollie's face as he sped past her to his bedroom and she didn't want to spoil it. Nessa shook the sheets over the bed.

"You must be feeling better now you're clean," she said to Ruth. "Let's get you out of the house."

Nessa decided on a round walk, across the fields to the village and back along the river. Ollie complained about the wet grass soaking through his socks and Ruth tried to chivvy him the way Rich did, making jokes about mud monsters and sock thieves. He never once laughed and he stopped every five steps to adjust his heels or pluck a real or imaginary stone from his Crocs.

They took the tourist track to The Ravages. At the viewpoint, Ruth sat at a picnic table with her back to the waterfall and looked down on Black Coombe Cottage. From this distance the mossy lawn looked like worn velvet, brown and threadbare around the picnic table. The crows on the roof were flecks of jet.

She turned to Nessa, her heart pounding in her throat. "Oh, God! I can't keep track of anything. Mum was coming for lunch and she'll be at my house right now. What am I going to do?"

Nessa grinned back at her. "Celebrate! You've let her down for once in your life." She threw back her head and laughed. But Ruth dialed Angran's number with shaking hands.

"Where are you?" Angran said. "I'm starving!"

"I'm at The Ravages. I'm so sorry, Mum, I didn't mean—"

"The Ravages? You're not going to do anything stupid, are you?"

Ruth swallowed. She could hear the clatter of the falls behind her, the riot of gushes and sputters as the water hurtled over the rocks. "Something stupid?" she murmured. "Is that what you—" She faltered, afraid to go on.

"I can't hear you," Angran barked. "What's happening?"

Ruth watched Ollie and Nessa making their way down the steps toward the pool. They were peering over the bank at the foaming water. Ruth explained that Nessa had come to the house and got her out of bed.

"She forced you? Doesn't she know you need some peace and quiet?"

Ruth looked at the shielded windows of the house and thought of the shadowed rooms inside. She remembered the smell of Angran's bedroom when she was a child, damp floorboards and cold coffee, and the shape of her in the bed, the covers mounded over her hips. Ruth had longed, sometimes, to push her hands into the folds and feel the warmth of the sheets against her skin, but she had never dared.

"I can't do this, Mum."

"I know you can't. You need someone there who knows how you feel."

From the path below, Nessa called, "Come on, Ruth! Ollie wants some clean socks!"

"I'll sort it out," Angran told her. "Just get back home as soon as you can."

But it seemed to take forever to walk along the river. Nessa wouldn't cooperate. She kicked through fallen leaves, and, once they'd left the falls behind, she tried to teach Ollie how to throw skimmers into the stream. She turned to Ruth, cheering, when Ollie sent one bounding over the water. Ruth wiggled her fingers in acknowledgment, but as soon as they turned away she let the smile sag on her face. She could hear them giggling, but she had no desire to find out what was funny. She really didn't care.

She had felt like this before: she had sat through dinner parties with her mouth clamped shut, wearied by the banter. And when Ollie was newborn and their friends came visiting with flowers and knitted hats, she had hidden in her room, claiming to be catching up on sleep, when really she was lying motionless beneath the covers, hardly daring to breathe.

What if it never stops? she thought now. *What if I go to bed tonight and never get up again?* It was possible, she reckoned, that one day she would turn her mind to Rich and find that she didn't even care that he was gone. She had hated herself for this before. Now she knew that everyone else would hate her too. They'd count up Ollie's missed days at school, the skipped meals, the plates piling up in the sink. They'd stand there, all of them, at her bedroom door, just as she had stood at Angran's, and each of them would suffer when she turned away.

"Mum was depressed, wasn't she, when we were kids?" she said to Nessa, as they came to the picnic place. She kept her eyes averted from the water lest she saw a rat swirling in the current. "Do you think that's where I get this from?"

Nessa leaned against an oak and looked up into the branches above. Ruth saw the sharp outline of her chin, certain and defined against the complex shadows of the bark behind.

"You've just suffered a horrendous loss," she said. "Of course you feel awful."

But Ruth could not be sure that the cold weight in her belly, the drag in her thighs, had anything to do with Rich. It was more to do with rats in the water and the shadows in Angran's house. Grief, with its sharp and urgent pain, seemed bright in comparison, and she wanted it back.

"Why is it," she said to Nessa, "that I'm so bothered by Mum and you're not?"

Nessa shrugged. "I dunno. Maybe I was more defiant from the start. All that running off to the woods, it used to enrage me. I know you thought she was going to do herself in, but I didn't think it would ever really happen. You should give her that credit at least."

Ruth, thinking of the thudding rats, wasn't sure that any credit was due. Those nights spent shivering in her mother's bed, waiting for her to return from the woods, had blighted her life. "I don't know what scared me more," she said, "Mum's anguish, or the thought that she might never return. I'm sure it's why I feel so useless now."

Nessa shook her head. "You're feeling useless because you've stopped getting out of bed and brushing your hair."

"You hated it when she ran off too, Ness. You can't say it hasn't affected you."

"Yeah, I can," Nessa pushed back, but she wouldn't meet Ruth's eye. She began talking about being strong, how she'd had a good life because she'd never been scared of anything. "It's better to be angry, if you ask me. Do you know what pissed me off back then? The way she moaned about Dad but never made any effort to find out where he was."

Ruth tried to remember their father. She pictured a stubbly chin and a smell of cigarettes in a knitted jersey, but she thought she might have invented that. Nessa had memories of strumming his guitar. She'd said that when he sang lullabies he'd fall asleep himself.

"I never believed Mum when she said he didn't do anything for us," she said. "I was furious not to have a dad anymore."

Ruth looked at Ollie, who had moved away from the river into the field. He was standing on one leg, holding one of his Crocs and frowning into it. She didn't think he was furious. She didn't know what he was. Numb, perhaps, or bewildered. Searching for answers he'd never find. She hoped he wouldn't end up like her, tainted, hollow and heavy with indifference.

When they arrived at the house they found Angran inside. She was kneeling on the hall floor with her back to the door, surrounded by cardboard boxes and bulging bin bags. There was dust in the air, and the bookshelves in the hall were empty. She did not turn around as they entered, or look up as Ollie edged past her to the stairs.

"What are you doing?" Ruth asked. She could see a pair of Rich's jeans in a bin bag, the ones with a curry stain on the knee. She had embroidered a pattern of autumn leaves over the yellow splotch in the fabric. "Please don't throw anything out, Mum," she said.

"It's no good your being here on your own," Angran replied. "We've had a long enough trial." She reached for a stack of books and began thumping them into a box.

Nessa gaped at Angran. "You don't mean—" she said. "Moving her to your place? Today?"

"I don't see why not. At least it's quiet there. No one forcing her out of bed before she's ready." She unrolled a length of parcel tape and tore at it with her teeth.

"I can't believe this," Nessa said. She turned to Ruth, eyes wide, but Ruth didn't dare to respond. She watched Ollie on the landing easing a fresh pair of socks over his feet.

"I've packed up your wardrobe already," Angran said, slapping the tape onto the lid of a shoebox. "But your clothes were all mixed up with Rich's. It was a mess."

"Tell her," Nessa said. "Tell her it's not what you want."

Ruth's mouth was dry. She was halfway up the stairs now, holding the banisters with both hands. She saw the letter from the school on her bedroom floor.

"I have to think of Ollie," she said. "It'll be better for him." It sounded like a plausible reason, but she didn't really believe it. She didn't care where she went. As long as there was a bed and she could lie in it, with the curtains closed and the duvet drawn over her head.

Nessa

She looked at Angran's back. She saw her spine poking at the fabric of her T-shirt. She saw two ragged holes at her collar where she must have ripped a label out. She looked old. The skin on her arms was crumpled and it swung from her bones as she reached out for the books and brought them to the box at her side. It would be easy to lift her, Nessa thought, grab her by the armpits and drag her out of the house. She hadn't thought in this way since she was a teenager, when arguments had flared almost every week. Nessa had hidden in her room then, biting her nails, wondering what it would feel like to punch her mother, whether it would hurt her knuckles if she hit bone. How tempting it was, she thought, to give in to that now. To stride up to Ruth's bedroom afterward, dusting herself down: *Right, that's her sorted. You should do the same.* That would be grabbing life with both hands, all right.

The parcel tape made a shrieking sound as Angran un-rolled it at speed and wound it around another box. "If you're going to hang about here, Nessa, you can help with the packing. There's a ton of it to do."

She hauled another empty box across the floor. Nessa leaped forward and grabbed it by the rim. "Stop!" she shouted. "Just stop!" She flung the box away from them. "It's the worst thing Ruth could do, going to live with you. It'll finish her off!" It wasn't what she meant to say, but it was too late now. The adrenaline had surged through her and the words came spitting from her lips. "You never even liked Rich. I bet you've been dancing on his grave." She watched with satisfaction as the color drained from Angran's face. Ruth appeared at the top of the stairs, gesturing for her to stop, but the words had a force of their own and there was no hope of halting them. "You never liked any men," she said, turning her attention back to Angran, who was scrabbling to her feet. "Just because yours ran away, you thought they'd all do the same. You were jealous of Ruth having Rich. You wanted her miserable and lonely like you."

"Please, Nessa," Ruth cried, running down the stairs. "Don't listen to her, Mum."

"Oh, I won't," Angran said. The color was back in her face now, spots of red at her cheeks. Her eyes were fierce behind her glasses. "You think you're so clever," she said to Nessa, "but all you are is angry. I don't think that's made anyone happier—do you?"

Several retorts came to Nessa's mind:

You're just as angry as I am.

You won't make Ruth happier moving her to your stinking house.

How are any of us supposed to be happy when you never showed us how?

But none came out. The words that had flowed so freely moments ago were clamped in her throat. There was only a tiny voice, quavering somewhere far away.

"Is that why you kept running off to The Ravages when

we were little? Because I was angry all the time?" The voice was so small she didn't even know she had spoken.

Angran's answer was as loud and strident as before. "I don't know what you're talking about. I never ran off anywhere."

Nessa looked down at her hands. She tried to clench her fingers into fists, but they wouldn't go. "You did run off," she said, but she was backing to the door now, and her voice was too faint to be heard. It was she who had sent Angran to the woods, all those years ago. All that grabbing at her clothes and screaming through gritted teeth, it was ugly and wrong. She looked at Ruth, who was sitting hunched on the bottom stair, head resting on the newel post.

"I'm sorry," she mouthed, but Ruth's eyes were closed. Nessa could not think how to help her now, not without grabbing and pulling, making everything worse. She let herself out of the house and drove slowly home, her throat tight with unspoken words.

It was only later that she remembered Ollie. She thought of the socks in his chest of drawers. He'd have to know where they were. He'd have to be sure they were clean, laid out correctly in the top two drawers. Someone would have to haul that chest up the stairs if he was going to sleep at Black Coombe Cottage and she doubted that Ruth or Angran would have the strength to do it. Here at last was a sensible use for her grabbing hands. She strode out to her car and drove back to Ruth.

Angran

MOVING ALL OF Ruth's things to Black Coombe Cottage turned out to be a lengthy job. It was hard work, stacking the furniture in the hallway, lugging boxes of sewing supplies and bedding up the stairs, but Angran did it willingly over a period of a fortnight while Ruth lay, still and silent, in the spare room. She'd never had a chance to fit a door into the gap between the bedrooms. The hole was on the narrow side, rough-edged and leaking dust, but Angran didn't see how she could do anything about it now. She had no intention of banging about in Ruth's room while she slept.

"Peace and quiet. That's what she needs." She said this to Ollie and kept him downstairs with his sudokus until bedtime. She said it to Nessa when she came visiting, wanting to open Ruth's curtains or drag her downstairs for her meals. And she said it to herself, remembering how she had longed for it when it first dawned on her that John would never return. In those days it had been unnerving to hear the girls' footsteps pattering over the bare floor-boards at night, their fidgeting at her bedroom door. Ruth especially seemed to stand there for hours, slurping at her thumb in her mouth. If there had been someone on hand,

Angran thought, to see to her children, as she was seeing to Ollie now, she might have been calmer with them. All that misery, roiling in her blood, she might not have unleashed it if they'd only left her alone. She still shuddered when she thought of The Ravages at night. Ruth at least would not go that way. Not if she was hidden upstairs, lying in the dark.

So it pained her to discover one morning that Ruth had been on the phone to Marjorie, inviting her to visit the next day.

"I don't want that woman here," Angran told her. "No one has apologized yet for the terrible things they said to Ollie."

Ruth was out of bed, a scratty cardigan pulled over her pajamas. She was kneeling on the landing, rummaging through bin bags of rags and tea towels.

"*She* didn't say anything to Ollie, Mum. And, anyway, all that seems like ages ago now."

It was true that since Rich died, Gerald's attitude seemed to have changed, but the new Gerald wasn't any better, as far as Angran could see. He just phoned Ollie all the time and talked nonsense. Angran had been hoping to catch him on one of these calls and wrest an apology from him. Either that or invest in a phone that would block his number.

"You'll end up feeling awful if she comes here," Angran said now. "You're too tired and you'll want to be tidying the place up first and pretending you're all right. She won't approve of you going back to bed in the day."

Ruth pulled a clot of loose thread and hair from the frayed edge of a floorcloth. "I've been looking for my quilt," she said. "It's not in any of these bags. Can you remember where you packed it?"

"Why are you fussing about it now? You're warm enough without it."

The cloth unraveled in Ruth's hands, leaving a mess of grubby thread in her lap. "You're right," she said. "I'm too tired for everything. I don't think I can cope."

Angran helped her back to bed, guiding her through the stacked boxes and slumped heaps of bin bags. "Shall I ring Marjorie, then?" she asked, drawing the curtains against the light. "Tell her not to come?"

"I'll do it." Ruth sighed, shuffling down under the covers. "But later. I can't do anything now."

It turned out, though, that Ruth forgot to phone her, or never meant to in the first place. Angran couldn't get out of her which it was. Ruth would only say that Marjorie loved Ollie and she didn't want to deprive him of that. She stayed up late that night shifting boxes around, stacking them into neater piles. She claimed to be searching for the quilt, but Angran suspected her of trying to tidy the place, attempting to bring it up to Marjorie's house-proud standards. In the morning she found Ruth in the kitchen, ironing her dress, telling Ollie to smile at his grandma if he could manage it, and to speak to her nicely.

"Of course I'll smile," he said. "I'm not stupid. And, anyway, I need to ask her something, so I'll be as nice to her as I can."

Angran peered into the sink where some washing-up water was gulping at the plughole as it drained away. "You shouldn't teach him to be false," she said to Ruth. "That doesn't help anyone. You ought to know that by now." Ruth pulled the dress over her head.

"Mum, there's a difference between being genuine and

being rude. Ollie's not the only one who needs to remember that."

Angran wanted to ask her what she meant by that, but Marjorie's car was already crunching into the driveway and Ruth was rushing to the door. Angran saw that the zip of her dress was still open at her side as she pulled Marjorie into an embrace.

"Well, I bet that's not genuine," she muttered to herself.

Ollie stood in the hall, watching. "Is your vase very beautiful, Other Grandma?" he asked.

Ruth laughed. "You have to give her a chance to arrive, Ollie," she said. They trooped into the kitchen and Angran noticed how Marjorie's eyes darted toward the propped ironing board, the heap of Ruth's saucepans at the end of the table and the bulging carrier bags on the windowsill.

"Have you arrived now?" Ollie asked.

Marjorie opened her handbag and drew out a pack of puzzle books. "These are for you, darling."

He laid them aside and drew a crushed envelope from his pocket. "I'm doing another puzzle now. I need to know about your vase, Other Grandma. Is it very beautiful?"

Angran had no idea what he was up to. He had taken to questioning people lately, odd queries about the meaning of life. Vases, she thought, were not a good line of inquiry. She didn't want any discussion of the vases that had been smashed in the past, or of the one Rich had given her, hidden at the back of the cupboard. So she smiled briskly at Marjorie and said: "Any chance you could put a brake on all these phone calls your husband's been making?"

Marjorie blinked at her. "Phone calls? Who to? He doesn't use the phone these . . ." Her voice faded as her gaze fell on Ollie. He was clasping and unclasping his fingers, clenching his teeth. "What is it, dear?" Marjorie said, stepping toward him. "Is something wrong?"

"Your vase, Other Grandma," Ollie began, but Angran saw that Marjorie was about to stroke his shoulder. She held up the flat of her hand.

"Don't touch him," she said. "You'll set him off."

Ollie turned on her, lips pulled tight across his bared teeth. "It's you that's setting me off, Angran. You're talking over me." He was grabbing at his knees now, tugging at the fabric of his trousers. "Everyone says I have to speak nicely, but *you* never do. You're just rude to everyone."

He stamped off along the passageway. At the hall he turned to shout again. "I'm trying to focus here. And none of you want to help." He clattered up the stairs and slammed his bedroom door.

Ruth put her hands to her face. "I'm failing him," she said.

"I'm sure you're not," Marjorie said.

"But he keeps going on about this focusing. There's something I'm not getting."

Marjorie put her hand on Ruth's arm. "Well, there must be something we can do to help."

Angran turned away from them both and went to the back door. "I doubt it," she said. "Sometimes people just need to be left alone."

Outside the air was damp and there was a smell of claggy earth, a rotten undertone of backed-up drains. It had smelled like this when she moved here forty years ago and it had never truly gone away. It made her tired at times, despairing even. She didn't know if it was just the rain that stirred up something underground or if she had made some fundamental mistake when she laid the pipes in the bathroom. She had hardly been able to think straight, with the girls crying all the time while John gallivanted around the world.

"Don't think about that now," she said. "Irrelevant."

She went to fetch her axe. She thought it would do her good to split a few logs and work up a bit of a sweat on Ruth's behalf. As she left the kitchen she had spotted Marjorie reaching for Ruth's hand. "Simpering doesn't achieve anything," she muttered. She was the one with Ruth's best interests at heart, the one looking ahead, providing fuel for the winter. Each jolt of the axe was proof of it, every split log stacked up by the hearth.

But when she returned to the house an hour later, she found Marjorie with a righteous glow all of her own. While Ruth had been occupied with Ollie, Marjorie had cleaned and tidied the kitchen. The carrier bags were gone from the windowsill, the ironing board was stashed away, and Ruth's pans were lined up in order of size on top of the dresser. Ruth was beaming.

"It seems lighter, somehow," she said. "And spacious."

"I've chopped a lot of logs, you know," Angran said, but Ruth did not turn the smile on her. She opened her arms instead and drew Marjorie into yet another embrace. Angran saw that the bin was bulging, the lid propped half open. She dusted the splinters from her hands and went to investigate. It was crammed with tins of beans, bags of flour, a crumpled tube of tomato purée.

"What a waste," she said. "We can't afford to throw food away."

"Oh, you mustn't eat it," Marjorie stepped away from Ruth. "It's all out of date."

Ruth giggled. "It's from my house, Mum. Trust me and Rich to have a cupboard full of rotten old stuff."

Angran tugged out a bag of porridge oats. "Don't be silly. No one's going to get food poisoning from this." She placed it on the floor and retrieved a tin of pineapple and some kidney beans.

"But the cans are crushed," Marjorie said. "The seal will be compromised."

"Nonsense. I'll have to go through all this now, and I'm exhausted, you know, after chopping all that wood."

Ruth came over and began putting the cans back into the bin. "Don't bother, Mum, it's fine. I would have chucked them all myself if I'd had a chance to check them back at the house."

Angran took the cans out again. "Well, it's a good thing you moved here, then, isn't it? It's time you learned to be frugal."

"Oh dear, oh dear," Marjorie said, her hands fluttering about her face. "I didn't mean to cause trouble. I could write you a check for the cost of the lost food. I was only trying to help."

Angran grasped at a packet of self-raising flour. "I don't know why everyone thinks they can just barge in and decide what's good for Ruth. They never ask me first, but I'm her mother. I know how she feels." She flung the flour onto the floor. The bag split and a white cloud rose up between them. "You think it's a good thing, coming down to visit," she went on, "but my Ruth was up late last night, tidying for you. She's exhausted now. Can't you see it in her face?"

"I can't see anything," Marjorie said, coughing and waving her hands in front of her. "Where's your hoover? Let me clear this up for you."

"Don't you dare," Angran said. "Ollie's just got himself worked up and the hoover is the last thing he needs. You see, I know things like that about Ruth's life. That's why I'm here. You think you'd be helping with the hoover, but you'd be making everything worse. Even if it didn't set Ollie off, the noise would give Ruth a headache on top of everything else." She bent over the bin and pulled out more tins and a pack of corn flour, stained with grease. Through the dissipating cloud of flour she saw Marjorie backing away toward the passageway.

"Please forgive me," she was saying, and by the time Angran had clambered to her feet she was gone.

"So rude," Angran called after her. "I was explaining something to you and you walked away." She followed her outside and found her hunched in the car already, with Ruth leaning into the window to speak to her. "Tell her not to come again," Angran said. "We can do without all this fuss." Marjorie started the engine and Ruth stepped away. There was flour in her hair and in the creases of her dress. "And tell her to stop Gerald phoning too. I'm sick of it."

"I think she's got the message," Ruth said. She waved weakly as Marjorie backed into the lane.

"You look terrible," Angran said to her. "You need to go and lie down."

Ruth brushed the flour from her dress and nodded. "I think I do."

Angran thought she wouldn't mind lying down herself, closing her eyes and blocking out the lot of them. "Well, thank your lucky stars there's no one to come bothering you now," she said as Ruth walked away and disappeared into the shadowed hall.

Ruth

SHE LAY IN the dark of her room for a while, hoping for sleep. Through the hole in the wall she could hear Ollie on his bed, the occasional boom in the springs of his mattress as he thumped or butted against it with his head.

"Would you like me to sit with you?" she called to him.

"Get lost."

If Rich were here, Ruth thought, he would have gone to him without asking. Not that it always helped to have him making jokes and asking questions about Chelsea strikers while Ollie sobbed or stuffed his sheets into his mouth. And not that Rich had behaved perfectly himself: sometimes he would growl at Ollie, or stride about the room remonstrating, and if Ruth tried to intervene he would growl and remonstrate with her. But now, as Ruth lay motionless under the weight of her bedcovers, she scorned herself for accepting Ollie's refusal so readily. One of the things she had loved best about Rich was his unabashed belief in his own goodness. He never doubted that people would be pleased to see him, that his presence was anything other than positive. But Ruth had never felt like that: she was afraid she'd be a disappointment, that it was not comfort she offered but darkness instead.

The wind shuddered in the eaves. From the sitting room came the sound of Angran stacking logs against the wall. It reminded her of something, the low steady thud of it, something murky and unpleasant, a dream, perhaps, but she couldn't remember what it was. Her mouth was dry and sour.

She wondered what Marjorie would say to Gerald about the split bag of flour and Angran's screeching voice, and whether it would, in some strange way, turn him against Ollie again, or if he would even understand what had occurred. But perhaps Marjorie wouldn't speak of this incident at all. When she had backed away from Angran ranting in the kitchen, her expression, as she skirted the flour bag and picked her way over the crushed tins, was not one of outrage, as Ruth had feared, but of embarrassment.

"I'm so sorry," Ruth had said, but Marjorie wouldn't meet her eye. There was flour on her wrists and in a sheen across her handbag. She didn't shake it off, and Ruth wondered if it was a kind of delicacy that prevented her—that it would be rude to acknowledge it was there.

"Perhaps you should come to us, next time," Marjorie had said, as she started the car. "My house is a bit of a mess these days, but . . ." Her voice faded as Angran appeared at the front door. She gave Ruth a tight little smile as she backed onto the track.

Ruth couldn't imagine visiting her. She had been found out. Even if she arrived with her clothes ironed and her nails clean, and if Ollie was polite and agreed to remove his Crocs at the front door, Marjorie would know where she had come from. Rich no longer provided a front.

Downstairs the thudding of the logs went on. Ruth

closed her eyes and it came to her, the dream of dead rats in the river. The black log, slick with slime, the flow of the water choked. She had thought at first that the dream was about bereavement, the black line across the water signaling the finality of death. But now, as she pictured the swollen bodies of the rats, she knew it was about depression. There was meaning, she thought, in bereavement. There was congruence. To walk about with aching arms, because you yearned to wrap them around the man you loved, was real and sensible. To feel that the air you breathed was grainy and gray and weighing you down was not. There was movement in grief too. It was a current, bubbling beneath her conversations and smiles, and it might burst over her if she thought of the golden hairs on his knuckles or caught the scent of him in a T-shirt folded in a drawer. But depression brought all feelings to a halt. It killed them off and slammed them up against the bloated log.

She sat up in bed and swung her legs over the side. The river would be brimming now and she was drawn to it. Not to The Ravages, but to the picnic place, where the sun had shone on the flooded field and Rich and Ollie had shouted numbers to the canopy of trees. She had not stepped into the water that day. Now she yearned to feel the push and rumble of it on her skin.

She crept downstairs and pulled on a pair of Angran's wellingtons. The trees swayed and roared overhead as she climbed the hill. She took the steps to the pool and followed the path downstream toward her house. The river was lively beside her, rattling over the stones, and when, at last, she came to the picnic place, she ran right in, bending to the water and scooping it to her face.

It was the movement she wanted, the constant force of

it. She let it rush into her boots as she waded in deeper, her leggings cleaving to her skin. Rain pattered on the leaves above her. Fat drops fell from them, pocking the still waters and spattering onto her face and arms. She listened to the gushes and trickles echoing and funneling around her. Deeper still, she thought, and she crouched. Cold crept over her groin and she gasped at the bite of it. Her dress spread across the surface and billowed in the current.

She felt mad. If anyone saw her they'd think she was peeing in the river. They'd think she was a crazy woman and maybe she was, but she couldn't have cared less. Here, with the water pummeling and pounding at her back, she felt she was honoring Rich at last. If only she'd waded in on the day of the picnic. She could have splashed over to that rotten log and shoved it hard. How glorious it would have been to kick it away, laughing with Rich as the water plunged toward Angran on the shriveled mud below. How outraged she would have been, spluttering as it hit her and flowed on by, constant, relentless and never still.

She lay back in the water. The trees dripped above her. The splashes on her face were like tears, but with the force of a god behind them. She pushed her head under and there was a jumble of noise. It was love and grief and anger rushing together, a muscular current that dragged at the sand beneath her feet.

She came up for air and heard a shriek. Angran was in the shallows. Her glasses were splashed, her wellingtons slapped against her shins.

"Get out of there!" she shouted. She reached over and dug her fingers into Ruth's arm. Ruth scrambled to her feet. Rivulets spindled from her clothes as she tried to shake herself from Angran's grip. "You gave me the fright of my life," Angran yelled, pulling her to the bank. Ruth looked back at the water, swirling in her wake. Cold air shrank against her skin and she began to shiver.

"Where's Ollie?" she said. "You haven't left him on his own?"

"Nessa's on her way over. I had to follow you, Ruth. What was I supposed to do, when you disappeared into the woods?"

Still Ruth stared down at the water tumbling over the stones. If Rich was here now, she thought, he'd be laughing. Or he'd be tugging her back into the water. She remembered the day they had visited Angran with news of her pregnancy. Angran had been afraid for her that day, she realized now. She must have known what was lying in wait for her when the baby came, that she would be dragged down into despair. All her admonishments— *You're not ready to leave home, you won't cope with a child, you can't trust men to look after you*—were not judgments on her weakness, as she had thought. They were attempts to protect her from the horror of the dead rats and the log.

"Are you listening?" Angran said. "This is exactly why I wanted you at home with me. Exactly what I wanted to avoid."

Ruth shook her head. She saw now that from the moment she had met Rich, Angran had tried to hold her back. It had been a battle for Ruth just to love him. What if Angran's worries had spoiled their love? Perhaps Ruth could have loved him more and didn't dare.

"No," she said to Angran. "I'm not listening. I hadn't finished here. You've ruined it."

Angran froze. Her mouth was half open, her glasses

stark and rigid against her face. Ruth turned away from her, and stumbled back toward the path.

"Wait!" Angran cried behind her, but Ruth kept walking, her wet dress heavy on her skin, bubbles sucking at her feet inside her boots.

When they arrived at the cottage, Nessa was there, with Ollie pale and trembling behind her. He stared at Ruth, focused on the dripping hem of her dress.

"Were you on your own for long?" Ruth asked him.

"I had no choice," Angran said, before he could reply. "I *had* to leave him. I thought you were going to do something stupid!"

Nessa's eyes sought Ruth's. "You weren't, were you?"

Ruth thought of the current pushing at her scalp, the way the grief had surged through her, like water out of a dam. The way her love for Rich had come rushing after it.

"No," she said. "It wasn't something stupid. It was a good thing to do."

"That's a turn of phrase, isn't it?" Ollie asked. "Something stupid?"

"Yes," said Ruth.

"No," said Angran, at the same time.

Ruth gazed at her. She thought back to when she was little, to the nights spent in Angran's empty bed, shivering as she waited for her to return from The Ravages. "Well, you've proved it now, haven't you?" she said. "We know exactly what you were thinking of when you used to run off to the woods."

"What was she thinking of?" Ollie said. "Tell me what it means."

"But I was at the river because I want to live," Ruth

continued, "not to end it all." She pulled at her wet clothes, lifting the dress over her head and furling her pants down over her thighs, water squirting from the rolls of fabric. "I was thinking of Rich and how wonderful it was to love him. He's the one who died, you know. I'm completely alive." She was naked now and shivering. She left them gaping at her and went to run a bath.

She heard them all scattering as soon as she left the room. The kitchen door slammed, then Angran's boots echoed in the passageway. Ollie was scampering about, shouting something about being alive. She couldn't know if he had understood the conversation, but she hoped he had not. *I'll have to tell him*, she thought, *that I will never leave him.* She ran the bath, and as the steam warmed her skin, she planned a little speech. She would tell him that she was sadder than she'd ever been today, that she was raging with it, that it ran through her, like the water at The Ravages. Then she would explain that she welcomed it. She wanted more rage, more tears, because love came with it too. All the love she had barely dared to feel when Rich was alive, it was boiling in her now and she wanted it, more and more and forever.

Nessa

SHE HAD FELT a tingling in her palms when she looked at Ruth, dripping in her dress. She had felt the same tingle at Rich's bedside when she pressed her palms to his feet. She had thought it was the life force humming there.

"I'm completely alive," Ruth said, and Nessa had to run outside and press her hands to the wet grass. They had told her to do this on the massage course, to place her palms against the ground after each massage, to make contact with the earth. She had found it phony and sniggered about it with Ruth. "There can't be any science behind it. They must think there's some kind of magic in the earth."

And yet the solid ground beneath the grass felt like an answer to a question that was forming in her hands. At the instant of Rich's death, with her palms against his feet, she had felt a sting in her hands, a sudden flare. Marjorie, stroking his shoulders, had startled too, as if she had been pricked. Nessa had only to think back to that moment and a kind of fullness kindled in her hands. Now, kneeling on the lawn, she felt she was honoring it at last.

The trees growled in the wind. Nessa lowered herself onto her belly, pressed her face against the grass. It smelled loamy and the blades shifted and crackled faintly against her skin.

"I'm completely alive," Ruth had said, and Nessa had been awed by her calm as she said it. If Nessa had made a statement like that, she would have ended up dancing about and stretching her mouth into a clownish grin. But Ruth had held a sadness in her voice and she seemed to treasure it as she spoke. "Rich is the one who died," she had said.

"Rich," Nessa murmured, sobbing into the grass. Would anyone ever dance and grin again, knock back cider and laugh at the fizzle of it on their tongues? Maybe they would not. But this tingling in her hands was here to stay. Rain pricked on her back as she spread her arms wide against the earth. Rich had given her a shawl. She wanted to wrap it around her shoulders now, feel the fibers shush across her clothes. It was not only the fun she wanted to remember. There was the tenderness, the tranquility she had witnessed as he died. This burgeoning in her palms.

Above her the bathroom window opened. Ollie leaned out and tossed something into the wind. She rose to her feet and called to him, but he slammed the window shut. In the flowerbed below she saw scraps of torn-up paper. She picked them up and noticed words on them, blurring as the ink began to bleed in the rain. She made out some names, *Angran, Mum*, then a whole phrase: *life with both hands*. The paper turned pulpy in her grasp, stained now with earth from her fingers.

The back door opened and Angran glared from the step. "What are you doing out here?" she called. "Ruth's already given me the fright of my life. No need for you to go charging off, too."

Nessa pushed the mushed-up paper into her pocket and looked down at her hands. She wondered if she should place them on her mother's shoulders. Could she pass on this sense of peace, this awe in the presence of the life force? Or would she find a different sensation in Angran's shoulders, something jagged and sharp? Upstairs, a door slammed.

"I don't want to get sadder and sadder!" Ollie yelled. Something metallic clattered across the landing and he screamed.

Nessa pushed past Angran and ran to him. She found him at his bedroom door with a box of kitchen implements upturned at his feet. He held a cheese grater pressed against his arm.

"Go away," he said, as she made her way past the stacks of bags and boxes. Through his open bedroom door she saw the chest of drawers on its side, socks spilling onto the carpet. Beyond it was the empty skeleton of his bed frame, the mattress slumped at an angle across the floor.

"Would you like me to sort your room out for you?" she asked, hoping to distract him so he would loosen his grip on the grater. "Remember how I did it before?"

Ollie hunched away, pressing it harder into his skin. "You can't sort anything out," he said. "No one can. The puzzle's gone wrong and now you all think I'm stupid."

Ruth appeared at the bathroom door, pulling a dressing gown around her. "No one thinks you're stupid," she said, but Ollie just yelled back at her: "Yes, you do! Because I'll never find out now what it means to be alive."

He started on a story, confused and faltering, about a vase and some bubble wrap and some boxes he'd swapped before they were made into parcels. Nessa couldn't follow the thread of it. She could only stare in horror at the grater rocking against his arm, at the white speckles on the skin where the blades pushed against it.

"You're not focusing!" Ollie bawled. He yanked the grater from his arm and flung it toward her. She ducked just in time and it smacked into the banister and clattered down the stairs.

"No, Ollie!" Ruth cried. "That's dangerous!" But Nessa shook her head. If he was a pupil in her class he'd be out of the door by now, marched to the head teacher. But something kept her still, the tingling in her hands perhaps, or the tears stinging in her eyes at the sight of his speckling skin. She wished again that she had the shawl with her, to wrap around her shoulders, to keep her calm and quiet while she listened to his story again.

"Come and lie down," Ruth said to him, heaving the mattress back onto his bed. "Tell us exactly what's wrong."

Ollie pulled his jumper up over his face and gnawed at it. "I'm staying here," he said, but Ruth nudged him over the spilled pencils and torn sudokus and he threw himself onto the bed. He started on the story of the vase and the boxes once more, his voice muffled this time through mouthfuls of jumper. Nessa looked into Ruth's face, expecting to see her own confusion reflected there. Instead she saw a spark of laughter.

"So the vase got sent to Angran?" Ruth said. "Oh, God, she would have *hated* it."

"It's not funny, Mum," Ollie said. "There's nothing funny about being wrong."

Ruth pressed her lips together. "No, of course not," she said. "But it's not your fault, Ollie, it's Dad's. He promised he'd check the addresses on the boxes, make sure everyone got the right parcel."

Nessa began to understand what had occurred. "Don't worry," Ruth was saying now. "I'll let Angran know. We'll get the shawl back from Other Grandma, and then it will be fine."

"Don't be stupid!" he said, scrabbling at his jumper again. "Other Grandma didn't get the shawl. I *told* you. I put it in the necklace box."

Ruth looked at Nessa with her hand over her mouth. "Shit," she said. "So every present was wrong."

"That's what I said!" Ollie wailed. "I told you I was stupid and now the puzzle will never be solved."

"There never was a puzzle," Ruth said, but Nessa could see he hadn't heard her. It wasn't that he'd stopped paying attention, she realized, as she watched him shuffling about on the bed: it was that there was too much clamor in his head to let it in. He was shouting about Rich's birthday now, how he'd thought there would be a party, how no one came to visit anymore, and no one asked him questions about the Premier League.

"I'm going to sort this," Ruth said. She reached for Nessa's hand and, for a moment, Nessa thought she felt a flare in her fingertips. "He has to know that he's been heard."

Ollie rubbed his head back and forth across the mattress. He was still talking about puzzles and sadness and being alive, but his words were beginning to slur. There were gaps between the statements, moments of stillness before he reared up and began again. Soon his voice faded. His clawing fingers fell still and he flopped against the mattress, asleep.

Nessa listened to the wind in the eaves, the spattering of rain on the roof, still holding Ruth's hand. From the kitchen came the smell of frying onions. Ollie sighed and shuddered, sinking into a deeper sleep. Ruth put her head on Nessa's shoulder.

"Which present did you get?" she whispered.

"The shawl," she said, imagining it sliding from her shoulders now that she knew it was not meant for her.

Ruth groaned faintly. "Can't we just pretend it was supposed to be that way?"

Downstairs they heard the clang of a saucepan dropped on the stone kitchen floor, a sudden curse from Angran.

"We have to admit to our mistakes," Nessa said. "Or we'll end up like her."

Ruth squeezed her hand. "At least she's making us some dinner."

"Even if she's scraping it up off the floor right now."

They began to laugh. They had to clamp their mouths shut so that Ollie didn't wake. Ruth, rocking back and forth, found one of his clean socks on the floor and stuffed it into her mouth.

"Don't," Nessa squeaked. "He'll never forgive you."

They crept out onto the landing, the laughter still shaking their bellies.

"You know what Rich would have done," Ruth said, after a while. "He'd have had a gathering. Got everyone over here and admitted to the whole thing."

Nessa looked about her at the mess of boxes and bags on the landing, the sewing machine and the stacks of chairs cluttered against the wall. Her vision of a party on the beach, with a bonfire and a sound system, shimmered away among the shadows. But she did not try to grab it back.

This would be Ruth's little gathering and she did not want to interfere.

"Are you up to it?" she asked.

"Probably not." She rubbed her face and sighed. "Not while I'm depressed. But I think I have been all my life, in some way, you know. Depression just might be me."

Nessa's hands were tingling again. She put her arms around Ruth and held her in a long embrace. Ruth shifted away, and poked at Nessa's thigh.

"Have you wet yourself," she asked, "with all that giggling just now?"

Nessa felt her jeans, found the soggy mush of paper soaking through her pocket. "I might have done." She grinned. "I can't be invincible forever."

Part 3

Ollie

MY DAD DIED. Mum says that every time I start shouting and pulling my mattress off my bed it's because he died. It's not true. I used to shout before he died. But Mum looks for meaning in everything and that makes her get things wrong.

I made the puzzle go wrong. I want to put it right now. Mum says saying sorry puts things right. She's wrong about that. Angran trod on my book of sudoku once and wrinkled the pages. She said she was sorry, but I threw the book away because the creases made the numbers look ugly and I didn't get that satisfied feeling when the sudoku was completed. She saw me stuffing it into the bin and she said: "Ollie, don't be silly. I've said sorry."

I said sorry to Auntie Nessa when she told me she got the shawl. She said: "It doesn't matter, Ollie. That shawl means a lot to me now."

Whatever it means to her, it's wrong. My dad wanted her to have a necklace. She won't know what it means to be alive unless her present is right.

My dad died. We're supposed to be having a party for his birthday. It's my chance to put the puzzle right. I threw his list of presents out of the window and now I have to try to write it out again. I have to remember every gift and who was supposed to have it. Then I have to work out what they received by mistake. It's like a puzzle, sorting out which box each gift was sent in, and which box it should have been in. But I can't make it clean and neat like a puzzle. Other thoughts keep getting in the way. I keep remembering my dad, on the night we packed the boxes. I was rolling up the shawl to fit in the smallest box and my dad was telling Mum not to worry. He said: "Life's too short." Usually that's a turn of phrase, but for him it was true. I'm scared that it's the answer to the puzzle.

Ruth

SHE WOKE IN the early hours to the sound of scratching somewhere in the room. She lay still, eyes closed, thinking of mice with tiny skeletal claws, scrabbling through the skirting-boards. They'd be burrowing into the bin bags, she thought, chewing up the bedding. There were five black bags heaped against the wall beneath her window, a crinkling mound that shifted and slumped whenever she brushed past. She was sure her sunflower quilt was balled up in one of them, but she hadn't yet retrieved it. She thought it might be tangled up with Rich's shirts, an embrace of soft cuffs and empty collars that she couldn't bear to witness.

She had made that quilt when she first moved in with Rich. She'd brought home scraps and remnants from the theater and laid out shapes on the kitchen table. Sometimes she'd left them there for days and they'd had to eat their meals on the sofa or in bed. She still owned some of the sheets from those days, stained with curry or tomato ketchup. Nessa had tutted when she'd seen the quilt taking shape.

"Flowers," she'd said, "on a bloke's bed?" But Rich had

loved it, had dragged his friends up to the bedroom to admire it. Ruth remembered rushing up the stairs ahead of them to kick away the dirty underwear that had been left on the floor. On the day they moved into their house the quilt was the first item he'd unpacked, as soon as the moving van had gone.

But now it was bundled up somewhere in the shadows of Black Coombe Cottage and the mice were at it. They would be shredding the satin petals into fluff for their pissy little nests.

She rolled over and blinked into the darkness. Something flashed in the corner at the doorway to Ollie's room. She rubbed her eyes and there it was again, a bright ripple across the raw plaster, spilling over the pocks and chisel marks, shrinking into shadow. She could still hear the scratching sounds, but there was more detail in them now: a tiny plastic rattle, a hiss that she recognized suddenly as a hand moving over a page.

"Ollie! What are you doing?"

"Shush, Mum, I'm focusing on this puzzle."

The shaft of light swept briefly over the doorway and she heard him scribble at the paper. He was sitting up in bed, wearing his head torch, she realized, and now it was shining downward onto his page.

"You can't do sudokus at this time of night. You've got school tomorrow."

"It's not a sudoku, Mum. It's Dad's puzzle. I made it go wrong and now I'm putting it right for the party."

Ruth closed her eyes. She had an urge to call for Angran. *Help me, Mum. Make this stop.* She considered shuffling down under the covers, pulling them tight over her ears so that all she could hear was the sound of the fabric shifting against her skin, the rush of her blood through her head.

"Ollie," she said, trying to keep the edge from her voice, "we haven't set a date for a party. We might not even have one."

He did not reply. She heard his pen moving steadily over the paper. She couldn't think what he was writing or what he thought he might discover from this puzzle. Surely the only thing he could learn was that she had failed him. She should have known what he was up to with this puzzle from the first. If she'd paid him more attention after Rich's death, listened to his questions, asked him just once why he kept squinting down at that crumpled envelope, she could have unraveled the knot of it and released the grief inside.

Shadows stretched and bucked across the walls as Ollie shifted on his bed. Ruth understood now why Angran had turned away from her in the night when she was small, why the sight of her at the foot of her bed would have seemed like an emblem of her unsuccessful mothering. She could hear Ollie coming for her now. The beam of the torch was swinging over the floor as he shuffled sideways through the doorway, head down, shoulders raised, careful not to touch the rough walls.

"Grandpa's wrong present," he was saying. "What was it? I can't work out what got sent to him."

Ruth grasped at her bedclothes. "Please, Ollie. You have to stop this now. It was all a mistake, my love. There never was a puzzle."

"But I can't stop," he said, looking up and blasting the torch beam into her eyes. "I have to know what it means to be alive."

Across the landing, Angran's bedroom door swung open. They heard her stomp to the bathroom, let out a long groaning fart that echoed in the toilet bowl. Ruth wanted to laugh, but she swallowed it. Ollie might fling the pen at her, she thought, and accuse her of not focusing. Worse, he might screech out a list of all the failures she had inflicted on him since Rich died, the skipped meals, the missed school, this disastrous move to Black Coombe Cottage. She hadn't dared to ask him what he thought of it all and she wasn't sure she was up to finding out now. She felt for her bedside lamp as Ollie yanked the torch from his forehead.

"I've got it, Mum!" he cried. "It was the candles. That's what Grandpa got." Now the room was flooded with light. He thrust the paper into her hand and clambered up to kneel on the bed beside her. "Write it down, Mum. I've done loads of lists but they keep going wrong." She looked down at the paper, but she was still blinded by drifting spots and flares where the torchlight had blazed against her retinas. "Go on, Mum," he urged. "Write *Grandpa*, then *picture*, then *candles*. You have to put arrows between them."

In the bathroom, the toilet flushed. Angran came to the bedroom door. She was wearing her faded old gardening shirt, grass stains on the cuffs, loose threads dangling over her naked thighs.

"Why aren't you in bed?" she said to Ollie.

"Angran, I'm doing the puzzle." He bounced on his knees and the bed rocked. "And I needed some help. So I came through that door, Angran. Isn't that why you made it? So I could get help in the night?"

Ruth glanced toward him. Her eyes were clearing at last

and she saw that his cheeks seemed warm and full. She remembered that Rich used to comment on the changes in Ollie's face. He said that, in meltdown, Ollie looked haggard, but when he was happy, his flesh seemed to plump out from his bones. The difference never seemed so obvious to Ruth. On her darker days, she thought it was because she never really saw him happy, that her very presence shriveled him. Only Rich, making up songs and juggling balled-up socks, saw the jolly-faced child. But here he was now, round-cheeked and content, jabbing with his finger at the page.

"That door is for when you're screaming," Angran said. "Not for puzzles and—" She stopped when Ruth held up her hand.

"It's all right, Mum," she said, coming to a decision. "This is something he needs to do now."

Angran turned away. "Well, just keep your voices down. I've got work to do in the morning, things that need doing in this house."

Ruth looked down at Ollie's paper, saw lists of names and presents, scrawled arrows, question marks and scribbles.

"Do you think different-colored pens might help you with this?" she asked. She reached for her phone and searched for a website with a stationery sale. "You know, a red pen for Angran and her present, a blue one for Other Grandma. I'll buy you some, if you like."

Ollie shuffled up next to her and peered down at the phone. "For the colors of their thinking?" he asked. "I'd have to have a gold one for the answer, though."

Ruth wasn't sure what he meant, but she tapped on a packet of sparkly pens anyway and added them to her basket. She wondered if she was being irresponsible, reckless even, with his feelings. This could be leading only one way—headlong into more grief when he discovered that there never *was* a puzzle. But if she explained that to him now, she thought, she would be depriving him of the adventure along the way. And it was true, too, that with or without the adventure, the grief would come for him anyway.

"Hey, Ollie," she said. "What about index cards? Shall we buy some of those too?"

The mattress bounced as he replied. "People could write their answers on them." He picked up her phone and began scrolling down the page. "And can I have some White-Out? For if someone writes it wrong?"

In the doorway between their rooms, a piece of grit pattered down the wall and tinkled across the floor.

"You have to let things go wrong sometimes," she said to him. "That's when the best adventures happen."

Ollie frowned at her. "I don't want it to go wrong," he said. "I want White-Out."

Marjorie

MARJORIE WAS ON her knees when the post arrived. Gerald had switched off the freezer overnight and now there was a stink of prawns in the utility room and a puddle on the floor. He came to her with the letters in his hand. She took hers and kept her face turned away, too upset about the freezer to smile her thanks.

It was a note from Ollie, written on an index card.

> *Bring the hand necklace to the party. You will find out what it means to be alive.*

Now tears sprang to her eyes. What party? Ruth had said nothing of a party the last time she phoned. Nor had she received an invitation. She didn't want a party anyway. Not if Gerald was going to remember that he wanted an apology from Ollie. Not if Ruth's mother would be there, with her smudged glasses and muddy knees, her sharp, haranguing voice. She dabbed at her eyes with her fingertips. In the dining room Gerald was striding about, growling and banging the bureau drawers, but she didn't go to him. She had just spotted a checkbook at the back of the freezer, the pages shrinking into pleats, and she knew he must have put it there. Which was worse? she wondered. Loving an old man who was losing his mind, or loving a boy whose mind was so off-beat he sent out letters that made no sense?

Bring the hand necklace to the party.

The necklace was upstairs in the drawer of her dressing table. On the days when she couldn't hide it beneath a high collar, she had taken to coiling the beads around the silver hand and pinning them into place on a doily. She liked to slide the drawer open whenever she passed, see the metal glinting in the shadows. Sometimes she paused to trace the spiral with her fingertips, to feel the delicate patterns of the silver against her skin. Each time she shut the drawer she felt she had glimpsed something of Richard, the light in his eyes, perhaps, or something more nebulous: the feeling she had when she sat beside him or the smell of him as a boy running in from the garden to gulp down a glass of milk. It made her heart lurch and she had thought for a while that she ought not to do it. But that glimpse of silver each day kept her going. She didn't want to take the necklace to a party. She didn't want to see the beads clattering across anyone else's fingers, the filigree hand swinging wantonly in the air.

She rose to her feet and dropped the sodden checkbook into the bin.

"Marjorie!" Gerald cried from the dining room. "Why did you hide the—the things, the bloody—" Something heavy dropped onto the table and skidded across it. She heard it thump to the floor.

She looked again at Ollie's note.

You will find out what it means to be alive.

She had a feeling she knew already. It was the jolt in her blood when she woke each morning and remembered that Richard was gone. It was the drag in her feet, and the sag in the skin beneath her eyes.

"Please don't swear, Gerald," she called. "I hope you're not making a mess."

Being alive meant tidying up after Gerald. Here she was, mopping up water, the cuffs of her blouse wet and chilly where she had reached into the dripping freezer. Or it meant touching up her makeup every few hours because there was always something to make her cry.

There was another clunk from the dining room, then a curse and a groan. Marjorie dropped the letter and ran to him. She found him under the table, curled on his side, hands spread over his head. He was rocking and moaning to himself. One trouser leg was hoisted and his shin was bone-white and skinny. She lowered herself to her knees and ducked her head beneath the table.

"Oh, Gerald, please. Gerald, what happened?"

She tried to crawl to him, but her skirt kept catching under her knees. She pulled it free and bundled the hem into her waistband.

"Gave me a smack," he said. "Damn fool table." He rolled onto his back, hand over his eyes.

"Can you sit up?" she asked.

"Don't be a fool, I'll get another smack if I do that."

Her thighs quivered as she urged herself toward him. She could feel her cheeks hanging down, pulling inward toward her mouth.

Gerald rubbed at his forehead. "Be glad to be shot of the things. Got to barter them, you know."

"Shot of what, Gerald?"

"That tray of stinking candles. I told you to throw them away. Bartering's just as good, though."

Her arms were beginning to ache. She wondered if her knickers were exposed behind her.

"What do you mean, bartering?" she said.

He began patting at his jacket pockets. He drew out a till receipt, scrutinized it and then flicked it away.

"Don't, Gerald, you'll make a mess!"

A pair of nail-clippers came out next, a chocolate bar and a handkerchief with what looked like a blot of ink in the corner. He piled them up beside him and she blushed. He'd worn this jacket to Cedar Park last week, and after all his repeated calls to Ollie, she'd asked them to check through his pockets for his mobile phone when he arrived. A strip of orange peel was coming out now, foxed and curling.

Her arms could not support her any longer. She turned onto her side and lay beside him. The carpet smelled of dust, and lavender where a candle had rolled over it. Gerald reached for the chocolate bar and tore at the wrapping with his teeth. He broke off a square and passed it to her. She let it melt against the roof of her mouth. She wondered how long it had been in his pocket, whether it was out of date. This was the kind of thing Angran would do, lie about on the floor with her legs exposed, stale food in her mouth. But she couldn't imagine that Angran would be experiencing this soft flood of warmth in her chest. Nor would there be anyone beside her, tapping her knee, his eyes crinkling at the corners in the way Richard's had.

"Oh, Gerald," she said. "It's not a barter, it's a party!" The understanding came to her quite suddenly. "Ollie's having a party and he wants you to bring the candles."

Gerald passed her another square of chocolate. He gazed at her and she gazed back at him, at his dear familiar face, the pouchy skin on his jawline, old man's skin now but still as meticulously shaven as when they were young.

"I'm not going to a party with those bloody candles stinking the place out," he said.

Marjorie giggled. "You mustn't swear," she told him, but her heart wasn't in it. She thought she could hear a dripping sound from the utility room. "We'll have to go," she said. "Ollie wants it and . . ." she paused for a moment, nervous ". . . we've got to do our best for him."

"Richard's son," Gerald said. His eyes crinkled at the corners again, but this time it was not Richard she thought of, but Ollie with a book on his knee, looking up, delighted because one of his sudokus was complete.

Gerald

WITH HIS HEAD on the carpet, the arm of his glasses dug into his cheek. It hurt when he shifted the chocolate around his mouth. He didn't even like chocolate. Never had done, too sweet and too . . . What was the word? *Soupy?* No. *Loopy?* No, that was him and Marjorie, lying about on the floor like damn teenagers, some dreadful music churning through the room. Who came in and put the radio on in his house? A burglar? Was that why they were hiding under the table? No, it wasn't that or Marjorie wouldn't be smiling at him. *Gloopy.* That was chocolate for you. And since he'd had that smack on his head there was an awful noise in his ears. The usual burbling turned high and whiny, like violins out of tune.

"Maybe we should light some of those candles," Marjorie said. "Just a few. I wouldn't want Ruth to think they weren't appreciated."

The thing about flames, Gerald thought, *is that they're wobbly.* He didn't know why that mattered, but it did. He'd have liked to give Richard a telling-off. *What were you thinking of, son, making a present of those damn, stinking things?* But he was glad he never did. If Richard were here now, playing that ghastly violin music, or cutting up cheese

or whatever it was he liked to do, then it would be a damn
shame to reprimand him. Why not eat the bloody cheese
and let him tell you every detail of how it was wrapped in
a muslin cloth in a cave or whatever it was that he wanted
to say? Why not shake him by the hand and tell him he
was a jolly good son? Warm hands, Richard had, and a
proper handshake too. No limp fishes for him. But even if
Richard had been the limp-fish type, even if his palms had
been damp and even if, damn it, he'd had no control of that
son of his, well, Gerald would rather that than have him
dead.

Wobbly. Gerald was heading that way himself. Been like
it since Richard died, sniveling into his handkerchief when
Marjorie wasn't looking.

"Gerald!" Her face was suddenly close to him, blurred
because she hadn't given him time to shift his head and
work his varifocals. "Are you crying?"

The violins in his head swirled to a crescendo. He swiveled his neck and brought her into focus. There were little
tracks on her face, spoiling her . . . her . . . He couldn't
think of the word, but he could see that she had been crying too.

"Well, I do feel a bit wobbly," he said. How the word
pleased him. Had Richard said it to him once? Just the sort
of nonsense he'd come out with, talking with his mouth
full. He wanted to light the candles. The ones he'd found
had rolled off somewhere, but he didn't know where.
Makeup. He was thinking of makeup. Marjorie's makeup
was smudged. Her hair was a mess, half of it scrunched
against the carpet. Maybe she was feeling wobbly too. He
reached for her knee and tapped it gently: one, two, three.

Angran

THE VASE WAS on a high shelf in the kitchen cupboard. She had pushed it to the back, crammed behind the sprigged tea service.

"Stop," she said to her shaking hand, as she reached for it. "Ridiculous."

But the vase rattled against the teapot as she withdrew her arm through the pathways of crockery.

Bring the vase to the party. You will find out what it means to be alive.

"Parties," she said. "Did I ever agree to having a party here?" She wasn't going to let that Alan and Tom in her house, or Michael Wardle, prancing about and whinnying. It was bad enough that Rich's parents would have to come. She pictured Gerald walking across the driveway, pulling at the knot of his tie. Would she rush out and demand an apology before they could proceed? Or would she wait, teeth gritted, until they had endured the cake cutting and the toasts, and wrest it out of him as he left? She would not be able to enjoy the party either way. But perhaps she had never enjoyed Ruth's parties anyway. She had attended them all, had admired the paper pompoms hanging from the apple tree, or the bunting strung across the garden, but the guests were often disappointing.

"Isn't she wonderful, my daughter?" she'd say to them. "Hasn't she made it beautiful here?" But it was always Rich they wanted to praise, for his choice of music, for treating them to all that expensive cheese. Why had she bothered to go? Because she loved her daughters and she wanted them to know. That was what it meant to be alive. To keep a watch over the people you loved, never to let them forget it.

Angran placed the vase on the kitchen table. The shadow of the rock had not long receded from the garden and sunlight came lancing into the room.

"At least I've never smashed the thing," she said.

The glass sparkled in the sun. Angran blinked and squinted at the bright spots dancing on the walls around her. An image came to her, sudden and sharp. Rich at a party, many months ago, setting out cheese on a marble slab, Ruth laughing out loud as he arranged the wedges with the points facing outward, a sunburst of cheese.

"You're a genius," Ruth had cried. "I'm going to use that for a cushion cover. I've been meaning to do another cheese cushion—this is the design." She had laughed again, but it was not the snickering laugh she shared so often with Nessa. It was a shining bellow, vivid as the bright scarf in her hair.

Now Angran touched her fingers to the lip of the vase. Long ago, she had laughed like that with John, but she never liked to remember it. Was that why she had never seen the value of it in Rich? She moved her hand over the scalloped rim and the chip in the glass snagged on her skin. With her fingers in her mouth, she felt like a child: a small one, lost and forlorn. She had not cried since Rich's death, but now tears were pooling at the rims of her glasses and her nose was hot and dripping.

"I welcomed him into our lives," she said to herself, thinking of the meals Rich had cooked for her, the holidays she had shared. But she knew, too, that she had never shown gratitude for the joy he sparked in Ruth's life.

Bring the vase to the party. You will find out what it means to be alive.

Angran blew her nose. There should be cheese at this party, she decided. She would pay for it herself and buy more than was strictly necessary. She would place it on the marble slab at the center of the table, arranged, of course, like a sunburst. She did not expect that Ruth would laugh at it in the same way. But later perhaps, on a quiet evening, when the fire was lit and Ollie asleep, she would remember her plans for the cushions, reach for her sewing box and cut out some triangles of yellow cloth.

Angran removed her glasses and wiped the tears from the lenses. The vase was a blur now, pink and shimmering in the sunlight. It glowed before her like a dawn.

Nessa

SHE SAT WITH the shawl wrapped around her shoulders, one corner pressed against her mouth. She didn't want to relinquish it. Nor did she want to find out what it meant to be alive. Not Ollie's version anyway. It was a puzzle that Rich had set him, he said. There was a clue in each present, and the combination of them all would provide the meaning of life.

"You've got to tell him he's mistaken," Nessa had said to Ruth. "As if Rich would ever get it together to organize a thing like that."

"I've tried, I've tried," Ruth had said, but she couldn't have tried hard enough, because this letter had arrived now, even before Ruth had set a date or invited anyone to the gathering. Ollie's version of what it meant to be alive was going to involve thrown socks and a whole lot of upset at this rate. Some party that would be. Hardly a celebration of Rich's shining life.

And yet, she thought, drawing the shawl more tightly around her shoulders, thrown socks had been a large part of Rich's life and he'd never shirked from comforting his son. Perhaps a bit of upset at this party would be a fitting tribute to Rich after all. As fitting, anyway, as any event at Black Coombe Cottage could ever be.

There was another card inside the envelope: *Don't forget to bring the picture from the hospital.*

She drew the shawl tighter still. She'd forgotten she'd agreed to go to the ward and explain that there had been a mistake. She had hoped she wouldn't have to, had even considered finding a similar picture online, buying it and hoping no one noticed the difference. It was a mad thing to do, to wrest a gift, a bequest even, out of the hands of the deserving. But then this whole enterprise was mad and, if Ruth was to be believed, it was Rich's fault the presents had ended up in the wrong hands. Him with his slapdash approach to life. *It'll all work out in the end,* he'd say. She couldn't begin to imagine how this would ever work out. Perhaps, she thought, it would be the best tribute of all, to go to the hospital and embarrass herself, to let the whole ridiculous mess of it unfold. She thought of the half-finished letter he'd written for Ollie. *I think you will be a brilliant man. You will be very funny, very clever, and also rather strange.* So perhaps Ruth was right after all, not to force Ollie away from this puzzle. She was giving him the chance to be the man his father had imagined, to turn out just like him: funny, clever, and incredibly strange.

Ollie

MY DAD DIED. It's raining. There are snails on the paving stones, swollen and shiny, like Mum's face when she's been crying about my dad. She cried a lot this morning because it's his birthday. He was born forty-nine years ago today. Now he's dead and we're having a party in the rain. Except it's not really a party. Mum says it's more of a family gathering. I'm sitting at the front door of Black Coombe Cottage with a cardboard box beside me. The rain is clattering on the porch roof and sometimes the drops spin off the edge and prick my feet through my Crocs.

The box has got the vase in it. When Nessa arrives she's going to open the lid and put the picture and the shawl inside. Other Grandma and Grandpa will add the necklace and candles, and the puzzle will begin.

I can smell the drain and it's like rotten eggs. Angran says she tried to sort it out, but there's nothing she can do if the rain stirs it all up again. I can hear her walking up the passageway behind me with plates rattling in her hands. The clacking of them hurts my ears. We've put up a trestle table in the hall for all the party food. She's stacking the plates on it now and shouting to Mum.

She says: "Where's the box of cheese, Ruth? I thought you brought it up here."

I turn around to look at her. She's got her best shorts on, bright red with flowers on the pockets, embroidered by Mum. She gave them to Angran last Christmas and Angran said: "For God's sake, Ruth, you know I'll spoil them digging in the garden." Mum said she should keep them for best, but Angran said she didn't have best, she wasn't that kind of person.

My dad died. I think it's turned her into that sort of person because she's wearing those shorts for his birthday. I say to her: "Hey, Angran, do you like shawls?"

I can't wait for Nessa to come so I can give Angran the shawl. It's not a turn of phrase that I can't wait: I actually can't. That's why I'm asking Angran about it now as she comes to the door. She says: "Shawls? Not specially." Then a car arrives and it's Other Grandma and Grandpa. I can see the loose skin in Grandpa's neck swinging about as he clambers out of the passenger seat, and I smell Other Grandma's perfume as they walk up the path. Angran steps out into the rain and says: "Water under the bridge."

I think this is a turn of phrase because there isn't a bridge here. All the water is dripping off the porch roof and making little shiny puddles in the gravel. I point at my cardboard box as they walk toward me and I tell them to put their presents inside. Angran says, "When they're ready, Ollie. Give them a chance," but Other Grandma winks at me.

She stops to lift the lid of the box and peep under it. She says: "Oh, look at that. What a beautiful vase!"

Marjorie

THE AIR AROUND the cottage was heavy and fetid. It made her reluctant to smile, to open her mouth too wide and breathe it in. But she smiled anyway when she saw Ollie, so bright and eager at the door. She had never seen him like that before, so animated, so ready to talk.

"This is the box for your presents," he cried, and Marjorie wanted to ask him all about it, to stop and examine the pretty vase she'd glimpsed inside. Angran, though, had other plans.

"Come out of the rain," she ordered, eyes gleaming behind the lenses of her glasses. Marjorie did not dare to disobey. She held on to Gerald's arm and followed Angran through the shadowed hall to the sitting room, where she flicked her hand toward an arc of mismatched chairs before the hearth. "Sit down," Angran said. "Grab a moment of peace before Ollie starts in on you with his puzzle."

Marjorie sought out the chair with the firmest seat and eased Gerald into it. The room was chilly. The windows were deep set, beaded with gray droplets of rain, and everything was dark—the wood of the mantel, the black beams of the ceiling, even the cushions, covered with brown felted wool. Angran knelt at the hearth and began rattling through a basket of kindling.

Gerald leaned forward in his chair and tapped Marjorie's hand. "Bit of a stink around here," he whispered. "I think they're all b—" He paused, tugging at his tie. "You know, b—" he tried again.

"Don't keep searching for the word," Marjorie whispered back. "You know it makes it worse."

She wondered if the word he was after was *bastards*. She almost wished it was. She wasn't supposed to laugh when he swore, but sometimes her chest swelled with childish giggles. The lightness of it, bursting through her grief, was thrilling.

"Bohemians," he said now, sinking back, blinking.

"Nothing wrong with bohemians," Angran said. She blew on the grate and flames crackled into life. Outside, a car crunched on the gravel and down in the hall there was a flurry of greetings and exclamations as Nessa arrived. Marjorie heard Ruth gasping over a cake, discussing a lost box of cheese. Ollie kept interrupting them, with questions about necklaces, shawls and pictures. Before long he came running into the room.

"I need the necklace, Other Grandma," he cried. He was clutching the cardboard box to his chest and it clunked and rumbled as he shifted from foot to foot. "Auntie Nessa's here. She has to see the necklace."

Marjorie put her hand to her throat where the wooden beads were warm beneath her collar. "I have to take it off?" she asked.

"Yes! I've got a card for you and a card for Nessa. You've got to write your answer down."

"What answer?"

"About the vase. It's brilliant that you like it, Other Grandma. That means the puzzle's going to work."

Angran rose from the fireplace, joints cracking. "Ollie," she said, her voice sharp. "You're confusing them. They don't know about your puzzle."

"I'm trying to explain!"

The fire was roaring now and sparks flittered onto the stone hearth. Marjorie thought about Richard. She had heard Angran speak to him in the same admonishing way. *Rich, when will you ever learn to think ahead?* Richard had always shrugged at her or laughed. But Ollie was shrinking away, head down, fingers curling around the edge of his box.

"You've got to give people space," Angran went on. "They've only just got here. There'll be plenty of time to look at the presents later."

"He wasn't bothering me," Marjorie tried.

"You haven't seen him when he gets going. We've had days of this, Ruth and I. Necklace this, shawl that. He looks happy now, but he'll get anxious before long and once that—"

She was interrupted by Gerald. "What the blazes is going on?" He cleared his throat and staggered to his feet. "Well," he said, blinking, "anyone going to tell me?"

Marjorie wanted them to ignore him. If they could just smile now, talk gently among themselves, he would forget why he was fussing and sit down again. But Angran and Ollie were not the types to talk gently. Angran was frowning at him now, arms folded. Ollie was advancing toward him, rummaging in the box.

"Do you want to see your picture, Grandpa?" he began, but Marjorie put her fingers to her lips.

"Don't worry, Ollie," she said. "Of course you can have the necklace." She unhooked the clasp and drew it out from under her collar. "Please be careful with it," she added, as she slipped it beneath the lid of the box. "I've grown to love it very much."

Ollie beamed at her. "Auntie Nessa!" he called. "I've got it!" He skipped to the door and turned to smile at Marjorie again. There was a glimpse of Richard in his face—his eagerness, his delight in each small triumph of the day. She knew that Gerald had seen it too. He was grasping at the arms of the chair, his eyes clouded with tears as he lowered himself down.

At the hearth, Angran unfolded her arms. "Marjorie," she said, "you didn't have to do that." It could have been a reprimand, but there was an unexpected softness in her voice.

Marjorie wanted to tell her, suddenly, how easy it had been to console Richard as a boy. He was always weepy in the first days when Gerald left for sea, but a hand on his head would calm him, or a few sweet words whispered into his ear. In the hospital, when Richard's breath turned hoarse and jagged, she had put her palm on his shoulder and whispered to him. His breathing had softened and slowed. This moment, the proof of their bond, had carried her through the worst days of bereavement.

"Ah, well," she said, smiling up at Angran, "it's always heartwarming, isn't it, to give comfort to a fatherless child?"

Angran blinked at her. "Oh—I suppose," she began, and for a moment Marjorie thought she saw a quiver in Angran's chin. Marjorie reached out a hand, but then Ollie scampered back in, the box rattling on his hip.

"Auntie Nessa thinks the necklace is wonderful," he announced, brighter now than ever. Marjorie looked back to Angran, ready to share another smile. But Angran was polishing her glasses on her T-shirt, eyes down, biting her lip.

Ollie

MY DAD DIED. People have come to celebrate his birthday and they're surprised because there's no cheese on the table. When Nessa arrived she said: "We can't have a party for Rich without cheese."

For a moment I thought that everyone would go home because the box of cheese had gone missing. I thought I'd never get to swap the presents back and find out what it means to be alive. But then I showed Nessa the necklace and she gasped. She said: "Oh, my God! Where did you get that?"

I told her it was the present from my dad. I told her to give me the shawl and answer the question on the card, but she didn't listen. She just stood there with her hands over her mouth, saying: "I can't believe he remembered. I can't tell you what that means to me."

I said: "You have to tell me what it means. That's the whole point."

It looks like we're still having a party anyway, even without the cheese. We're gathered in the sitting room now, listening to the Beach Boys. Mum is sitting next to Grandpa. She's holding his hands, telling him about the scattering of the ashes at The Ravages. He says: "Nothing prepares you to see your own son dead."

I wonder if he'll stop saying that when I've completed the puzzle. I wonder if Mum will stop sniffing all the time and blowing her nose. But I'm not close to solving it yet. No one has written out their answer, and when I ask them to do it they just smile at me or sigh.

Angran comes into the room with a tray of tea and the flowery teacups she keeps at the back of the cupboard. The index card I gave her is poking out of the embroidered pocket on her shorts. I say: "Have you thought about the shawl yet, Angran? Do you want to write your answer down?"

She bangs the tray down on the hearth. She says: "Christ, Ollie, this nonsense with the puzzle is getting on my nerves. Your mother should never have let you begin."

The Beach Boys CD finishes at that exact moment and it's really quiet in the room. Mum reaches for Angran's hand. She says: "Can't you be gentle with him, for once?"

But I don't want her to be gentle, I want her to help me with the puzzle. She won't, though. Her neck has gone tight. She's stalking out of the room and Mum is chasing after her. Angran says, "Leave me alone" and we hear her boots on the stairs and the slamming of the bathroom door.

It's even quieter in the room now. Auntie Nessa looks at me and says: "Are you all right, Ollie?" Then she says she's had an idea and beckons me to follow her out.

I take the box with me down the passageway. I'm hoping her idea is something she's going to write on the card. I'm hoping she's going to use her teacher's voice to make the others write on theirs too. But when we get to the kitchen, she starts rattling around in the dresser drawer and she says: "Why don't you take a break from the puzzle for a bit and help me sort out the drains instead? It might be just as satisfying. I don't know why I haven't done it before."

She takes a wrench from the drawer and walks out into the garden. The rain has stopped and her footprints are dark on the wet grass. She turns at the hedge and calls to me to follow, but I don't. I'm too cross. I go to the leather armchair, sit down and look into the box again.

That's when I see the crack in the vase. It makes me feel sick. The rain has stopped, but I can still hear it rushing in my head. There's a chunk gone from the rim and a jagged gap across the middle like a lightning strike. I drop the box at my feet and kick it. It skims across the floor and spins off under the kitchen table. I hear glass splintering as it rams into the legs of a chair.

Gerald

HE PRESSED DOWN with his hands on the armchair and heaved himself to his feet. A fierce bubbling surged in his ears as he rose, and a pain shot through his hip, but he was up, standing, and he hoped the wobble in his legs didn't show.

Not that anyone was looking. Marjorie was bending over the tray on the hearth, mopping up some milk, and the others seemed to have wandered off somewhere through the shadows of the house. Perhaps they'd gone to perform some kind of ritual among the dripping leaves of the garden. That was what bohemians did, wasn't it? Danced about with twigs in their hair, banged drums to conjure up the . . . the damn . . . He couldn't think of the word, but he didn't care. It was about time, he thought, that someone took charge of things here. No point in dancing. Better to help the boy with his puzzle.

"Where are you going?" Marjorie said, advancing toward him with the crockery rattling on the tray.

Spirits. That was the bloody word.

"You can't drink spirits now, Gerald. It's not that sort of party."

He didn't know what sort of party it was. He'd thought there'd be speeches, people tapping their glass with a spoon, declaring Richard a fine figure of a man. But it wasn't that. And it wasn't the sort where you drank spirits and laughed out loud to hide how damn miserable you felt.

He made his way into the passageway toward the table of food.

"Shall I make you up a plate?" Marjorie said, at his elbow. He looked at the bowls of salad. Bitty stuff, herbs, nuts, bastards to pick out of his teeth. He turned away and scanned the dark hall in search of the candles Richard had given him. If they were going to have rituals around here, he wanted one of his own. Light the wicks, sit there quietly, watching the wobble of the flames.

"Wobble," said a voice in his head. "Be more wobbly." It was Richard's voice and he strained to hear it. Was it the last thing he'd said before he died? Bloody stupid thing to say if it was. All the same, he wanted to hear it again. The laughter in it, the muffled tone, as if he were speaking with his mouth full.

Marjorie went clattering off to the kitchen with her tray. Gerald went to the open front door and stepped out into the damp air. The drains smelled of egg and raw meat, but at least it was lighter out here. If Ollie had come out here it would be easier to find him. Something was troubling the boy, the meaning of life or some such. Well, Gerald knew a thing or two about life. Perhaps it was time to share it, man to man.

He walked around the corner of the house, noting as he went the messy herb garden and the dead roses in the hedge, their heads weighed down with rain. Nessa was squatting on the lawn. Her frown was dark on her brow as she peered down at the earth. Either she was starting this ritual of theirs or, judging by her look of concentration, she had found the meaning of life that Ollie so desperately wanted.

"Nothing prepares you," he found himself saying, "to see your own son dead."

He wanted an answer to that. Not people looking away, pretending they hadn't heard. Not people saying, *Hmm, ah, well, it gets easier with time.* Poppycock, that. What did they think, that because he forgot his words sometimes, he would forget his damn son, lying there dead? Ruth, holding his hands just now, had given him an answer of sorts. She'd held his hand and talked of a waterfall where they'd scattered Richard's ashes. She told him they'd seen a . . . some bird . . . a . . . It didn't matter what bird it was, flying off through the trees. What mattered was the force of the water surging over the rocks. That was what he'd felt at Richard's bedside. A roaring in his head, a swirling and gushing in his chest as he'd stared down at Richard's twisted mouth beneath the oxygen tube. That was the thing he wasn't prepared for. That was what Ollie needed to know.

He looked away from Nessa into the tangle of trees around the rockface. *Heron.* That was the bird. Great raggedy things with wobbly necks. The place was full of herons and crows, the scruffs of the bird world. Well, maybe he was scruffy too, walking in the grass with the turn-ups of his trousers damp against his ankles, tears on his cheeks, sniveling like a child.

"Be more wobbly." The voices were back, and through

the gurgles in his ears he heard the waterfall, hissing in the woods ahead. He was prepared for it now, for the rush and bubble of it, for the force of his grief. Nothing to be scared of, not if you wobbled along with it. Could he say that to Ollie if he found him? No harm, he supposed, in giving it a try.

Ollie

MY DAD DIED. His brain went wrong and it hurt him. I know it did because he made a sound like a cow. I heard it, grinding in his throat. I saw his arms scrabbling at the air. What if his brain was hurting when he set the puzzle? It might have made the answers into something horrible. What if he never set me a puzzle at all? Just thinking of that makes my ears rush. It sounds like The Ravages and that's where my dad is—all the bits of his burned-up body squashed into the mud. I don't want to think about it. I'm going to take the presents to The Ravages instead, and throw them into the water. I might as well. The vase is broken, and I don't want to do the puzzle anymore. Not if it's all been made from a hurting brain.

I go upstairs to find some spare socks in case my feet get wet on the walk. I see Mum on the landing rattling the bathroom door. Behind it, Angran's voice is hard and echoing. She says: "Leave me alone, Ruth. There's nothing wrong. I just came up for a pee."

Mum presses her forehead against the door. She says: "Why do you always have to run away when you're upset? You never let us sort anything out."

She's lucky I'm not carrying the box of presents. I'd

have thrown it at her if I was. I hate it when she argues with Angran. It's like there's no one else in the world except Angran, even if I'm standing there, trying to tell her something important. I give up on the clean socks and I go back downstairs. I don't even care if my feet get wet now. I see the box of presents under the trestle in the passageway, shoved to the back, deep in the shadows. I think I must have kicked it there. I slide it out and take it to the garden, where it smells like Camembert and dog food. Auntie Nessa is poking at the drain with the wrench. Grandpa is standing on the lawn. I run past them both and climb over the tumbled-down wall. Grandpa says: "Hey, boy, wait for me!"

My socks are wet already. They're tight against my feet and they squeak against my Crocs, but I don't care now. I had a plan. Everyone was going to write the meaning of their present on their card. Then they were going to stand up and read from them one by one so I could focus on solving the puzzle. That won't happen now. All the presents will be smashed instead, deep down in the dark rushing river.

Angran

SHE WAITED UNTIL Ruth had finally left the landing, then flushed the toilet and splashed her face with water. She looked out across the woods at The Ravages, the fall thicker now after the rain, white ruffles against the black rocks. In the garden below she saw Gerald limping about by the wall. He was peering after something in the wood and she couldn't tell if he was swaying or if there was a bulge in the glass that made him look quavery. No doubt he had taken refuge from Ollie's constant pestering about the puzzle. It was time, Angran thought, to put a stop to it. She'd had enough of him running to her with that box beneath his arm, shoving that shawl into her hands. How she hated that mossy green wool. It was the color of rain and dark mornings, waking in the shadow of the rock, the color of her misery, of all that should be pushed down and forgotten.

She scrubbed at her face with the hand towel. It seemed obvious to her that Rich could never have organized this puzzle for Ollie, even if the idea had occurred to him. It was true that he played elaborate games at times, but they were haphazard and unplanned.

"Buffoonery," she said to herself, wincing at the harsh

fibers of the towel as it scraped over her skin. "Nothing so clever or precise."

But Ruth had encouraged Ollie with this pestering from the start. She'd bought him envelopes and index cards, and shrugged away Angran's misgivings.

"When was the last time you saw him excited like this?" she'd asked. "Certainly not since Rich died. Maybe not ever. It's like he's suddenly come alive."

Now Angran tossed the towel to the floor. Glad as she was to see Ollie engaged with something other than a su-doku, she was certain that this particular endeavor could only end in disaster. More than anything, Ollie hated to be wrong and Angran wanted to save him from that pain.

There was a cry from the garden. Angran looked out to see Nessa squatting in the grass. There was a stick in her hand and she was poking at something in the ground. Ruth came rushing up to her, bright skirt fluttering around her legs. More unnecessary fuss and flap, Angran thought, as Ruth let out a cry of her own. They were looking into the drains, she realized. It was not a stick in Nessa's hand, but a wrench. She must have pried open the inspection panel and now they were putting on a performance, laughing and bending at the waist as they pretended to retch.

"Hey!" Angran shoved at the window and shouted down to them. "What do you think you're doing? I've told you not to interfere." The air was thick with the reek of rotten egg.

"Come down," Nessa called. "You've got to see what it's like."

"I don't want to see. Leave it alone."

And yet she left the bathroom, hurried down the stairs and marched out into the garden anyway. She had thought many times of lifting the inspection panel herself, but she had never dared, lest she let loose a deluge of filth, flowing over the garden and threatening the house.

"Stop that," she scolded, as she approached, and Nessa looked toward her, still poking at the pipe.

"No," Nessa said. "Why should I?" She narrowed her eyes and, for a moment, Angran quailed.

"Please," Angran tried, as brown sludge swelled and bulged at the lip of the stoneware pipe. "Why have you always defied me? I only ever tried to make you happy."

"Really?" Nessa said, withdrawing the wrench. "I didn't think you knew the meaning of the word."

Angran flinched. She stared at the wrench drooling into the grass. She could tell that Nessa wanted to flick the muck toward her, watch it spatter onto her face. If Rich was here, she thought, this would have played out differently, and for a moment there was a tiny clench in her heart, a sort of inward gasp at the loss of his benign presence in their lives. She pictured the way he'd have chased them around the garden with the wrench, how they would have shrieked and giggled, their voices echoing, bright against the rock. But Angran had killed off any fun they might have had. Just as she always did. No wonder Rich had chosen her a dull green shawl, and not the vase, with its joyous scattering of light.

"Let me do it," she said, holding out her hands for the wrench. The iron was warm where Nessa had gripped it and the gloop in the pipe, when she pressed on it, was spongy. Something bubbled up toward her and she startled, breath quivering in the back of her throat. How cursed the cottage seemed now. She wished she could fathom up memories of her children running barefoot on the lawn, crushing the rose petals to make scent, lacing daisy chains through their hair. But what came to her now were the arguments when Nessa was a teenager, some so fierce Angran had run to her room and locked herself in. She'd stay there until dark, shrinking beneath the bed-clothes, even as Nessa banged on the door, sobbing out apologies. She remembered how the air in her room was thick and heavy in her lungs, how each breath seemed to press her deeper into the mattress. She had thought she was betraying her daughters if they saw her like that. But the failure, she realized now, was not the depression, but the pretense that it had never occurred.

Hands shaking, she poked at the pipe once more. Something suckered and she heard a click, wet and slick as a lascivious kiss. Next came a gulp. Deep underground water gurgled and the sludge gave way beneath the wrench.

"Done," she cried. There was a gushing in the pipes. She looked up to share her triumph with her daughters, but they were gone. There was only an empty lawn before her, and, beyond it, Gerald on the far side of the wall, moving into the shadows of the trees. She let the wrench fall from her hands.

"Ruth!" she called. "Nessa! I've cleared the drains!"

Her voice echoed against the rock. It brought memories to her, the cries of her little girls when she ran from them in the night.

"Don't think about that now," she told herself. "Irrele-vant." Except that it was relevant. She had been denying it for too long. She ran across the lawn and found them walk-ing to the front door, arm in arm, and she pulled at Ruth's shoulders to turn them around.

"The way I've been," she said, "I can't go on anymore." Ruth stared at her, her brow wrinkling in something that looked like fear. "I feel so terrible," Angran continued. "I've failed you, I know." She nodded toward the woods, meaning to apologize for all the times she had run off and left them, but she stopped short as she noticed Gerald, high on the path, heading toward the viewpoint. He was grasping at a branch. She thought of his polished shoes, the treacherous mud, the precipices he would encounter if he strayed. She let go of Ruth's shoulder and pelted down the garden.

"No, Mum! Come back," Ruth called after her, but Angran was already stepping over the wall, scrambling up the path after Gerald.

Ollie

MY DAD DIED. There's mud on my hands. It smells sharp and dirty and I can feel it pulling at my skin. My feet won't stay where I put them. They slide about, bumping into roots and rocks. Twigs work their way under my heels and poke at my skin, as I try to find my way to The Ravages.

There are other people near me in the woods. I can't see them through the trees but I can hear them calling. Grandpa's calling for me, Angran's calling for Grandpa, and Mum, somewhere down below, is calling for Angran. I'm not calling for anyone, but I feel like calling for my dad. I'm going to chuck his box of presents into the river. I'll stand at the top and watch the white gush of water smashing it down into the pool. Mum says I don't have any imagination, but she's wrong. It's easy to imagine the picture splitting in the water, the beads on the necklace spinning apart. Shards of glass will snag on the shawl. I have to imagine all this because I'm not going to see. It's all going to happen deep down where the water's black and bubbly. The puzzle will come to an end. I won't have to think about meaning anymore.

My dad died. I don't want to know what that means.

Mum is here. She's running up from Angran's garden

and she's panting hard, bits of spit at the corners of her lips. She says: "Ollie, what are you doing here?" Then she says, "Have you seen Angran? I'm scared that she's going to—" and she claps her hand to her mouth before she finishes her sentence.

I say, "Going to what?" but she doesn't answer. She just turns her head and stares into the trees.

She says: "You'd better go home, Ollie. There's nothing good going on here."

But I don't go home. I follow her to the top of the hill. The woods have turned dark and the leaves are shivering. I don't want to go to The Ravages on my own anymore. I call: "Wait for me, wait for me, please."

She stops at the top, but she's still looking all around her, into the trees one minute and then down the steps toward the pool. There is steam in the air and a smell of moss and thick mud. She says: "What is it, Ollie?"

I say: "My dad died."

Mum looks at me then. Her arms drop to her sides. She says: "Oh, God, Ollie, you're right."

I don't know what I'm right about, but I don't really care. I've been wrong all day and now I'm right at last.

Mum beckons me toward her and we make our way to the viewpoint and stand there together. We're close enough now to look over the edge of the waterfall and into the froth below. We stare down at the black pool that seems still at first until you notice the current snaking underneath, pulling the bubbles to the edge, to the next fall, and then the next, all the way down to the stream that runs through the picnic place. Mum takes a long, slow breath. She says: "Yes, your dad died."

So that's what I'm right about. It's the only thing I've

ever been right about. The sound of The Ravages keeps on pushing through the air. I'd thought it would sound like the rushing in my ears, but it doesn't. There's more detail in it. There are drips and gurgles and deep-down gulps and things that sound like laughter and things that sound like engines bubbling on.

Mum says: "Oh, Ollie. Whatever happens now, we'll always be the people who lost your dad. We'll have that with us forever."

My arms ache where I've been grasping the box. I hold it out toward her and say: "Can you throw that over, Mum?"

Just then Angran appears. She's running toward us from the picnic tables and her breath is loud. She doesn't stop to talk to us. She thumps right past and heads down the steps, skidding away from them suddenly and sliding down the bank to the pool. Mum screams. She says: "Oh, my God, Ollie, this is it!" Then she follows her down and scrambles onto the bank. I can't keep up with her. I keep slipping about on the mud. My dad died.

Ruth

She had no plan in her head, or any idea what her mother might do. Dive down onto the rocks headfirst? Stand beneath the falls with her mouth wide open, choking on the gush of water in her throat? It seemed unlikely now that anyone could die at The Ravages. Had she misconstrued, after all, those hints about doing something stupid in the river? Was it just a fearful fantasy she had harbored all these years? But she could not let it go.

"I can't go on," Angran had said, in the garden, and it had brought the fantasy back to Ruth in full force. Now it was carrying her down the bank, juddering and sliding, calling for help. Angran was ahead of her and she, too, appeared to be powered by some other force, compelling her toward the rocks at the edge of the pool.

"Have you seen him?" Angran shouted over her shoulder. "He might have lost his way."

In her fear, Ruth thought wildly, *She's crazed, talking nonsense.* The sinews in Angran's neck were taut and shadowed as she peered into the water.

"Stay there!" Ruth cried. "I'm coming!"

She had a vision of herself, careering toward Angran and skidding past, tripping on the jagged rocks and plunging into the froth. It wouldn't feel like drowning, she thought. It would feel like fighting. She'd be thrashing about in there, clothes twisting around her in the current, black water surging around her throat. When she had stepped into the river at the picnic place the water had been a salve, renewing her connection with Rich. Here, the blast of the falling cascade and the crash of the backwash seemed to charge her with rage, as if it were bursting in her blood, bright and mighty. She grabbed Angran by the elbow and roared, "How dare you scare me like this?"

Angran whirled around to face her. "Like what?" she shrieked back. Her glasses slipped on her nose. She tried to push them back, but Ruth had grabbed her by the shoulder and was rattling her bones.

"You know exactly what!" she shouted. The glasses bounced down Angran's face. They snagged for a moment on her chin and clattered onto the rocks.

Behind them on the bank, Ollie cried out. Ruth saw him clutching the box to his side, mouth open, face pale against the dark trees.

"I'm scared," he wailed.

Angran snatched herself away from Ruth's grip and began feeling for the glasses at her feet.

"It's OK," Ruth called to Ollie. "Everyone's safe now."

"No, they're not," Angran said. She rammed the glasses onto her face. A lens was cracked, and a cobweb of fissures obscured one of her eyes. She glared with the other. "Gerald's out here somewhere in his ridiculous shoes. I've been searching for him, but now, thanks to you, I can't see a thing."

"Gerald?" Ruth said.

Angran craned her head, straining toward the trees.

Ruth saw the same urgency in her face that had enraged her moments before. But now she understood that Angran had not been intent on hurting herself when she had hurtled toward the pool. She was bent on rescue.

"Shit, Mum," she said. "We'll have to look for him together." She climbed the bank to Ollie and squatted before him.

"I need you to run back home," she said. "Go straight to the house and tell Nessa that we're out here, looking for Grandpa. It's important. Go as fast as you can." She saw his lips quiver. His fingers curled around the edge of the box.

"I want to stay with you." His voice was hardly more than a whisper. "My dad died."

"I know. No one's going to forget that, and we'll all come back, alive, as quick as we can."

Angran let out a wail. She was staggering toward them, hand to her face over the smashed lens. "I saw him, I'm sure I did. How can I get to him if I can't see a thing?"

Ruth squinted into the undergrowth, following Angran's gaze downstream. She thought she saw something moving, ducking behind a tangle of briars. She stood up and held out her hand.

"I'll guide you," she said. She watched Ollie climb the bank to the steps and she grasped Angran's hand.

Ollie

MY DAD DIED. Mum told me to run home again, but I'm not going to. She thinks Grandpa is farther down the river, but she's wrong. I saw him earlier at the tourist track. He wasn't slipping around, like they said he would be. He was walking with his hands behind his back and talking to himself. I expect he was saying that nothing prepares you to see your own son dead.

I'm sick of carrying this box around. It's time to throw it into the water. My feet slide around in my Crocs as I climb the steps back up to the viewpoint. The sound of the water is high up here. It's like panicky breaths and the moss along the sides is shaking about in the spray. I go right to the edge, where the water curves over like an escalator and I hold the box out at arm's length. I hear Grandpa's voice behind me. He says: "Careful there now."

He stands at my shoulder and looks over. He says: "So this is The Ravages, then. It never stops, does it? Couldn't make it if we tried."

My arms start shaking from the weight of the box. I say: "Shall I throw it in?"

But it's a stupid question because I don't care how he answers. I let it go and the box twists open in the air. I stagger back because there aren't any presents inside, there is cheese. The lid flaps apart and a big wedge of Stilton splashes into the pool, spins around and disappears. Then the box falls in and the Cheddar floats out from under it. A round cheese smashes into a rock, a white one speeds past it over the lip of the next fall. Grandpa says: "There he goes." That's what Auntie Nessa said when the heron flew by and I still don't know what it means. My dad wasn't a heron and he wasn't a cheese. I look down at the frothing pool and I think it means he's gone.

We stand for ages watching the water and listening to the gulps and bubbles. Grandpa says: "I know what it's like, you know, when you've got something to say and no one understands." I think the only thing I've got to say is that my dad died. Grandpa says: "You're trying to work it all out, aren't you, lad? It's time we gave you some . . . some . . ."

I think he's trying to say it's time to give me some help, but I can't be sure. Lots of other words would fit in there. Money, or presents. It could even be something bad like a clip around the ear. After all, he did once say I needed discipline. I say: "Some what, Grandpa?" but he shakes his head.

He says: "Gone, I'm afraid. Feeling a bit wobbly."

I've heard him talking about being wobbly before. It's probably a turn of phrase, but then I think that I'm feeling wobbly too. It's the rock I'm standing on, wobbling under me. My feet skid forward in my Crocs. My toes stub into the end of them and my heels skitter behind them. I'm teetering on the edge of the rock now and panic shudders in my legs, like the roar of The Ravages rising up toward me.

Grandpa's arm thumps across my chest. He shouts, "I've got you, lad, I've got you!" and he drags me back. It's so fast and hard that I slam into him and he hauls me, floundering, back onto the path. Back and back we go, scuffling and shuffling, my knees folding inward as he pulls me from the edge. He says: "That's it, Ollie, you're a good boy." Then his legs collapse. He drops to the ground and I fall too, jammed against him. We roll together into a heap. My head is wedged up under his chin, his legs are under my ribs. He says, "You really are a good boy, you know," and his voice quivers. I can hear him hissing through his teeth, groaning now, and his breath is hot across my scalp.

Nessa

SOMETHING POPPED IN the fire and sparks showered from the hearth. Nessa stamped them out. She lifted the fire-guard from a hook on the mantel and placed it before the flames. The smell of the drains was gone. Somewhere, deep underground, water would be running through the pipes now. She wished Ruth was there, to marvel at it and laugh. But Ruth had gone chasing after Angran, with something that looked like panic in her eyes.

"She's not going to do herself any damage," Nessa had said, clenching her fists to stop herself grabbing at Ruth's sleeves. "You've got to stop being scared all the time."

But Ruth, blinking toward the trees, had said she wasn't scared. She said she was ready to tackle anything and started on some story about the river; how, when she'd gone to lie in it fully clothed, she'd felt the power in its flow.

"Well, don't go climbing into the pool at The Ravages," Nessa had said. "This is Rich's day, remember, not yours and not Angran's either."

Ruth had started running then, down the lawn to the broken wall. She claimed, as Nessa scrambled after her, that going to The Ravages was all about Rich. She was facing her fears, she said, seeking out the experience, instead of hiding away.

"All this darkness in me, it's just an age-old terror of Angran's pain. I'm sure it held me back from loving Rich. I'm going to deal with it now. Then I can feel all the love I need. God, Nessa, I just want the full force of it now."

Nessa's hands had started to tingle. She had thought for a moment that she should follow Ruth and cheer her on, but she saw that there was something private in Ruth's passion. If her love for Rich was truly at the heart of this venture, she should not intrude. So she turned back to the house instead, hoping to honor Rich in some other way. Marjorie, she thought, might want to reminisce a little, about Rich's slapdash approach to life or the way he liked to pour wine into a glass from a great height. Even Gerald might be happy to laugh about Rich's Hawaiian shirts. But when she had come to the sitting room she found the flames crackling in the hearth and the chairs empty.

She stood before the fire now, wondering if Ollie had given up on his puzzle at last. She realized she had no idea where he and his box of presents had gone either. He had been agitated, she remembered, when she was searching for the wrench in the kitchen, but she hadn't really been paying attention. The trouble was that he was always agitated about something, socks usually, or the noises people made when they were eating. She understood that he couldn't always stop himself and she had learned, too, that it didn't necessarily help to respond. But perhaps it was time to offer him a subtler form of care, to notice him more, to sit with him quietly as if she had the shawl wrapped around her shoulders. She stepped away from the fire. It was time to find out where he had gone.

She tried the kitchen first, but it was Marjorie she found there, standing at the sink, soap suds dripping from her fingers.

"The last time I tidied up for your mum," she said, "she got a bit cross with me. I hope I haven't caused any problems now."

Nessa laughed. "Oh, you don't need to worry about her. She's gone stomping off to the woods, saying that she failed us all."

Marjorie dried her hands and regarded Nessa, her brow wrinkled. "But that's awful if she thinks she failed you. You're her loved ones."

It was not a reprimand, but Nessa felt chastened all the same. She looked down at the floor and saw the box of presents there, shoved up against the wall.

"The puzzle," she said. "Oh, Marjorie, I feel awful, you know, that I didn't really help with it more."

She lifted the box onto the table and Marjorie came to stand beside her. "Well, maybe we can set the gifts out nicely. Then you can go and find him and start it all over again." Nessa looked into the box. She saw the shawl there, the soft, dusky folds of it. But snagged on the fibers were shards of broken glass.

"What a terrible shame!" Marjorie cried. "That beautiful vase!"

Together they spread the shawl over the table, and picked out the pieces. Outside the wind hummed in the woods, and a sweet silence settled between them.

"Was Gerald all right in the sitting room?" Marjorie asked, when they were done. "He usually dozes off about now."

Nessa shook her head. "He wasn't there."

"He must have been in the lavatory. Perhaps I'd better go and check on him."

Nessa felt herself grow hot. She knew he wasn't in the bathroom. She'd have heard the taps sputtering and the banging of the pipes. Besides, she remembered now that she'd seen him in the garden when she had opened the drains. Marjorie was on the stairs now, calling for him. Nessa took the binoculars from the box and ran to catch up with her. In the bathroom she went straight to the window. There was no one in the garden now. Beyond the wall the trees were almost bare, the undergrowth black and shadowed. She looked up at the white blur of The Ravages and, beside it, a knot of people at the viewpoint. Marjorie had noticed them, too, and she grabbed the binoculars from Nessa's hand. Nessa thought she could see Angran's red shorts, Ruth's bright dress, but the way they were moving made no sense. They seemed to be bobbing, standing for a moment then sinking down.

Marjorie gasped. Her hand clutched Nessa's elbow. "Ambulance," she said. "Something's wrong."

Nessa dialed and gave directions to the crew. Then she took the binoculars from Marjorie and looked out at The Ravages again. This time she saw that Ruth was leaning into Angran, her arm around her shoulders.

Ollie

MY DAD DIED. It's midnight. Mum's slicing up my dad's birthday cake even though it isn't his birthday anymore. I'm not going to eat any. Auntie Nessa thinks it's the icing that's putting me off. The cake was decorated to look like a cheese board, with yellow wedges of marzipan and a bunch of grapes made out of fruit jellies. Auntie Nessa keeps picking bits off, telling me it doesn't taste anything like cheese. I want to say, *I'm not stupid, you know*, but I think she's trying to be kind.

My dad died. He died in the hospital and we all went there again tonight. Grandpa went in an ambulance. A jeep came up the track and he was put on a stretcher. He didn't make the cow sound, like my dad did, and he didn't claw at the air. He said, "Terribly sorry, terribly sorry," and it was hard to hear him over the sound of The Ravages and the engine of the jeep.

Everyone kept asking me if I was all right. I said, "My dad died," but I think that was the wrong answer because it didn't stop them asking me again.

Now we're in the sitting room, and Angran's lit another fire. She's wearing her spare glasses with thin wire frames. She's got a tray on her knee with the broken bits of vase on it. She's squeezing glue onto the snapped edges and it looks like snot. The vase is going to look stupid when she's finished. There will be big jagged lines across it, studded with lumps of snot. Mum says it will be art. I think that's because it will have meaning, but I don't want to know what the meaning is.

My dad died. Last time I was at the hospital I had to go into a room and see him with his hands puffed up and shiny, and a stupid white tube stuck in his mouth. This time I had to see the nurse and have my arm squeezed tight in a blood-pressure pump. Auntie Nessa came in with me. She'd brought me some dry socks from home and she said she was proud of me, but I don't know why. As we left the nurse's room she got a piece of paper out of her pocket. I thought it would be her answer for the puzzle, but it was the letter my dad had started writing to me before he died. She said: "I'm sorry, Ollie. I shouldn't have kept this. It's yours."

I looked at the weird scribbly writing on the back and none of the phrases really made much sense, but I was glad she gave it back to me. I think she was trying to be kind then too.

We went back to the lobby after that. We waited for Grandpa, and the water-cooler went on and off fourteen times. I felt it buzzing across the floor and it made my feet ache.

Now everyone is making eating noises as they chew the cake. The box of presents is on the floor. People keep looking into it, saying how wonderful the presents are, how they'd have been happy with any of them, just because they came from my dad. Auntie Nessa pours herself another glass of wine. She says: "Well. It looks like we're starting the party all over again."

Everyone laughs, but I don't think it's funny. At the party everyone was going to take the gift my dad chose for them. They were going to write their answers on the cards and stand in a line, reading from them, one by one. Then I was going to solve the puzzle. That's not going to happen now and there are lots of reasons why. Because Grandpa can't stand up on the knee he had bandaged at the hospital. Because no one wrote anything on their cards. Because there never was a puzzle anyway and I'm stupid and wrong.

My dad died. I keep saying it, but it never makes any sense. It sounds like a turn of phrase, but it's not. There isn't any extra meaning. It only means he died.

Ruth

SHE LOOKED AT Ollie and thought he was going to start screaming or he was going to be sick, one of the two. A wave of longing for Rich washed over her. She wanted his easy smile, the way he could heave himself up from his chair, heavy-limbed but eager all the same, even when faced with Ollie's gritted teeth and rising screams.

Ollie pressed his fingertips around the ball of his knees. His fingernails whitened and she heard a small groan, tight at the back of his throat. She yearned for Rich, but the truth was that he was often useless with Ollie in meltdown. He brought too much of himself into the fray. He winced if Ollie punched the wall, cried out if he grabbed a puzzle book and tore the pages.

"You only need to witness him," Ruth had told him, more than once. "You're adding to his woes if you get upset yourself." But Rich could not hide his horror if Ollie yelled that everyone hated him or that he wished he'd never been born.

"I can't stand to see him so distressed," Rich would weep. "Can't we just love him into happiness?"

Ruth had read enough to know that she was right about this, but secretly she admired Rich for his wholehearted response. Shutting down came easily to her; it felt cold and unkind. It was too close to depression and she wished she did not have to offer it to her child.

Now she heard a shudder in his breath. She willed the others in the room to help her, but Angran was bent over the vase, dabbing at the glue with a rag. Nessa was staring into the flames, eyes drooping, and Marjorie and Gerald were smiling into each other's eyes. Gerald put his hand on Marjorie's arm, tapped at her gently with his finger.

Ruth pulled herself to her feet and went to the door. She called to Ollie to join her but she didn't really expect him to come. In his current state he was more likely to screech, she thought, or grab a slice of cake and hurl it at the wall. But he raised his head to look at her. She saw that his eyes were smirched, swollen with tears, his lips puffy and wet. In the next moment he was on his feet and hurtling toward her. He butted into her ribs, grabbed at her dress and stayed there with his knees pushing into her.

A hug, she realized. Her first in many years. He was all hard edges, skinny ribs, chin jutting at her solar plexus, elbows poking her hips. She staggered back and found herself shoved toward the passageway. She didn't know how hard to shove back, whether to root herself and gather him to her, or lurch about, accepting everything on offer.

"My dad died," he said.

"Yes," she replied, and the strange, pummeling hug went on. Somehow they came to the kitchen and when they stepped into the light they drew apart.

She went to the back door and pushed it open. Cool air brought the smell of wet earth and moss. Nothing from the drains. She called Ollie to her, and once again he came. There was a dripping in the trees and, behind it, the distant hiss of The Ravages. He pushed a piece of paper into her hands. It was the letter from Rich and her heart clenched at the sight of his writing. *Sky the color of apricots. Heart full of golden sky.* She looked out into the garden, saw the dark hulk of the rock, the branches black against the night sky. *Open your arms to the sunrise.* I can't, she thought. Not here in Black Coombe Cottage, where the sun doesn't climb above the rock till noon.

She smiled down at Ollie. "It's almost morning," she said. "We've been up all night."

Ollie shrugged. "I don't care."

She wished she could hug him again, soften to him, her hand on the back of his head, but she knew the moment had passed. "Do you *ever* care about the dawn?" she asked him. "Or is it just tonight that you don't?"

He looked down at his Crocs, shuffled his feet in and out of them. "Don't ask me two questions at once."

The trees shifted in the wood, a soft shushing in the branches.

"I care," she said, and was surprised to find that this was true. She understood now just how much Rich had loved the pink flush of a sunrise. She knew, too, that she could not witness it here at Black Coombe Cottage. But she cared deeply that it happened all the same. She would not see the silent apricot rays glisten on the wet grass, or the many diamond droplets in the dripping trees, but she knew they were all shining anyway. And now that Ollie had come to her with his awkward, grabbing embrace, something had changed with him too. There would still be many tedious conversations ahead, about sudokus, socks and footballers' names, and they would all appear to be empty of depth and meaning. But it did not follow that the meaning was not there. Somewhere beyond the rock, the sky at dawn would be aglow; when she thrust her hand into a sock and agreed that, yes, there was a loose thread hanging from the seam, it would be an act of love.

She had asked Rich once why he found it so easy to make Ollie laugh.

"Oh, I don't know," he said. "I just muck about. It doesn't always work." Ruth had thought at the time that she had never learned to muck about. You couldn't, if you thought it might send your mother rushing out of the house and into the howling woods. Now, though, as she looked out across the garden and up at the twilight sky, she realized that all the terror was gone.

"Let's get up early one day and watch the sun rise from the viewpoint," she said to Ollie. "Would you like that?"

"No. It's stupid." His hands hovered over his knees.

"Yes, it probably is," she said. "But let's do it anyway." She watched his fingers from the corners of her eyes, bracing herself for whatever might happen next.

He shrugged. "All right," he said. "If we must."

Ollie

MY DAD DIED. He used to make hot chocolate if we stayed up after midnight. He used to put cream in it and marshmallows and, for himself, a capful of brandy. Angran doesn't have marshmallows, cream or brandy, but Mum decides we should make hot chocolate anyway. She pours two and a half bottles of milk into the saucepan, shaking out the last drops from each one.

She carries the tray into the sitting room and Angran frowns at her. She says: "You've used up all the milk, haven't you? Silly girl. Now we'll have nothing for the morning."

Auntie Nessa is sitting with her eyes closed and her feet stretched out in front of the fire. Now she sits up and says: "Chill out, Mum. I can run and get some when the shops open."

Other Grandma speaks at the same time and she says: "We don't mind black tea, do we, Gerald?"

Angran's frown is so tight it makes her spare glasses slip down her nose. She says: "But, Ruth, you just didn't look ahead! You're worse than Rich."

Now it goes very quiet in the room. Everyone looks at their hands or their knees. Mum stands very still, holding the tray tightly, and I see the bulge of her arm muscles under her dress. Suddenly she smiles. She says: "Do you know what? I'm going to take that as a compliment."

Everyone starts moving again. I hear Other Grandma's tights crackle as she crosses her ankles. Auntie Nessa flops back into the chair and yawns. Mum hands a cup to Angran, and Angran says: "I suppose you're right. Rich made lovely hot chocolate. Maybe yours will be just as good." Then she dips her mouth to the cup and slurps. When she lifts her head her glasses have steamed up and there's a bubbly brown mustache on her upper lip. She takes another slurp, louder this time, and grins. The chocolate mustache stretches thin and the bubbles start to pop. Auntie Nessa chuckles. Angran slurps again and Mum starts to giggle too. Then Other Grandma joins in and even Grandpa smiles. I think it sounds disgusting, like the sink in the upstairs bathroom. I say: "Why are you all laughing?"

It makes them stop. Mum says: "Oh, Ollie, you really are sad tonight, aren't you?"

I say: "That's not the answer! Tell me why you're laughing."

Auntie Nessa grins. I see her eyes slide toward Angran. She says: "Because Angran's a big idiot and it's hilarious." There's a silence in the room again, but it only lasts a moment, until Auntie Nessa makes a snorty sound with her nose. Then everyone laughs again until Auntie Nessa claps her hands like a teacher. She says: "Right. Let's answer him properly. Me first, and we'll take it in turns. Ollie, I was laughing because it feels good. You've always got to do what feels good, you know. It's the only way to live."

She turns and points to Other Grandma. Other

Grandma says: "Me? Oh, I don't know. I suppose I was laughing because I'm so relieved." She puts her hanky to her eyes and says: "I was so worried about your grandpa and I'm just so glad he's all right."

Auntie Nessa points at Angran next. She holds the broken vase up to the light, and peers through it. There is still chocolate smudging around her lip. She says: "I wasn't laughing, actually. But I was having fun. There hasn't been much of that in my life, you know, but I was thinking of your dad just then. He found fun in everything."

When Auntie Nessa points at Grandpa, he stares up from his chair and his neck stretches out so he looks like a tortoise. He says: "Is this some kind of party game we're playing? Don't know the bloody rules."

Other Grandma giggles again. She squeezes his hand and she says: "We're telling Ollie why we were laughing. Have you got anything to say?"

He does, but I don't really understand it. Something about how we should all be more wobbly. When he's finished, everyone looks at Mum, but she just puts her hands over her mouth and blinks down at the box of presents at her feet. Auntie Nessa says, "Oh, come on, Mrs. Meaning-in-everything. Surely you can tell us why that was funny," but Mum keeps shaking her head.

She pushes the box of presents to the middle of the room with her toe and says: "Hey. Don't forget about these."

They all lean forward and look into the box. I'm about to tell Grandpa to take the picture of the boat but I see his hand, all speckled and shaking, grasping one of the scented candles. Auntie Nessa says: "They smell lovely, don't they?" She lights one and places it on the mantelpiece.

Grandpa sits back in his chair and stares at the flame. Other Grandma picks up the necklace. She fastens the clasp around her neck and then she unbuttons the collar of her blouse so we can see the silver hand glinting in the firelight. Nessa spreads the shawl over her knees and strokes it, like a cat.

My dad died. I don't want to think about it anymore, but everyone else does. They sit by the fire for an hour talking about him. But now it's time for bed. I don't think I'll sleep because Mum says we've got to give up our beds for the guests. That means I have to lie on the sofa and the cushions are scratchy against my cheeks. Everyone's bumping around the house, pulling airbeds out, calling to each other about pillow cases and whether the bathroom is free. Mum keeps rustling around in the bin bags that are still piled up on the landing. She keeps pulling things out and stuffing them into Angran's old army rucksack. She's got a carrier bag full of my socks. Grandpa makes little groaning noises as he goes up the stairs with Other Grandma. Auntie Nessa stubs her toe against a box on the landing and swears. Mum comes down, switches off the light and lies on the airbed. I know I won't sleep with her there. Every time she turns over I can hear it puff against the carpet. I say: "When will I get my own bed back, Mum?"

She doesn't answer the question. She just wriggles about, sending wafts of rubbery air toward me. Then she sits up and rests her chin on the arm of the sofa. She says: "I never told you why I was laughing earlier, did I? Do you want to know?"

I don't say yes, but she tells me anyway. She says: "I was laughing because I love everyone here. I miss Dad unbearably, but the more I miss him, the more I feel love. Isn't that amazing? Isn't that enough to make you laugh?"

I don't answer her questions. I shuffle away from her instead and sit hugging my knees in the corner of the sofa. There's a wet, clicking sound somewhere in the room. It's the sound of her tongue against her lips and the snot slipping in her nose because she's started to cry. I say: "Why are you crying now, then?"

She doesn't answer for a while. Then she says: "I'm crying because I love everyone here. I miss Dad unbearably." She says exactly what she said before, using exactly the same words, and now she seems to think it's hilarious. She says: "Go on. Ask me why I'm laughing now. I'm laughing because I love everyone here . . ."

I push my sleeping bag down over my knees and I say: "I'm never going to get to sleep if you keep saying that over and over again."

Mum sits up and lets the plug out of the airbed. Over the sound of it hissing she says: "Come on, then. I was going to do this in the morning. But there's no time like the present." She gets up and walks into the hall, beckoning me to follow. She has found the box that had the presents in it, and she's filling it now with mugs, a kettle, the binoculars and some of the cushions she made that look like different sorts of cheese. She rolls up the air bed and the sleeping bags and piles them on top of Angran's rucksack. She says: "Have you worked out what we're doing yet? We're going home."

Ruth

SHE DROVE HIM through the lanes with the mugs rattling in their box on the back seat. The trees overhead were black, crowding toward the car. Ollie fidgeted in the seat beside her, winding his fists into his jumper.

"It'll be rubbish at our house," he said. "There's nothing in it."

They left the woods and moved through the village. In the navy sky the clouds were moon-colored, light pushing through them. She wanted to tell him that it wouldn't be long before she filled the house with beautiful things again. It was what she did best, making a room bright and abundant. But she couldn't be sure if he cared about that. "It'll always feel empty without Dad," she said.

When they arrived, Ollie walked through the rooms with his shoulders hunched up, clenched fists pulled in toward his belly, as if he were afraid to touch anything. Ruth went up to his bedroom. She remembered how Nessa had dragged his chest of drawers up to his room at Black Coombe Cottage, set out his socks in his drawers, his puzzle books beside the bed. He had screamed at her but it had been the right thing to do, to make his room as ordered as they could. Now she realized she didn't have any of his furniture, only a carrier full of socks and the cheese cushions for a bed. She laid the cushions on the floor and emptied the bag of socks, placing them in a neat row beneath the window. It wouldn't be right, but nothing was right anymore, now that his dad was gone.

She went to her own room. She saw the hollows in the carpet where the legs of the bed had dug in, a scum of dust at the lip of each one. She spread out the airbed in the space between them and felt a longing to lie down. It would never go, she thought, this desire for her bed, and the urge to block out the world. Some days, she knew she would have to give in. But perhaps this would not be the disaster she feared, not if she could remember that she had lain in the river too, and felt the current surge against her and ripple over her skin. Giving in was not the same as giving up, whatever Nessa might think.

Downstairs, Ollie moved from room to room, the sound of his footsteps resonating against the bare walls. She took the binoculars from the rucksack and then the quilt, holding the fabric to her face. It smelled musty; a lonely smell. She would have to wash it on the next sunny day, and spread it out on the lawn to dry.

She and Rich had moved into this house on a golden day at the end of the summer. She was newly pregnant then and her sense of smell was acute. She remembered the sweetness of the hay drying in the fields and the dust in the lane settling after the moving van had driven away. She had gone up to their bedroom to lie on the mattress on the floor. She had known it was pregnancy that made her limbs heavy, but even so, there had been something familiar about it at the time, and she had been afraid that she was giving way to an urge she would always be expected to overcome. Depression wasn't something she had a name for then, but she knew now that it often hovered around her, a speckling of gray behind her eyes. She remembered lying on the mattress, listening to the river and to the sound of Rich shifting boxes downstairs. Finally he had come to her with the quilt in his arms and spread it over her.

"Have we done the right thing?" she asked him.

"Too late now," he said, shuffling in beside her.

They were still, looking up at the ceiling.

"You don't think we're too close to Mum?" she asked.

At that moment the sun came out and fell across their bed. On the ceiling, golden coins of light, reflected from the satin petals, glowed, dancing as the quilt shifted with their breath.

Rich felt for her hand and squeezed it. "It feels like a million miles away from Black Coombe Cottage to me," he said.

Now she spread the quilt over the airbed. In the garden she heard the cackling of a magpie. Out beyond the apple tree the sky was softening into a lighter blue. It was still too early for the sun to shine across her bed. But it would come to her soon, she thought. The sun was on its way.

Ollie

IT'S STRANGE INSIDE our house. Our footsteps echo in the empty rooms and it smells of dust and dry leaves. There's a cobweb in the kitchen sink. I can hear Mum moving around upstairs, lots of bumps and shuffles and things being dragged across the floor. At first I try to guess what's making each noise. There's a creak that sounds like the door on the airing cupboard, a thump that might be a book or cup dropping out of her hands. After a while I stop trying to understand it all. I'm too tired. I'm just glad I'm in the house with her and I don't care about the meaning of every little sound.

I go upstairs and she's in her bedroom, pumping up the airbed with the foot pump. I say: "Are you going to bed?"

As usual, she doesn't answer my question. She says: "I'm tired. Aren't you?" The quilt is spread out over the half-pumped airbed. It's a mess of yellow folds and creases. I tell her she's always going to bed. I say what Nessa says, that she'll rot in there and it won't do her any good. Mum laughs. She says: "Yes. Sometimes that's true. But at least I get to snuggle down under this quilt. I made it for your dad, you know. Look at the gorgeous colors. Don't they make you feel glad to be alive?"

I walk away to the window. I say, "That's what Dad said when—" and then I stop because I'm itchy under my fingernails and I have to squeeze my hands hard against the sill. Mum stops pumping the bed.

She says: "What did Dad say, Ollie? When?"

I don't answer because it's two questions at once and I hate them both. I look out at the apple tree in the garden. There's a magpie strutting along one of the branches. I can see his markings, smart and defined, like the frames of Angran's black glasses or the grid of a sudoku on the page. I say: "He never set me a puzzle, did he?"

Mum comes straight back with her answer. She says: "No, Ollie, he didn't."

I don't know what to do then. Mum starts up with the foot pump again. I say: "How will I ever know, then, what it means to be alive?"

Mum keeps on pumping, each thump of her heel like a heartbeat. As the bed swells, the creases fall from the quilt and the petals of the sunflowers open out. She says: "Maybe it's something you have to keep looking for, all of the time."

I see then that she's brought the binoculars, that they're lying on the floor beside the bed. I pick them up and focus on the magpie in the apple tree. He cackles and dips his head. His tail bobs against the branch and I see that it's not completely black. There's a blue sheen streaking through his feathers. It's like a secret hidden in the shadows. He opens his wings and flaps into the sky. I see the fan of his wing tips in the air. They are bright white at first, but when I follow them, they turn pink as he catches the glow of the rising sun.

Epilogue

HE KNEW THEY were at his bedside, though not in the sense of being certain, or being able to call their faces or their names to mind, or even knowing what a face or name might be, or that he was there himself to know about these things. And yet he knew. He knew enough to sink away, when a soft voice said, *You can let go now, Rich, everything is fine.* The words had no more meaning for him than a silk scarf draped across his skin, but that was meaning enough and he drifted down into the slow caress of oxygen in his blood. The voices billowed and swayed around him. They were a tide, drawing away, pulling him in, drawing away.

There was a circling within him. A thread of light, a river. Somewhere, the sun was rising and the light on the water was peachy and gold. He felt the banks break, spreading, soaking away. The glow hung in the vapor for a while before it faded into clear, bright air.

ACKNOWLEDGMENTS

WITH SADNESS, I offer my first thanks to Susan Kamil. I was so lucky to have her wrangle with this book. Her influence is there on every page and I'm so sad she never saw it finished.

Massive thanks to Clare Conville and the team at C&W, who have made my dream come true. Susanna Wadeson, you have made this book so much stronger and deeper than I could have imagined, I can't tell you how grateful I am and how much I've learned from you. Huge thanks also to Clio Seraphim for your heroic takeover from Susan, and to Eloisa Clegg for your insightful guidance to the end, and to everyone in the teams here and in America.

I would never have got through this process without the hilarious and intelligent company of Clare Dornan, Ken Elkes, Agnes Halvorssen, Kate Morrison, Tannith Perry, Penny Price, and Ilana Winterstein of the BFN. Thank you to other writing friends Kate Simants, Emma Smith-Barton and Amy Wilson, who talked me through some of the strangeness of this experience, and to Kate Brown, who was so generous with her time and insight.

Thank you so much, Nic Fryer, Bev Gibbs, Mandy Jones, Jo Knight and Helen Leach, for reading early drafts and giving encouragement and invaluable feedback. I'm grateful for the help of many more friends: Barbara, Pete, Eirlys, Ella, Faith and Sarah, for all the listening as I've fought my way through. Many thanks also to my colleagues at Bristol Register Office for their belief in me, to all those who talked so frankly about bereavement, to my book group, and all my other wonderful friends, who kept me going in so many brilliant ways. Barry and Kate, Emma and Joe, thank you for lending your houses when I needed them.

Simon, Manu and Lem, I could not have done this without your patience and support. My love for you sparks all my best writing.

Anna Kline, I wrote this book for and because of you. Immense gratitude to you, Ezra and Evan: you lived this. And biggest thanks of all to Nick Futrell, who really did know what it means to be alive.

This Shining Life

Harriet Kline

A Book Club Guide

An Essay from Harriet Kline

I HAVE BEEN lucky enough over the years to have friends with a great instinct for living life to the fullest. These people are a joy to be around. They laugh easily, they're generous, they never seem disappointed by the way things turn out—a walk in the rain is just as much fun for them as a carnival on a sunny day. They're not scared of trying new things or making an utter fool of themselves. I picture them at the top of a slide in a children's playground, whooping as they go down, even as they overshoot the end and land in a heap on the grass.

I am not like that at all.

I have also been lucky enough over the years to have friends who don't know what we are supposed to make of this life. I love to be with these people too. They'll talk late into the night about their deepest fears and mine. They admit to making terrible mistakes and laugh about them too. Every botched social interaction (and there are many) will be a learning opportunity and the source of an entertaining tale. At the playground, these people won't dare to climb the slide. They watch from the bench, but they notice everything—whether that whoop as someone speeds down has a hint of fear in it, or how long they stay in a heap at the bottom before they pick themselves up and run to the top once more.

I am exactly like that.

For a long time I wished I was different. I believed the slide riders had easier lives with access to more joy. They understood something about living that I did not, and I could not glimpse what it was. And then one day I did—but it was probably the saddest day of my life. A dear friend, someone who rode the steepest slides at the highest speeds, was dying, and I had the honor to be present at his death.

What I discovered that day was not that the slide riders had access to more joy but that they had access to more of everything; they accepted whatever was offered and they let it into their lives. As I sat with my dying friend, holding his hands, stroking his hair, I had no choice but to accept that he would be gone forever. Perhaps it was a bit like being on a slide, this journey toward the awful moment of his death. So I accepted each breath as it happened, each shudder, each tiny rattle at the back of his throat. The saddest day was also the most real and the most lived. What made life so precious was this ability to experience and to feel. It was as simple as that, and for my friend it was gone.

I vowed to carry this discovery with me through my life. It would be my tribute to him. I remember, three days after his death, I returned to my family and we all went out to play table tennis. This was usually a trial for me: my hand-eye coordination is appalling, and my skill is worse than useless. But that day, I returned each serve effortlessly—even with some grace—and my children were agog. It was as if I had tapped into the source of some magical flow. Suddenly I saw the point of sport. I'd found it rather meaningless before, but now I saw that it celebrated this flow—an ability to live in the moment and use it to win. I saw that music did this too, and dance, and a good conversation, even a perfectly cooked meal. I was on the slide at last, I thought. Whooping my way down.

Of course it didn't last. Where at first my grief had been pure and strong, it soon got tangled up with the usual angst; I couldn't cry in front of certain people. I decided I was crying in the wrong way, too loudly or too quietly, too caught up in my own loss when there were others who were suffering more. I made mistakes at the funeral, forgetting, when I read a poem aloud, that it was about my friend and not about my beautiful delivery. I found myself attending to slights and mishaps and not to the bereavement itself. I was at the top of the slide, it seemed, but I was clinging to the safety rail, with a queue of irritated people jostling behind me.

It was this process of returning to my old ways that I wanted to explore in *This Shining Life*. I had a phrase in my head. *No one grieves in a vacuum.* As I watched my loved ones on their journey through bereavement, I noticed that they each brought their own pain to it; sorrows that had less to do with their loss and more to do with the way their own lives had turned out. And it was these sorrows that impeded the acceptance of their grief.

I invented some characters, each with an obstacle between them and their bereavement. There were seven of them at first, and I planned to write two short stories for each one. I would show them turning away from their feelings in their first story, and moving toward acceptance in the second.

It didn't work. The pattern was too repetitive, and there was no uniting narrative to draw the reader in. The characters needed to interact. It was no good if they accepted their own feelings but never got the chance to accept each other's. I pulled the guts from the stories and wove them into one joined-up tale.

It still didn't work. The problem with writing characters who don't ride slides is that they're boring to read. They don't do anything. Their minds are active, but their lives are dull. I'd invented one woman who did little more than sit about shivering and deriding herself for things she hadn't said. She did once stick her hand in the waterfall, but she shrank away from the spray. She was the character most like me, and she had to be cut. Once I removed myself from the story, it took on a life of its own.

But it still didn't work. There was a hole at the center of the book. I'd written about all these grieving people, but the man they were losing had no voice. I had been afraid to write from the perspective of a slide rider. I'd only glimpsed for a few sad days what it might be like to live like that. I was afraid to write about dying too, going back to the sorrow that created the story. In the end, Rich's scenes were the easiest to write of all of them. Perhaps it was because I had to accept the reality of death to write them, and this put me back on the slide.

Rich's scenes brought the book together at last. But I discovered something else as I worked it into shape. Though I had glimpsed what it might be like to be a slide rider, I knew I'd never be one myself. But that didn't mean I wasn't living life to the fullest. My experience of clinging to the safety rail at the top of the slide was as rich and valid as the experience of letting go. The sorrows that stood between my grief and me were still worthy feelings in themselves. In writing about them all, and inventing characters who do this, I came to love those feelings and accept them too, to feel they are all part what it means to be alive—even if I'll never play a decent game of table tennis again.

Questions and Topics for Discussion

1. The novel opens with Rich in his element—at a party, surrounded by family. How did this introduction shape your first impression of him as a character, especially in light of the next time we see him, receiving his diagnosis?

2. What do you think of Harriet Kline's choice to structure Part 1 as alternating between the adults' undergoing Rich's diagnosis and last weeks, and Ollie's narrative after his father's death? How did it inform your reading experience?

3. Ollie's chapters give us the first glimpse into life after Rich dies. What do you think the refrain that opens each of his chapters—"My dad died"—says about the way he is processing his grief? How does his fixation on solving the puzzle fit into this?

4. How do Ruth and Nessa differ in the way they see the world? How does this inform the ways each of them grieves? Were there similarities in their personal journeys, despite how different they seem as people?

5. Compare Angran to Marjorie and Gerald. How do you think Ruth and Rich were each shaped by their parents? How do you think this has informed the way they parent Ollie?

6. How has Ruth's relationship with Angran informed who she is as a person, especially in terms of her mental health? How is her depression portrayed in the novel compared with Angran's own experiences when Ruth and Nessa were growing up?

7. How do you feel about the final scenes of the novel, especially in terms of seeing all of these characters together under one roof? What do you think lies ahead for Ollie and his family?

8. What was the most significant change you saw in each of these characters by the end of the novel?

9. Even though Rich didn't really intend for there to be a puzzle, Ollie's quest to try to solve it was transformative for him, and for his family. What did he, and the other characters, learn from this undertaking?

10. What does the phrase "golden thinking" mean to you? If you had to pick a color for your thinking, what would it be?

HARRIET KLINE works part-time registering births, deaths and marriages, and writes for the rest of the week. Her story "Ghost" won the Hissac short-story competition and "Chest of Drawers" won *The London Magazine* short-story competition. Other short stories have been published online with *Litro, For Books' Sake* and *ShortStorySunday*, and on BBC Radio 4. She lives in Bristol, England, with her partner and two teenage sons.

harrietkline.com

This book was set in a Monotype face called Bell. The Englishman John Bell (1745–1831) was responsible for the original cutting of this design. The vocations of Bell were many—bookseller, printer, publisher, type-founder, and journalist, among others. His types were considerably influenced by the delicacy and beauty of the French copperplate engravers. Monotype Bell might also be classified as a delicate and refined rendering of Scotch Roman.

RANDOM HOUSE BOOK CLUB

Because Stories Are Better Shared

Discover
Exciting new books that spark conversation every week.

Connect
With authors on tour—or in your living room. (Request an Author Chat for your book club!)

Discuss
Stories that move you with fellow book lovers on Facebook, on Goodreads, or at in-person meet-ups.

Enhance
Your reading experience with discussion prompts, digital book club kits, and more, available on our website.